This book belongs
to Jessica Loveday

THE
DRAGON
QUINTET

THE DRAGON QUINTET

Edited by
Marvin Kaye

TOR®
fantasy

A Tom Doherty Associates Book
New York

This is a work of fiction. All the characters and events portrayed in this book are either products of the authors' imagination or are used fictitiously.

THE DRAGON QUINTET

Compilation, Introduction, and Afterword copyright © 2003 by Marvin Kaye
Interior illustrations © 2004 by Stephen Hickman
"In the Dragon's House" copyright © 2003 by Orson Scott Card
"Judgment" copyright © 2003 by Elizabeth Moon
"Love in a Time of Dragons" copyright © 2003 by Tanith Lee
"Joust" copyright © 2003 by Mercedes Lackey
"King Dragon" copyright © 2003 by Michael Swanwick

A Tor Book
Published by Tom Doherty Associates, LLC
175 Fifth Avenue
New York, NY 10010

www.tor.com

Tor® is a registered trademark of Tom Doherty Associates, LLC.

ISBN 0-756-34911-6
EAN 978-0-765-34911-8

Previously published by Science Fiction Book Club of Bookspan

First Tor hardcover edition: April 2004
First Tor mass market edition: May 2006

Printed in the United States of America

0 9 8 7 6 5 4 3 2 1

CONTENTS

INTRODUCTION
Firedrakes Fierce and Friendly

Dragons are a rich, ongoing, thoroughly disparate myth in both western and eastern culture. They abound in literature and legend, from St. George through Beowulf, Siegfried, and Don Quixote, with a rebirth of interest in twentieth-century fantasy fiction.

If dragons are complicated creatures, and they are, it might have something to do with the etymological complexity of the word itself. According to Webster, there are two lines of derivation, the first being the Middle English, Old French *dragon* or *dragun,* which in those tongues derived from a word meaning "a place to stand," from which somehow arose "standard," as in an agreed-upon measurement; how this connects with dragons eludes me, but the dictionary states it as a possible etymological root. The more familiar and more likely root is the Greek *drakon,* a serpent, though that, too, is a bit enigmatic, since Webster avers it arises from *derksesthai,* literally "the seeing one."

If that is not confusing enough, the dictionary enumerates many different definitions, for example, a fierce person and/or watchful chaperone; a saurian of the genus *draco,* commonly known as the flying dragon or flying lizard; a constellation of the northern hemisphere; a kind of pigeon; a short musket with a dragon's head represented at its muzzle; a soldier so armed, also known as a dragoon; a large serpent or snake; any of various plants, such as the green dragon, so named because of its mottled stem that is reminiscent of a snake's skin, and a heraldic device.

Dragons have also been equated with the Devil; the Satanic serpent is the etymological source that Bram Stoker drew upon when naming his famous vampire *Dracula*. The dragon/devil equation presumably arises from the fact that in the Authorized Version of the Bible, the word was used as the common translation for a number of different Hebrew words that are now understood to have meant many things, including "serpent," "jackal," or "old serpent," the latter presumably a reference to Satan, although the devil is a latecomer in the Bible; in the Old Testament he was not the same entity as in the New.

But nevertheless, the concept proved popular, and the dragon became the classic mythic creature that we know today: dangerous, fire-breathing winged serpents with great claws and tails, and scaly bodies impervious to weapons except for the beasts' soft underbellies. According to legend, they despoil villages, demand virgin sacrifices, and rob all and sundry of gold and precious metals, which they rest upon in their caves in greedy contentment. Difficult and dangerous to kill, dragons were nevertheless prized for magical properties attributed to their carcasses. Dragon blood smeared on the skin before battle made a warrior impervious to sword thrusts. One who ate a dragon's heart would learn how to understand the language of birds, and if one also dined on the serpent's tongue, one would enjoy the gift of glib speech.

In the Orient, however, dragons are perceived quite differently. They are more or less equated with the four elements of earth, fire, water, and wind, and are perceived as beneficent and wise protectors deserving to be honored, as they are every Chinese New Year.

One of the most intriguing things I have noticed in contemporary fantasy fiction that employs dragons is a tendency to cross-pollinate the characteristics of Oriental and Occidental dragons. Sometimes, as in the film *Dragonheart,* the creature is kindly disposed toward humanity (and its sequel mixes the myth-pool further by introducing two Asians steeped in dragon lore). Sometimes the dragon, though fierce, may yet engage in social converse, such as Tolkien's Smaug or John Gardner's old dragon in *Grendel.* Still, there are many examples of old-style dragons in twentieth-century fairy tales, as anyone familiar with *Weird Tales* is well aware.

The Dragon Quintet, conceived in the style of my previous and popular anthology, *The Vampire Sextette,* contains five long stories especially commissioned for this volume. The authors were given complete freedom to create whatever kind of story they pleased, provided only that each one contain a true, as opposed to a metaphorical, dragon.

As the stories arrived, I was pleased and impressed by the wholly different character of each tale. Nevertheless, a common bond may be noted in all of the stories: Not one of the protagonists is an Arthurian knight or otherwise hyperbolic hero. This is an egalitarian collection; its heroes and heroines are children, commoners, servants, slaves; most of them must work hard and are treated unfairly. Each one faces a mystery or an enormous problem that shapes and defines them.

As for the dragons, they are of all kinds and types. Some of them are evil, some are good, all of them are unusual.

In Orson Scott Card's "In the Dragon's House," we encounter a nurturing little creature (but what does it *really* want?). Elizabeth Moon's "Judgment" features dragon's eggs and dangerous though fair dragons. Tanith Lee, in a manner reminiscent of the story she wrote for *The Vampire Sextette,* manages to mix a subtle (and sometimes not so subtle) blend of eros in "Love in a Time of Dragons." A gamut of dragon behavior is reflected in Mercedes Lackey's "Joust," while Michael Swanwick's "King Dragon" is a sinister, truly repellent creature with a thoroughly original physiology.

I am grateful to my editor, Ellen Asher, and her genial associate Andy Wheeler for their suggestions, advice, and invaluable input in fashioning *The Dragon Quintet*.

—Marvin Kaye
New York City, 2003

THE
DRAGON
QUINTET

IN THE
DRAGON'S HOUSE

by Orson Scott Card

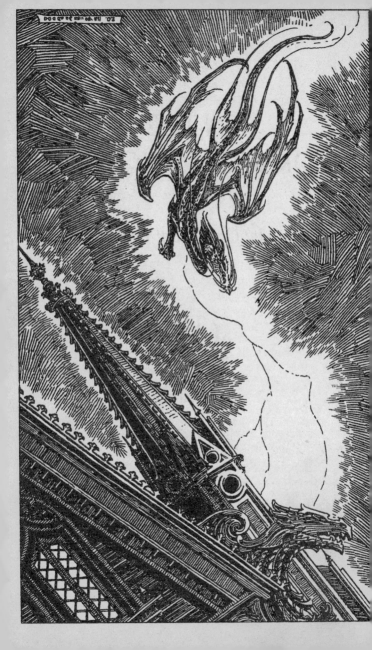

❧═◉═☙

Mix one oddly endearing family with one oddly unsettling old house and add something unspoken with wings, and you have the elements of this, our initial story, by Hugo and Nebula winner Orson Scott Card, gifted author of the award-winning novels *Ender's Game* and its sequel, *Speaker for the Dead*. A native of Washington State, Scott, as he prefers to be called, has written novels of fantasy, revisionist fable, and science fiction. His numerous short stories have appeared in *Amazing Stories, Analog, Isaac Asimov's SF Magazine, Fantasy & Science Fiction,* and *Omni.* His tale "Eumenides in the Fourth Floor Lavatory" is a classic of twentieth-century horror. "In the Dragon's House," though complete unto itself, contains the germ of a story that Scott intends to expand into a novel.

In a fit of romantic excess, the builder of the house at 22 Adams gave this lovely street of grand Victorian mansions its one mark of distinction—a gothic cathedral of a house, complete with turrets, crenellated battlements, steep-pitched roofs, and even gargoyles at the downspouts.

One of the gargoyles—the one most easily visible to those who approached the front door—was a fierce dragon's head. In a thunderstorm the beast spewed great gouts of water, for it collected from the largest expanse of roofs. But this wet wyrm was no less to be avoided than its mythical fire-breathing forebears.

Inside the house, however, there was no attempt to be archaic or fey. Electricity was in the house from the beginning. In fact, it was the first house in Mayfield to be fully wired during construction, and the owner spared no expense. Knobs and wires were concealed behind the laths, and every room of any size had not just one electric outlet but four— one in each wall. A shameless extravagance. What would anyone ever need so many outlets *for?*

As the house was going up, passersby were known to tut-tut that the house was doomed to burn, having so much fire running up and down inside the walls. But the house did not burn, while others, less well wired, sometimes did, as their owners overloaded circuits with multipliers and extension cords to make up for the electrical deficiency.

Between the gargoyle and the rumors of future fire, it was inevitable that the neighbors would call it "the dragon house." During the 1920s the moniker changed a little, becoming "The Old Dragon's House," for during that time the owner was an old widower—the son of the original builder—who valued his privacy and had no concern for what the neighbors thought. He let the small garden surrounding the house go utterly to seed, so it was soon a jungle of tall weeds that offended the eye and endlessly seeded the neighbors' gardens.

When helpful or impatient neighbors came over from time to time and mowed the garden, the old man met them with hostility. As he grew older and more isolated, he threatened violence, first with a broom, then with a rake, and finally with a cane that might have been pathetic in the hands of such an old man. But he was so fiery in his wrath that even the boldest man quailed before him, and he soon became

known among the neighbors as the Old Dragon. It was from
him as much as the gargoyle that the house seemed to derive
its name.

Finally, the neighbors went to court and got an injunction
compelling the man to control the weeds on his property. The
Old Dragon responded by hiring workmen to come and pave
the entire garden, front and back, with bricks and cobble-
stones so that the only living things in the yard were the insects
that wandered across it in search of likelier foraging grounds.

The old man lived out his days and when he died the
house went to a great-niece who called it, not "The Old
Dragon's House," but "The Albatross," and put it on the
market the moment it was certified as hers.

That was when Michael's great-grandparents bought the
place and turned it into the home he grew up in.

Normal Schwarzhelm had owned a chain of vaudeville
theatres and had married his favorite headliner, Lolly
Poppins. Just before vaudeville's collapse, Normal sold his
theatres to a developer who was turning them all into movie
houses, then invested the money and retired to Mayfield, the
smallest and most charming of the towns on his little circuit.

Buying the Old Dragon's House was not Normal's idea,
it was Lolly's. To her, it carried all the magic and romance of
the legitimate stage to which she had always aspired; her
twenty years of doing slightly naughty comic songs followed
by one tragic tear-jerking ballad had never been more than a
stopgap until she got her "break."

Her break had turned out to be Normal, who adored her
and indulged her and had a wagonload of money. Of course
he hadn't the power to get her into legitimate theatre now.
He was out of the business, and she was too old and too
well-known for her shtick, which was looking surprised and
confused at the double entendres in her own songs, followed

by a whooping laugh when she finally got her own joke. Nobody in legitimate theatre would give her the roles she coveted.

But the Dragon's House had a copious cellar and, with a little excavation and remodeling and an additional dose of heavy-duty wiring for the lights, she fitted out a little underground theatre where she could mount amateur productions to her heart's content. Which she did. She became the producer, the director, and a beloved character actress in a lively community theatre company that did everything from *The Trojan Women* to *Macbeth*, from *The Importance of Being Earnest* to *The Women*. It should not be hard to guess which parts she played.

She also brought in old friends from vaudeville to take part in her shows, putting them up in her home and feeding them generously while they were there—a way to help out those in need without it looking like charity. "You're doing *me* a favor," she would insist. "These local amateurs need to see what a professional looks like!" To fit all her guests, she had workmen divide most of the bedrooms into small but cozy chambers, and as she did, she had the plumbing and wiring brought up to code, so that despite its age and ancient look, the Dragon's House had all the modern amenities.

While Lolly rehearsed and performed in the cellar, Normal climbed the stairs to the attic, where he, too, had a plethora of new wiring installed to support his passion—electric trains. The walls of the windowless room were lined with tables, and from the south wall a huge table projected into the middle, leaving only a narrow corridor. All the tables were covered with train tracks, trestles, bridges, hills, villages, and cities, with the walls expertly painted as mountains and farmland and, on one side, a river flowing into the sea.

Lolly invited all comers to the basement to watch her plays, but no one ever saw Normal's trains except the family, and then only a glimpse once in a while when calling him down to meals or to meet with his lawyer or broker. His hobby was not for display. It was a world where he alone could lie. And over the years his fantasy life in the attic became quite an eccentricity, for now and then he would come downstairs and remark, "The dragon was lively today" or "We had quite a thunderstorm in the attic," as if the train layout had its own weather and the occasional mythical beast to liven things up.

"Next thing you'll tell us," Lolly would say, "the little tiny people will start packing their little tiny clothes in little tiny suitcases and buy teensy-weensy tickets so they can ride the train."

He would look at her like she was crazy and say, "They're not *real*, Lolly." And she would roll her eyes heavenward as if to ask God to judge which of them was mad.

Lolly's first three children, fathered by her first three husbands, had been born during her vaudeville days and therefore loathed the theatre, absolutely refusing to take part in her plays. But her two children by Normal, their son, Herrick, and their daughter, Bernhardt—Herry and Harty—had no bad memories of backstage life, and so they happily threw themselves into every play. They were the princes murdered in the tower, they were Hansel and Gretel, they were young Ebenezer Scrooge and his beloved sister. When they weren't in rehearsal they were romping among the costumes and props and old set pieces stored on the north side of the cellar.

When Normal and Lolly died no one minded that they left the house and all its contents to Herry and Harty. After all, they were Normal's only children, and it was generous of him to leave a bit over one hundred thousand dollars to each of Lolly's other three children—a lot of money in those days. Most of the money, though, went to Herry and Harty, who kept up the tradition of theatricals in the basement until the city inspectors told them that the public-safety laws had changed and there was no way to bring the cellar theatre up to code without demolishing the building.

It was a sad day in the Old Dragon's House when the public performances ended, and while they still had guests over and put on shows once in a while, the regular community theater company moved to the local high school auditorium and Herry and Harty were no longer the heart and soul of it as they had been. They still contributed financially from time to time, but by the 1970s they had turned inward—not recluses, but focused on the life of their house.

With all those bedrooms, no more retired vaudevillians to sleep in them, and few plays to occupy their time, Herry and Harty cast about for something useful to do. The idea they hit upon was to take in strays.

Stray children, that is. Runaways. Abused children. Orphans. They didn't take all—no, by no means, they were quite selective. For they knew that only a few children would respond to what they had to offer, and why waste time and effort with those they could not help? So they'd take a child in for a day or two, and if things weren't working, they'd pass him or her along—bathed, fed, with new clothes on their backs—to the social workers who would find them the ordinary sort of foster care.

There were always a few children, however, whose eyes lit up when they were given costumes to wear and lines to say, and now the occasional theatricals in the basement of the Old Dragon's House were performed mostly by children and teenagers playing all the parts, with local kids joining in and an audience consisting of parents and friends. The lost children thrived in that company. Most of them did well in school; all of them went on to do well enough in life. For when you've been in good plays, you know how to work together with others, do your own part as well as you can and trust others to do theirs, and that's all you need to know in order to do fine in a job or a marriage.

Harty had never married but stayed on in the house with Herry and his wife, Cecilia. And when Cecilia died of breast cancer, Aunt Harty became surrogate mother to the four children and soon thought of them as her own. They were already teenagers before the transformation of the house to theatrical orphanage but they loved what their home had become and didn't mind that when they came home for a visit there was rarely any place for them in the bedrooms. They might have slept in the big old bed in the front of the attic but Harty didn't like to have people traipsing through her papa's train room to get to it, and so they'd end up sleeping on couches here and there—and, eventually, as their own families grew, in the nearby Holiday Inn.

But Michael was not one of the grandchildren, who always had homes of their own in faraway cities and came to Mayfield only to visit. Michael did call Herry and Harty "Gramps" and "Granny" but it wasn't true. They were actually his great-uncle and great-aunt.

Michael's real grandmother was Portia Ringgold, Lolly's daughter by her third husband, a soldier who died of the flu after World War I. Portia was killed by alcohol in her fifties, though technically the cause of death was listed as "falling in front of a subway train." Michael's mother, Donna, was beaten to death by one of the "uncles" who came and went in her short, drug-addicted life.

Michael wasn't there for that sad day, however, for Herry and Harty had got wind of what was happening in their niece's life and had offered to take care of Michael "for a while" so Donna could "recuperate." That was why Michael had no memory of calling anyone Mother. He knew only Gramps and Granny, and his only home was the little room at the back of the attic. They put him there because, as Gramps said, "The kids on the second floor come and go, but you're with us forever."

And that was why Michael Ringgold grew up in the Old Dragon's House.

———————

At first, of course, he didn't know that was what the house was called. To him, it was simply "home." That's what Gramps and Granny called it. "I'm home!" "In our home we have certain rules." "We try to help these boys and girls feel at home." "This is a home, not a gymnasium!"

He wasn't aware yet that other people's homes didn't have theatres in the basement, or sad and angry children coming and going from time to time on the second floor, or locked doors in the attic from which strange sounds emerged at odd hours of the day or night, or a warm place on the back stairs where, when he sat very still, he could feel the *throb, throb* of a beating heart.

He did know, however, that Granny didn't like him to sit there in the warm place. Every time she saw him there, from earliest childhood, she would say, "What are you doing, boy? Why aren't you *playing?*" She would assign him some errand or, once he learned to read, make him get a book and read something aloud to her, which was nice; he was proud of being a reader, he didn't mind that.

What he minded was the interruption. So when he heard someone coming down the narrow hall toward the back stairs that led to his attic room, he would scamper up to his bed and pretend to be sleeping. It never seemed to fool them. He tried pretending to be just waking up, but it was no good. "You were sitting there again, you dreamy dreamy boy," said Granny. Or, "He was in that *place* again," one of the visiting kids would call out.

Finally, when he was four, one of the visitors took pity on him and told him how they knew. "It's a wooden staircase, you moron," he said. "They can hear your feet when you run up to your room."

Oh.

Michael learned then to take off his shoes before he went to sit in the warm place. Then when he heard someone coming he walked up the stairs very slowly, stepping only at the outside edges of the steps so there were no creaks. It worked. Now the only time he was ever caught in the warm place was when he fell asleep there, and that hardly ever happened.

Because even though it was, as Granny assumed, a place for dreaming, it wasn't sleeping dreams he went for. And it wasn't because sleeping dreams were scarier—no, he had no nightmares as frightening as some of the dreams he had in the warm place. It's that the dreams in the warm place always seemed to make sense. They didn't just go from one thing to another in the silly way dreams did.

They felt like memories. Like he was thinking back on things he had done before. And whereas in sleeping dreams he always saw himself as if he were watching his own body from outside, in these memories he only *felt* himself. His own body. Stretching, taut, exhilarating dreams of having enormous strength and yet being amazingly light and on fire inside, all the time. Dreams of flying. Dreams of falling down, hurtling toward the ground so fast that his vision went white and he came to himself gasping as if he had just woken up, only he knew at the end of one of *those* dreams that he had never been asleep, for through it all he also remembered seeing the faded wallpaper and the part of the heavy-curtained window that his eyes were focused on even as he was moving through or over another world, in another body.

He knew it was another body because when he was walking around in the house, toddling on his little legs and falling down or bumping into things, it was definitely *not* the body he had in those dreams. In real life he was not strong and he could not fly and he never, never felt the fire inside.

Maybe in a weaker child that might have been an irresistible drug, to have those dreams in the warm place on the back stairs. But Michael Ringgold was strong without knowing it. Not strong of arm—he was as tough as any kid, but no tougher, and no one would mistake him for a blacksmith's apprentice. His throw could get to first base and he could chin himself up into a tree, and he didn't think to try for more. But there was another kind of strength that he had in good measure without knowing it. Michael loved dreaming that he could fly with the heat throbbing inside him, but he also loved running around outside with the other kids, or lurking down in the theatre watching a play rehearsal or helping to paint the scenery. He loved trying to steal cookie dough in the kitchen when Granny's back was turned; he even loved getting rapped on the head with a spoon as he made it out the door with his mouth full, while Granny shouted after him, "You can get a disease from the eggs in that batter, you foolish boy!" ·

Michael had the strength to do what he chose to do, despite his own desires.

One night when he was seven he heard the sounds from behind the locked door. A humming sound, but with a bit of an edge to it. It sounded like Gramps's electric razor. Or a shower running somewhere in the house.

It wasn't quite dark yet because it was a summer night during daylight saving time, and so even though there were shadows in the room and he had never before dared to get out of his bed when the sounds were there, tonight he decided he had to know, and so—because he was strong—he simply ignored his dread and got up. He only wore shoes for school and for church, but even though his feet had calluses from running across asphalt and climbing trees and scrambling through brambles, his soles felt extremely naked and vulnerable as he crossed the little space between his bed and the locked door that led deeper into the attic.

He turned the handle.

It turned freely, but he still couldn't open the door.

The sounds did not stop, either. It was as if his little effort to pull the door open was not worth noticing.

The keyhole was the old-fashioned kind, like the one on the door to the basement. But unlike the basement keyhole, this one seemed to have been plugged with something so he couldn't see through it. Nor could he see anything under the door, which might mean that it was dark in the locked room, or it might mean that it, too, had some kind of obstruction to keep light from passing.

So all his courage was wasted. He couldn't get through, and he couldn't see in.

Only he wanted to see, and this was the time.

What did he have in his dresser drawer? Whatever he had

taken from his pockets all summer, stashed in the bottom drawer inside a cigar box. He chose two items: the tarnished baby spoon he had found by the creek behind the house, and the cheap little pocketknife he had gotten by trading four fine marbles to one of the boys who hadn't stayed long at the house because he kept making fun of the kids who were serious about rehearsing the play. It was Gramps's cut-down version of *Macbeth* but the boy with the cheap knife never cared about it even when he was assigned to play Banquo, which meant he got to be a ghost in the dinner scene. And then he was gone, and Michael suspected he was the only person in the house who remembered him now at the end of summer; and that was only because he had this crummy little knife and somewhere in the past few weeks it had gradually dawned on him that he had been cheated.

Well, the knife wouldn't cut and it wobbled in its handle, but maybe it could poke through whatever was blocking the keyhole.

And it did. One punch, straight through, and the blade broke and remained stuck there in the keyhole.

Great. Now when Granny came up to clean, she'd see the blade sticking out and know that he had tried to break in. Only he hadn't, he just wanted to *see*.

Well, no, if he had been able to jimmy the lock, he would have opened the door. That was the truth and if he couldn't tell the truth to himself then he really *was* a liar like that one visiting girl said he was, when Michael told her that he said his prayers every night without Gramps or Granny watching over him to make him do it.

I want to see in there. And I don't want to get caught for having tried.

So he used the handle of the baby spoon. It wasn't the best tool—needle-nose pliers were what he needed, and just imagine trying to explain to Gramps why he needed them. But the spoon handle did the job. By prying with it, he got the broken knife blade to wiggle and finally come loose.

And now there *was* a hole, so tiny and narrow—thin as a blade, of course—that he couldn't actually see anything through it except for one thing: There was light in that room. Bright light. Dazzling light. And all that buzzing, whirring, rushing. What was in there? Why would Gramps and Granny leave a light on in there?

There was a big attic window in the front of the house, and Michael had wondered for a long time whether the locked room ran the whole length of the house. But that wasn't the light of dusky evening coming through the key-hole, it was like a very bright naked bulb, a hundred-watter like the one in the basement storage room that you turned on by pulling a chain that Michael could only reach by jumping. If there was always a light in the locked room, it would be visible through that front attic window and if it was visible there had been plenty of overcast and stormy days when Michael had been outside and would have seen that the attic was lit.

So the locked room didn't have any window.

It's my brother in there, thought Michael. My secret brother, who already lived here before they brought me. The crazy one who actually killed my mother and they couldn't tell me about it because it was too terrible. He's chained in that room, only they don't know he's broken the chain and he's just waiting for me to open the door so he can grab me and tear out my throat with his teeth like a wolf.

Or maybe it's my mother's body in there, like Snow White when the dwarfs laid her out in a glass coffin to lie there looking beautiful till the prince came to kiss her awake, only the prince can't get there because the door is locked.

Or maybe the attic crawl space would get him there.

There was a low door in the wall at the foot of his bed that Granny said led into the crawl space. "We don't store anything there, it's just in case we get a dead rat or a bird's nest in there and we need to clean it out. Don't you go in there because the floor isn't finished and you'll put your foot right through the ceiling in the bedroom below and then we'll have to saw off your leg just to get you out." She said it with her I'm-pretending-it's-a-joke-but-take-heed look, and so of course he tried to get in there the second her back was turned. But even though he could turn the primitive wooden latch easily enough, when he tried to push the door open it jammed against something immediately and he couldn't even see in.

Now, though, standing at the locked door, he looked over at his bed, whose foot was jammed in under the slope of the roof so he sometimes bumped the ceiling with his feet when he turned over too quickly in bed. And in that moment, perhaps because he actually wanted to know it, he understood exactly why the door hadn't opened. It was bumping into the continued downward slope of the ceiling. The door didn't open into the crawl space, it opened into the room.

Of course, that meant to open it Michael would have to move his bed. He had never tried to do that on purpose before, just accidentally before he learned just how angry Granny could get when she caught him lying on his back in the bed and shoving against the ceiling with his feet. "If I wanted footprints on the ceiling I would have moved to Australia where they walk around upside down all the time!" she said. And then she shoved the bed back into place with such vigor that the footboard of the bed made two indentations in the ceiling, so the only real damage was what she had caused her own self. She hadn't liked it when Michael pointed this out to her, and so he learned a couple of lessons that day.

How quietly could he pull the bed out from the little door? And how far would he have to pull it before he could get through?

The answers were: with only a couple of slight scraping sounds, and about a foot and a half.

He was sweating from the exertion of pulling the bed when he stuck his head through the opening and looked around.

It was very, very dark. But the longer he leaned there, his body half in, half out of the crawl space, the better he could see. There was light coming up from the outer edges of the room—faint light, because it really was full dusk outside and soon there'd be no light at all.

He could see the rafters like corduroy, row on row, with thick dust piled on them like snow on a fence rail. He thought of falling down through the ceiling. He thought of getting half there and realizing it was too dark to go on and then having it be so dark he couldn't find the door to get back into his room. And then he'd feel a *hand* on his shoulder and a voice would say, "Hello, little brother . . .".

. . . and when he thought of *that* there was no way he was going in, not tonight. Tomorrow when it was light. And when the noises weren't coming from the locked room.

He pulled himself back into his little room. There was one horrible moment when a belt loop on his jeans snagged against the doorframe and he thought he'd been grabbed. But then he was through the door and he slammed it shut, fortunately not making much noise because it was such a thin door and it didn't actually have a jamb to bump against. Then he scrambled to his feet, got round to the head of the bed, and shoved it hard against the wall.

Nothing could get through that door without moving the bed and that would wake him up, so it was safe. Besides, he'd

slept in this room all his life and nothing had ever come out
of that little crawl-space door to get him anyway, had it? So
why was he lying there under his covers, constantly lifting up
his head to see if the door had moved? It had! No it hadn't.
But maybe it had.

And then he woke up in the morning and didn't even
remember about the crawl space until he was in the front yard
enjoying one of the last days of summer before second grade
started. He looked up at the front of the house and saw the
attic balcony and window and wondered, as he sometimes
did, whether his brother ever looked out the window at him
playing and hated him—and that was when he remembered
the crawl space last night. Only had it really happened?
Wasn't it just a dream? Well, today he'd go in there while it
was daylight and settle the question for once and all.

But he forgot about it again. He forgot it over and over
except when he was too far away or too busy with something
to bother running upstairs to do the experiment. He kept not
doing it until he was away at school every day and then he
really did forget. And then one of the visiting kids told him
that all houses made weird noises at night. "It's just wind
coming out of the toilet drainpipes," the girl said. "That and
the house settling down to rest at night." And now that he
thought about it, Michael realized that toilet drainpipes
probably all made sounds like that from the wind whistling
over them so it wasn't coming out of the locked room at all.
It was from the pipes, and that was that. Mystery solved. Of
course it wasn't his brother. He had no brother. That was just
a nightmare.

One night, halfway through second grade, Gramps
looked at him and said, "How tall are you anyway, boy?"

"Tall enough to pee standing up," said Michael, "but not
tall enough to shave."

The visiting kids at the dinner table laughed and snorted.

"I hate it that you taught him to say that," said Granny.

"I didn't," said Gramps. "It's just the simple truth."

"It is so crude to use words like that."

"You heard your Granny, Michael. We have to call it 'chin depilation,' not 'shaving.'"

"I'm this tall," said Michael, standing up beside his chair again like he did during grace.

"That's what I thought," said Gramps. "Birds' nests are in grave danger from you now, young man. You're soon going to have to duck going under bridges."

"I'll just step over them," said Michael.

"You're not that tall," said one of the kids, a serious boy with round scars on his arm.

"It's a brag," said an older girl. "They always brag."

"It's a joke," said another girl.

"Nay," said Granny, "'tis a jest, a jape."

Which was the cue for Gramps to do his gorilla act, saying "I beat on my jest because I am one of the great japes." Only when he had finished and Granny spooned him on the butt and he fled back to his chair did he finally come to the point.

"We have an empty room on the second floor," said Gramps. "I think you're too tall for that little bed in the attic now."

"I like it fine, Gramps," said Michael.

"Yeah, he lives up there with his pet chicken," said one of the older boys. Another boy immediately made a choking sound.

Gramps glared at them both and they wilted a little so Michael knew there was something bad or dirty about what they had said, though for the life of him he couldn't figure out what it was.

Gramps and Granny didn't do anything about it for a few weeks but then one day when Michael came home from school he found that his stuff had been moved down into the little bedroom right at the foot of the back stairs, directly beneath the attic room.

It broke his heart but he tried to hide it, and he must have done pretty well because it wasn't till he was crying alone in his bed that he heard Granny's voice saying, "Good heavens, Michael, why are you crying?"

But he couldn't answer, he just clung to her for a long while until he wasn't crying anymore. "I'm okay," he said.

"But whatever were you crying about?"

"It's okay," he insisted.

"It's not okay, and if you don't answer me right now I'm going to go downstairs to *my* room and cry until *you* come down and ask me why *I'm* crying and I won't tell you either."

"I just . . . I just guess I'm one of the visiting kids now, that's all," said Michael. "I don't mind, really."

"Why—that's absurd, you silly frumpus. Why would you think that?"

"'Cause Gramps said when I moved in that the kids on the second floor come and go."

"No, no—oh, you poor boy—you remember that? You weren't even three; how can you remember? But don't you see? He was trying to reassure you because we thought that you might think that being up in the attic meant we didn't love you as much as the other kids. But the fact was that the bed up there is a child's bed and you're the only person who could sleep in it and it was the only space we had for you then. Gramps moved you down here because you're bigger, that's all. But you're not going to come and go, Michael. You're our very own. Our last little boy of our very own."

"I'm not your own," he said. "You're not even my Granny. You're my aunt."

"I'm your *great*-aunt, don't you forget. Only we shortened that to Graunt, and then Graunty, and then Grauny; only that sounds so theatrical and phony that we changed it to Granny. So you see? I'm your Granny *because* I'm your great-aunt."

"And I suppose Gramps is short for great-uncle."

"Not at all. It's because he's grumpy. We called him Grumps when he was a boy and it stuck, only somehow over the years it just changed to Gramps."

"So what is *my* name going to change to? Over the years?"

"I have no idea," said Granny. "Won't it be interesting to see? Over the years? Because you are going to be here for years and years. As long as you like. Until the day comes when *you* want to leave. To go off to college or to get married to some nice girl."

"I'm not supposed to say 'pee' and *you* can talk about me marrying some girl?"

"Hardly seems fair, does it?"

And he didn't feel like crying anymore and after a while he liked being on the same floor as the visiting kids and some of them even became friends, because they were almost his age.

Now and then he still went halfway up the back stairs to the warm place. But after the first few weeks he didn't bother to go all the way up to his old room. It wasn't his room anymore, was it?

And down here, he never heard the sound of the wind rushing past the toilet drainpipes. He almost forgot about it. For years he almost forgot.

Seventh grade. The year that Granny and Gramps put on *Our Town, As You Like It,* and *Tom Sawyer.* The year that Michael Ringgold changed from clarinet to French horn because the junior-high band had fourteen clarinets and no French horn player at all. The year that everybody was Indiana Jones for Halloween, so Michael and Gramps worked for a week to put together a costume so he could go trick-or-treating as the Lost Ark.

It was the year when they had such a blizzard the day after Christmas that the whole town of Mayfield shut down. The snow was no burden at the Old Dragon's House, of course, because with a troupe of boys and girls on hand and plenty of snow shovels to go around, the front yard and sidewalk were soon clear right down to the cobbles and bricks. The kids were enthusiastic about the labor, too, because they carried the snow into the backyard in wheelbarrows and soon made such a mountain of snow that they could slide down it in all directions on sleds, inner tubes, and the seats of their pants.

It was great fun, and no one broke any bones this time, so the worst injury was probably the cut Michael got on his hand when his sled collided with another kid's snow shovel. He didn't mind—it was cold enough that his hands were too numb for the pain to be more than a dull throb—but the other kids began to complain that his blood was turning the snow all pink and it looked gross.

So he went inside and Granny almost fainted. In a few minutes she had Merthiolate poured over the wound and was stitching it up herself, a skill she had learned from her mother, who had done her share of backstage doctoring during vaudeville days. "Hold still so I can line up the edges of the wound so the skin matches up. Otherwise you'll look rumpled for the rest of your life."

"Will I have a scar?" asked Michael.

"Yes, you will, so I hope you're not contemplating a life of crime because it will make your palm print absolutely distinctive."

"I wish it was on my face," said Michael.

"I wish it *were* on my face," corrected Granny. "And why ever would you wish for such a foolish thing?"

"Scars are romantic."

"Romantic! Maybe once upon a time *dueling* scars were romantic. But sledding scars are definitely not. So I hope you're not going to go out and lie down on Mt. Snowshovel and let the sleds run over you."

"I never would have thought of it if you hadn't suggested it."

She finished covering his palm with a bandage and winding it around with tape. "All packaged up so nicely we ought to put a stamp on it and mail it somewhere."

"Come on, this bandage is so thick I can't even pick my nose."

"Well if you expect me to do it for you, think again."

"So are you going to help me get on some mittens?"

"Apparently you are suffering from the delusion that you are going to go back outside and open up this wound after I went to all the trouble to stitch it closed."

"That *was* my plan, Gran."

"*My* plan is for you to stay here in the kitchen till you warm up. Whose plan do you think will prevail?"

"How about if I go lie down in my room?"

"That will certainly do, though I must warn you that if I look out back and see you on Mt. Snowshovel again you will have a nice set of scars on your squattenzone and I *will* stitch them all skewampus so that everyone who sees your backside will laugh at you."

"Who's ever going to see my backside?"

"Never you mind who. I can just promise you that you won't want them laughing."

"I won't go outside again," he said.

"Not even just to watch," said Granny.

"Not even just to watch." And Michael meant it, because now that he was warmer he could really feel the pain in his hand and it was nasty, a deep, hard throb that made it difficult to think about anything else.

"Well, if you're really going up to bed, let me give you some cough medicine."

"I don't *have* a cough, Granny."

"This cough medicine has codeine in it," said Granny. "That's how it cures coughs—you fall asleep."

So he waited while she spooned the oversweet stuff into his mouth. He remembered that when he was little he liked it, but now it was way too sweet. It made him want to brush his teeth.

Up to his room he went, feeling just a little lightheaded by the time he got to the top of the stairs. And when he flopped down on his bed, the sudden move made his hand throb so hard that he almost fainted from the pain. He lay there wincing and panting for what seemed forever, refusing to cry. He finally worked up the gumption to get up and find a comic book to read but the light coming into the room wasn't bright enough to read well, and he didn't want the overhead light on because it would be too bright, so in the end he fell asleep with the comic book on his chest.

When he woke up he was lying on the comic book and his hand hurt even worse but differently, with the pain of deep healing rather than the pain of harsh injury. There was still light in the window but it was the dim light of a winter evening and he could hear the sounds of dinner being eaten downstairs. He must have slept for hours and he was hungry.

Pain or no pain, he had missed lunch and he wasn't going to miss dinner, too. He swung his feet over the edge of the bed, stood up and then sat right back down, his head swimming. He had apparently lost a lot of blood outside in the snow. But after a few more minutes sitting on the edge of the bed, he was able to stand up and walk rather feebly toward the door, leaning on things as he went.

In the doorway, though, he heard gales of laughter from downstairs and suddenly he wasn't hungry at all, or at least not so hungry that he wanted to go walking into the bright crowded kitchen with all the kids gathered around the table. Granny would make a fuss over him but the other kids would mock him and tease him and it just made him tired. He wanted to be alone, like an injured animal that crawls off into the deepest thicket in the woods in order to either bleed to death or heal.

He might have turned back into his own room but that wasn't where he wanted to go. Without naming his goal, he walked along the narrow hall to the back of the house and then slowly climbed the stairs to the warm place.

He hadn't spent much time there this year. Perhaps none. Perhaps he hadn't sat in this place since sixth grade. Or fifth. He didn't remember. He only knew that this was the sheltered place where he needed to go when he felt like he felt right now.

He sat down on the step where he had always sat, but now he was bigger and his body didn't fit into the place as it used to. It really *had* been a long time, and he was going through a growth spurt, Granny said, and his legs were so long they stuck out of the bottoms of his pants like Popsicle sticks.

He did not close his eyes because he never closed his eyes here.

Instead he let his gaze rest idly and unfocused on the wallpaper near the back stairs window and let the warmth of the place seep into him.

It came into him as it always did, in gentle increments with each throb of the heartbeat of the place. This time, though, the throbbing of the pain in his hand had its own rhythm that conflicted with the slower beat of the warm place, and it made him feel agitated at first, jumpy, restless. But then the warmth went to his hand and for a moment it actually burned, as if he had thrust his whole hand into a blazing fire and he cried out with the sharpness of it.

And then he was caught up into a dream. Not of flying this time. No, he felt himself sliding and slithering through a dark passage of cold stone, downward mostly, but he couldn't really see anything except shadows against a dull red glow that seemed to increase with each of his breaths and quickly fade. He would brush against the sides or roof of the passage and feel the chill against his crusty skin, but the chill could never get very deep because he had so much warmth inside him.

Then the cold rock opened up and he was in a large open cavern with stalactites and stalagmites and a different sort of glow, a deeper red. The air was very hot here, as hot as the pain in Michael's palm, so there was a sort of balance and it didn't bother him so much, it was just part of the place. He slipped among the stalagmites, feeling his body trail among them, bending easily around them, scraping on both sides but never injured. He had never realized how *long* his body was when he was in the dreams of this place, or how tightly and smoothly his arms could press up against his sides.

The underground chamber grew larger and brighter the

farther in they went, and the stalagmites soon ceased. Instead the floor under his feet, under his belly, was as bumpy and yet as smooth as the surface of boiling water, if you could harden boiling water into stone.

He came at last to a shore of an underground sea, only the sea was made of molten stone, seething and bubbling, smelling of sulphur. The blast of heat from the sea was worse than standing in front of Granny's oven when she had it really heated up to broil something. And yet instead of making him want to back away, to retreat to some cool place, it seemed to waken a fire inside him and he wanted to be inside it the way he wanted to plunge into a swimming pool on a hot August day. Not that the sea of molten stone would be cool, rather that the intense heat of it would bring this body the same kind of relief.

This body. What am I, when I dream like this? Not this boy, this weak walking boy clad in soft, easily sliced skin, not this cowering creature who slinks through the world creeping up back stairs and hiding from the laughter of his enemies.

Enemies. I have no enemies.

None who dare to show themselves, huddling little human.

Who are you?

I am the fire.

And with that thought, the body Michael wore in his dreams leapt up and spread its arms, its thin strong wings, and rose circling high above the sea of magma until he could sense, with senses he did not know he had, the roof of the great cavern, the crown of this bubble of air deep within the earth, and having reached the zenith of this dark sky he plunged down, straight down into the hot red sea and his mind turned white inside and Michael sprawled unconscious upon the stairs.

He became aware of himself again, stretched out across the steps, long and sinuous, his sleek feathery scales unperturbed by the wooden edges. His wings were folded up under him and his great jaws began to yawn.

No, that would be the other body, not this one. He stretched, and it was the arms of a boy that stretched. The hands of a boy that flexed, the eyes of a boy that opened.

It was dark, but it had been nearly dark when he had first crept to this place so that did not tell him how long he had been asleep. It couldn't have been long because Granny would have checked on him when the other boys finished dinner and, not finding him in his room, would have looked first in this place.

He rose to his feet and was surprised at how small and light he was. An hour ago he had thought himself rather tall and big; his man-height was coming on him these days, and he was taller than Granny, wasn't he, and almost as tall as Gramps?

He looked down at hands that were not wings and again he flexed his fingers and realized that the bandaged hand did not hurt at all. Not so much as a twinge. The only discomfort was the awkwardness of the thick bandage.

He brought the bandage up to his mouth to bite at the tape but then remembered that he had another hand and used those fingers to pry up the end of the tape and peel it away. Granny's thorough packaging was unwrapped in only a few moments and underneath it there was no wound at all, not even a scar. Only a few loops of black thread lying in his palm. He blew them away and there was then no way to tell which hand had been sliced.

Was this what happened when he plunged into the sea of fire? It made him whole?

You healed me?

But there was no answering thought as there had been in the dream. Just a faint buzzing, whirring, rushing sound.

Which Michael now knew with absolute certainty was not the sound of wind rushing past the standpipes and playing them like an organ. It came from inside the locked windowless room where a bright light shone though no one ever entered to change the bulb. It sounded like razors, like can openers, and he had to know, he had to see.

He was up the stairs in a moment, his eye trying to peer through the keyhole. The tiny slit he had made years ago was still there, and as before, it showed only dazzling light.

In moments he had the bed back from the crawl-space door and was through it. It was dark but he felt his way along the rafters, taking care to find the next one before taking his weight from the ones before. If there were spiderwebs or beetles he did not care; he was barely aware of the thick dust that rose from the rafters with each movement of a hand or foot. For one moment he thought he would sneeze but he held it in by holding his breath, for he did not want to set the house on fire.

Fire? I make no fire when I sneeze.

Who are you, who healed me? Whose body is it that I dwell in, who took me diving into fire?

There was faint light up ahead. Far ahead, the length of the house. It was a couple of lines of dim light, and when at last he got there he found that it was another crawl-space door, which was closed only by the same simple kind of latch as the door in his old attic room. He lifted the block of wood and the door opened easily at his push.

He was in the front room of the attic, the one that had the window and balcony overlooking the street. The only light in the room came from the streetlights outside—that had been enough to make the faint glow around the edges of the crawl-space door.

But he could still hear the noise from the locked room and there, opposite the window, was another door. This keyhole had not been blocked up—a bright glow shone plainly through it. And when Michael turned the handle and pulled, the door opened easily.

Four bright naked bulbs in ceiling fixtures made the dazzling light, and the razor sounds had come from five electric trains making their rounds along tracks that stretched completely around the room. The table surrounding the room even crossed in front of the doors so the only way into the room was to duck down under the table and come up the other side, in the midst of a miniature world of villages, train stations, trestles and tunnels, hills and farms and rivers and a distant sea.

Who had built this? Why didn't anyone ever see it? Why did they leave the trains running, with no one here to play with them?

In one corner of the room a mist seemed to gather. Michael watched it, fascinated. It was a cloud, he saw that now, emanating from the smokestacks of a tiny factory. No sooner had it formed than electricity began to spark from it. Michael felt his own hair standing up the way it did when you rubbed a balloon and held it near. The sparks crackled. A tiny bolt of lightning snapped from the cloud to a train track. There was a sharp cracking sound—miniature thunder. He could smell the ozone.

How was it done? He had never heard of a train layout with weather. A storm, of all things! No rain, but maybe that was coming.

The cloud kept jetting out of the smokestacks and now the whole ceiling was masked by it, so the light of the bulbs was dimmed. Lightning cracked here and there all around the room now, snapping down to the tracks. Each time the trains hesitated for a moment but then went on.

Michael caught a whir of motion out of the corner of his eye. He spun to look. A train? But the only train in that part of the room was nowhere near the motion he had seen.

He looked intently at the painted, lichened landscape and again saw movement as a dragonfly suddenly leapt upward from the ground near the mouth of a tunnel. It flew rapidly around the room, so Michael could hardly get a look at it. There was something wrong, though. It did not move like a dragonfly, really. It had the long tail but the wings were not a dragonfly's blur of translucence, they flapped like a bird's wings. Yet the skin of the tiny creature was as iridescent as a dragonfly's body, sparkling in the light, glimmering with each thread of lightning.

The creature did not shy away from the lightning, either. In fact it seemed drawn to it, darting toward each bolt as if it were drinking in the ozone that was left behind in the burnt air.

I know you, thought Michael.

"I know you," he whispered.

You don't know me, came the answer in his mind. You will never know me. You are incapable of knowing me, you poor worm.

You healed my hand. You took me flying with you and plunged me with you into the magma deep within the earth. "Thank you," Michael whispered.

In reply the tiny dragon lunged in the air just as a spark of lightning began to crackle downward and even though it happened in a mere instant, Michael thought he saw the dragon sparkle all over as if the lightning were inside it and it was the dragon that snapped downward to the electric track, leaving a trail of lightning behind it.

And it was gone.

The lights went out. The trains fell silent. Michael was in total darkness, surrounded by silence and the smell of ozone and another faint burnt smell.

You couldn't have died, thought Michael. After all these years that the trains have run in this room, and the lightning flashed, you couldn't have died on this very day when I first came here and saw you. It must be this way every time. You were reaching for the lightning. You must have reached for it, caught it like a surfer catching a wave, and ridden it down to earth. You must still be here . . . somewhere . . .

You are not really as small as the dragon I saw in this room. In all my dreams the one thing I never felt was that you were small.

But there was no answering thought. Only the gradually increasing light as Michael's eyes became accustomed to seeing in the faint spill from the streetlights outside the window of the front attic room.

Who built this room? There had been something, some mention, now that Michael thought about it, of Gramps's and Granny's father having electric trains—was it him, then? Yet how did he ever get a dragon to come here? He couldn't have made it. No man could make a living thing. The dragon was already alive, but it came here into the house and it has lived here all my life. I had the bedroom next to it. When I peered through the tiny slit in the keyhole, I was looking for the dragon.

When I sat in the warm place, I felt the beating of its huge, invisible heart. I felt its life come over me like a dream. I dwelt in its memories. It healed my hand.

What am I to this creature? A pet? A friend? A servant? A son? Its future prey?

Michael ducked under the table and left the train room,

closing the door behind him. He made his way back through the crawl space and emerged again in the bedroom of his childhood.

He went downstairs into the room he had been sleeping in and took all the sheets and blankets off his bed and carried them up the back stairs to his old room. He knew he couldn't sleep on the child's bed there, so he spread them out on the floor. He went back down and gathered all his other things—not much, really, just clothing and his schoolbooks and a few toys and games and tools. It took only three trips, and he had moved upstairs again.

Only then did he hear the noises of the kids bounding up the stairs to the second floor, the water running in the bathrooms, lots of chatter and laughter and a few complaints and whines. Now he remembered—there had been a dress rehearsal of the New Year's play, *As You Like It*. They must have covered for him—he had a couple of smallish parts, being too young to compete for the leads in a grown-up play. Granny must have thought he was sleeping and didn't let anyone wake him.

But now the rehearsal was over and everyone was going to bed and Granny would come looking for him, to see if he was hungry, to check on his hand.

He went to the head of the back stairs and started down just as Granny started up.

She looked down at the remnants of the bandage lying on the steps. "Why did you take it off?" she said. "That was foolish."

"It's all better," said Michael.

"Don't be absurd," said Granny. "It takes days for the wound to fully close, even with the stitches." She held out her hand. "Let me see the damage."

So he went down a few more steps, and she came up a

few, and he held out his hand to her.

"Don't be a goof, Michael," she said. "Show me the hand that you cut."

"This *is* the hand," he said, showing her the other as well.

She held both his hands palms up in hers and looked from one to the other, then up into Michael's eyes.

"What were you doing here?"

"I moved back into my old room," he said. "I want to live in my old room again."

"The bed's too small."

"I'll sleep on the floor."

"What happened to your hand, Michael?"

"I guess it wasn't as serious as you thought," he said.

"Don't be absurd. I should know how deep it was, and even if it was only a scratch it couldn't be healed like this. What did you do?"

"I came up to the warm place on the stairs," he said, "and I slept."

She looked in his eyes and perhaps she could see that he wasn't lying or perhaps she could see something else, something that forbade her to inquire more. Maybe she could see the dragon's eyes, just a glimpse of the dragon's eyes, looking out at her.

"I never came up here," she said softly. "After I was a little girl, and Mother sent me up to fetch Father for dinner, and I knocked on the door of his train room and he didn't hear me so I opened it."

"What did you see?" said Michael.

"What did *you* see?" she asked him in reply.

"Trains," he said.

"And?"

"Lightning."

She shuddered. "What did Papa do in there, Michael?"

"I don't know," he said. "He must have been very talented with . . . electric things."

"He was just an ordinary man. Rich, of course. Theatrical. He owned a lot of playhouses back in vaudeville days. But none of that should have let him create . . ."

"Weather," said Michael.

"You went inside," she said.

"It would be easier," said Michael, "if you gave me a key. I won't tell the other kids. I won't let anyone in. But now that I've seen it, you can't keep me out."

"It's dangerous," she said.

"So is crossing the street."

"That's an unbelievably inept analogy, Michael."

"I won't die in that room."

"Papa was only truly alive there," she said. "There were weeks when he hardly came out, and when he did, it was as though he was living in a dream. As though we weren't real. Only the train room was real."

"I know what's real," said Michael.

"I'll talk to Herry," she said. "To Gramps."

"I love you, Granny," said Michael.

"Because you think I'll give you what you want?"

"Because you're good," he said.

"If I were really good," she said, "I would move out of this house and take you with me and never let you come here again. If I really loved you."

"I'd come back," he said. "I grew up in the dragon's heart."

Tears came to her eyes. "Papa talked about dragons. It was part of his . . ."

"He wasn't crazy," said Michael. "They live in the fire. The fires under the earth are like home to them. And they fly the lightning. They soar into the storm and they search for the lightning and when they catch it just right they ride it down to earth."

"Don't tell me any more," she said. "You can't have inherited his madness. None of Papa's blood is in your veins."

"It's not madness."

"The house does it. Letting you sleep in the attic, I never should have done that."

"He came to the house because he loves the lightning and there's so much electricity here. In the theatre lights in the basement. And up here, in the tracks, the trains. That's all. It's not madness, it's real. He came up out of the earth because all the electricity called to him."

"How do you know this?"

"Because I've felt how he hungers for it. I felt it, too. That's what called me into the train room. That's what drew me, I know it now. He's all through this house. It didn't matter where you had me sleep. Once I felt his heartbeat here on the back stairs I knew him, Granny."

"And when was that?" she asked softly.

"The first day I came here," he said. "When you and Gramps took me up these stairs and told me I would live here forever. I felt his heartbeat as we climbed the stairs. That's how I knew that I was truly home. Because it was warm there. And I'd never been warm like that before."

"Why didn't you tell me what was happening to you?"

"I didn't know it myself until today. Until I said it out loud to you just now." He bent down—for he was standing two steps above her—and kissed her forehead. "I love you, Granny. I'll be safe here. I'll be careful. Don't be afraid for me. Look."

He held his hands out to her.

"He healed my hand. It really happened. He's looking out for me."

But even as he said it, he knew it was not true. Dragons don't look out for human beings. Dragon's don't care.

She pressed his hands against her cheeks. "God help us, Michael."

To which he had no answer. If God helps us, he thought, he does it through other people. It was you and Gramps who took me in when I needed a home—but maybe it was God who made you my great-aunt and great-uncle. It was the dragon who healed my hand—but maybe it was God who brought me to the house where the dragon lives.

Or maybe not.

"I'm hungry," said Michael. "Is there any dinner left?"

"Yes," she said, coming to herself again. "Yes, of course. I kept some of it warm in the oven for you. Shepherd's pie."

"Nasty stuff," said Michael, sliding past her, putting his arm around her, walking with her down the stairs. "I don't know why you work so hard to poison us with stuff like that."

"I saved you half a pie because I know how you love it," she said.

"Only half? When I didn't have lunch? What were you thinking?"

"Don't get smart with me."

"You want me to get stupid? I can do that."

"No, you can't," she said. "It takes *real* brains to do that."

It was an old joke between them, but it felt far more meaningful now. Almost portentous. But then, anything they said would sound that way, now that they knew each other's secrets. Some of them, anyway.

The dragon gargoyle on the house at 22 Adams pours water out of its mouth whenever it rains and it splashes on the cobbles of the garden, and in a bad storm it can soak the shoes of whoever is standing at the door. The house is so unusual—gothic amid Victorians, the garden cobbled and bricked, and the torrent of boys and girls running in and out of the house at all hours—that people drive from all over town sometimes just to see the Old Dragon's House.

None of them guess that every night in the back room of the attic the old dragon watches over the sleeping boy whose body is growing into one that someday he can use, someday he can wear, allowing him to emerge from the wiring of the house and bear a living body up into the sky, soaring once again on gossamer wings, his wyrmtail curling under him, seeking lightning in the storm so he can ride back down to earth. One ride per body, alas, for it burns up on the ride and shatters against the earth as the dragon within it plunges down into the earth.

But then, one ride on a single bolt of lightning is enough to keep a dragon going for a thousand years.

And the boy would love that moment when it came.

They always did.

JUDGMENT

by Elizabeth Moon

"Judgment" is a splendid tale of dragons, dwarfs, and myopic villagers who fail to read the heart of a protagonist whose destiny both torments and defines him. The fantasy credits of its author, Elizabeth Moon, include *The Deed of Paksenarrion* (originally published in three volumes) and *The Legacy of Gird* (originally in two volumes), as well as a number of short stories in anthologies such as *Sisters in Fantasy* and the *Chicks in Chainmail* series. She has written two books with Anne McCaffrey, herself a true dragon maven, in the Planet Pirate series, and a number of science fiction books. The first three of her Serrano novels have been reissued by Baen Books in a trade paperback under the title *Heris Serrano*. Moon's most recent work, *The Speed of Dark*, was released in January 2003 by Ballantine/Del Rey.

"That's odd," Ker said, picking up the egg-shaped rock. "I never saw a rock shaped like an egg before." It was heavy, like any rock, cool in his hand. Smoother than any rock he'd ever seen.

"You find rocks like that in the hills west of here, lad," Tam said. He sounded as if he'd seen many such rocks before. "Someone dropped it," he said, looking around as if he expected to see that someone. "Gnome. Dwarf. Rockfolk would have something like that. And what'd they be doing here, I wonder? Never saw them this near the village; they need rocky hills to live in."

"They wouldn't drop it, not they." Ker turned the rock, rubbing it with his thumb. Stories said the rockfolk had grasping hands that never let go what they held. "It's smoother than most rocks anyway. Like someone'd polished it."

"Carried in a pocket with a hole in it. A sack—"

"I reckon as it belongs to someone, then," Ker said, putting the rock back on the path. "Best leave it be."

"For someone to stub a toe on in the dark?" Tam picked it up, hefted it, ran a calloused thumb over the smooth surface. "You're right, lad, it is smooth." He put it down just off the path, near a brambleberry tangle. "Now no one'll kick it in the dark and call a curse on us for leaving a tripstone, but it's easy enough to find, if whoever dropped it recalls what way they came."

Ker nodded and walked on, down past the brambleberry tangle, taking the steps made by its roots and those of the yellowwood thicket, steps worn into hollows by the feet of those who went daily from the creek up to the cow meadows and back. Under his bare feet the warm earth turned cool, and then chill and damp as he neared the stream.

Tam followed; Ker could hear Tam's slower, more careful footfalls, the slight grunt as he came down the slope. Caution was in Tam's movements, in his words, as was proper for an older man, an Elder in the vill. Ker would not have worried about someone tripping on a rock in the path at night, though now Tam mentioned it, he knew he should worry. Others than humans used that path; the first humans here had found it bitten deep into the land, so that now the bushes and thickets towered over it, and here near the creek he walked between walls of fern and flowers. The people of light used it, and the people of shadow, singers and unsingers, and the people of earth, those of the law and those of the forge. A curse from any of these might bring desolation to humans within its each, and the curses of the Elders reached a long way.

Just beyond the old way marker, put there by no human hands in ancient times, he saw another of the odd egg-shaped rocks in the path. He made the sign to avert a curse. The rock remained. He stopped.

"Go on," said Tam from behind him, touching his shoulder.

"It's another one," Ker said.

"Another one what? Oh." Tam edged past Ker. "It's not the same color."

Ker had not noticed that; he had seen the shape only. Now he could not remember just what color the other one was. Stone colored, or he'd have noticed, but what color was stone? His mind threw up images of gray stone and brown, black stone and reddish yellow. This one was pale gray, speckled with dark.

"What if it is eggs?" he asked. "What if something lays stone eggs?"

Tam laughed, a harsh barking laugh. "What—you think maybe dwarfwives lay eggs?"

"I didn't say that." Ker stepped carefully around the rock. He wasn't going to pick it up this time. He'd averted a curse, or tried to, but handling things that might be cursed was a good way to catch bad luck anyway. He wished he hadn't touched the first one. "I only said—we found two. If they are eggs, what laid them?"

"They're not eggs. They're rocks." Tam bent down, picked up the rock, and shifted it from hand to hand. "This one's a little grayer. Heavier, not by much. Could be it has pretties inside. Some of them egg-shaped rocks over to

Blackbone Hill has pretties inside. Gems, or near as need be."

Ker shivered. Blackbone Hill had a bad reputation, for all that some claimed to bring burning stone and valuable gemstones out of it. Stories were told about what lay under Blackbone Hill, what bones those were. A dragon, some said, had been killed there for his gold, and others said the dragon had died of old age, and still others argued that the dragon had choked on magegold. Tam had always said the stories were fool's gold, that only rock lay under the grass.

"Was there as a youngling," Tam went on. Ker knew that; everyone in the vill had heard Tam's stories of his travels. "A long ways off, and not much worth the trouble, but for his pretties." He hefted the rock in his hand. "I've half a mind to crack this open and see if it's that kind. Had to trade all the pretties I found at Blackbone for food by the time I'd come home."

Ker shook his head. "What if it is something's egg? Bad luck, then, for sure."

"It's not an egg. Nothing lays stone eggs."

Nothing Tam knew of. Ker knew that he himself knew less than Tam, but surely even Tam did not know everything.

"We should ask somebody," he said, seeing Tam about to crack the rock egg against the old way marker that stood at the foot of the cut. The way marker came from the Elder People; it might be bad luck to break anything on it.

"Ask who?" Tam said.

That was the stopper. Tam knew more than anyone else Ker could think of; he was an Elder, but . . .

"Somebody," he said. "The singers, maybe?"

"Finders, keepers," Tam said, and his arm came down. The egg-shaped rock hit just on the edge of the way marker, and it broke open to show a serried rank of purple and white crystals.

"Pretties," Tam said with satisfaction. "Just as I thought.

Here, Ker—you can have one." He probed with thick fingers and broke off a single crystal spike, about the length of his finger from knuckle to nail. He held it out.

Ker felt cold sweat break out on his face and neck. He could not refuse a gift from his future father-in-law, not without risking a quarrel, but he didn't want to touch that thing, whatever it was. He whipped off his neck cloth, and took the crystal in that. "I don't want to risk breaking it," he said. It was partly true, but the partial lie made a bad taste in his mouth. For courtesy, he looked closely at the crystal. Cloudy purple, the eight facets glinting in the light, the point narrowing abruptly at the tip . . . it looked sharp, and he did not test it with his finger. Carefully he folded the cloth around it and tucked it into his shirt, snugging his belt so it wouldn't fall out.

Tam took off his own neck cloth. "Good idea," he said. "Best not break the pretties. They're worth more unbroken." He wrapped the fragments of the rock, and put them in his shirt. Then he started off, leading the way this time. Ker did not see the next egg-shaped rock until Tam bent over, halfway across the gravelly ford of the creek, and picked it up. He showed it to Ker—this one was greenish-gray, streaked with darker green—before tucking it into his shirt with a grin. "If this'n has pretties too, I'm set for a long time. It's easy to trade pretties for 'most anything at the Graywood Fair. I'll pick up the other one tomorrow or the next day."

No more worries about who might've dropped it, Ker noticed. He followed Tam into the village, turning aside to his mother's house as Tam went straight on to his own. He lifted the hearthstone that guarded their treasures, and laid the pretty beside the armlet of bronze, the bronze pendant with a flower design, the string of glass beads he would give Tam's daughter the day they were wed, and eight silver bits that would, at his mother's death, be his inheritance and pay his cottage fee.

Then he went to sit in the village square, holding the staff of his approaching marriage, and endured until nightfall the taunts and teasing of those who tested a bridegroom's will and temper. It was hard not to respond when Dran's daughter kissed him full on the lips, or Roder's son told everyone about the time he had eaten a woods pear so fast he'd bitten a grub in two without noticing it, then thrown up. But this was the way of it. Lin had spent her time sitting in the square and now it was his turn; as he had sat on the judicar's bench and watched her, so now she sat on the same bench and watched him for any sign of impatience, bad temper, or unfaithfulness.

When full dark had come, and no one more bothered him, he went home and slept as usual until—in the darkest hours of night—he woke with a start, staring about him, bathed in cold sweat. Fragments of a dream swirled through his mind and vanished. Lin's face. Flame. Darkness. A great roaring that was almost music.

His ears hummed with the noise, as if someone had smacked him in the head with a rock. He tried to lie quietly, breathe slowly, return to sleep, but the humming itched at his ears and quieted only slowly. At last he slept.

In the morning he remembered waking, but nothing of the dream except that it was unpleasant. Today he would again spend the hours until homefaring with Tam, and then sit in the village square in the evening. He rose, fanned the embers of the fire into flame, then fetched water to boil. Lin's mother, Ila, a guest in this house these five days, opened an eye and watched him, as his mother had guested with Tam for the days of Lin's testing and watched Lin. Ker measured grain into the pot, adding a pinch of salt from the salt-crock, then he left while the others rose. Tam was just coming out of his house.

"Guardians bless your rising," Ker said.

Tam grunted. "Guardians should bless my sleep instead. The water boils?"

"It boils," Ker said.

"Good. I'm hungry." Tam walked to Ker's mother's house, twitching his shoulders as if they hurt. Ker stood beside the door of Tam's house and waited, stomach growling, until Lin's little sister brought him a bowl of gruel and a small round of bread, lumpy and hard, the girl's own baking. Lin's would be better than this, he knew.

He ate it standing by the door, and the girl came to take away his bowl. He walked over to his mother's house, and waited until Tam came out, belching, his face red from the heat of the fire.

"Well, now, to work," Tam said. Today they would join the other men ditching a field near the creek, draining it. All morning Ker hacked at the soggy soil with a blackwood spade, careful not to strain it to the breaking point. Old Ganner, who'd died before Midwinter, had carved the blackwood spade years back, and traded it to Ker's father for a tanned sheepskin. Ker knew himself lucky to have it. Tam and the other men watched him as much as they worked themselves. No one liked ditching; it was hot, hard, heavy work that drew the back into tight knots, but the blackwood spade cut through the roots better than one of oak or ash.

Shortly after the noon break, Tam beckoned to Ker. Ker scraped the muck off the spade with the side of his foot and went to Tam's side. "Stay here, lad, and keep working. I'm going to check the cow pastures for us both," Tam said.

· Ker's head throbbed. He knew what Tam would do. He would try to find that other egg-shaped stone, and break it open for more pretties. His heart sank, stonelike, and he found no words.

"You have the shoulders for digging," Tam said. "It's young man's work." He grinned and clapped Ker on the shoulder, then turned away.

Ker stabbed the ditch with the spade, more in worry than anger, and the spade groaned. Sorry, he thought to the wood, and stroked the handle. He looked closely at the shaft, but the grain had not split. Blackwood, best wood, supple and strong . . . blackwood made good bows as well as digging tools.

Tam came back in late afternoon, his hands empty and his face drawn into a knot like Ker's shoulders.

"You didn't sleep much last night," he said to Ker.

How had he known? "I had a bad dream," Ker said.

"You followed a dream out through the dark?" Tam asked.

Ker shook his head, confused. "I didn't go out," he said.

"It was gone," Tam said, not naming it. Ker knew what he meant.

"I did not take it," Ker said.

Tam shrugged. "Someone did. Rocks don't walk by themselves."

"Maybe the one who dropped it," Ker said.

"Maybe. No matter. I have the other for pretties." His sideways glance at Ker accused, though he said nothing more.

They went back to the village then, and Ker spent another evening in the square, with Lin on the bench watching him and the young people standing around making jokes. Old Keth, Bari's mother, came and reminded everyone of the time he had spoiled a pot she was making, bumping her at her work. Lin's little sister reported that he had slurped his gruel that very morning, gobbling like a wild pig of the forest. He bore it patiently, as Lin had borne it when his mother told that Lin had made a tangle in the weaving.

That night he dreamed again: fire, smoke, Lin's face, noise. Again he woke struggling against that fear, and again his ears hummed for a time before he could sleep again. In the morning he knew he had had the same dream again, but still remembered nothing of it. That frightened him: To repeat a dream meant something, but he could not interpret a dream he could not remember.

That day he finished the ditch before it was time to sit in the square, and decided to cool off in the creek. Tam was talking to the older men in the shade of the trees. Ker waved, mimed splashing, and walked off to the creek. Upstream from the ford the creek had scooped out a bowl waist deep at this time of year.

Under the trees the sun no longer bit his shoulders, but the air lay still and hot. His feet followed the path as his mind cast itself ahead into the cool water. The scent of damp and fresh growth filled his nose, promising comfort. He came to the ford, where the water scarcely wet the top of his foot, and turned aside to the pool, stripping off his shirt and trews to hang them on the bushes to one side.

He eased into the water, murmuring the thanks appropriate to the merin of the creek, and splashed it over his head and shoulders. Something tickled his heart foot, then the other. Slowly he sank down in the water, crouching, until only his head was out. He had always loved the way the water's skin looked, seen from just above it like this. Its surface would have looked flat from above, but now, in the wavering reflection of the trees overhead, he could see its true shape, the grain of its flow. On his back, the current's gentle push, and between his legs the water flowing away downstream, past the village lands, beyond into lands unknown.

He let his eyes close and listened. No sound of breeze in the trees, no leaf rustle. Something moved on a tree trunk; he heard the scritch of claws on bark.

He had known Tam all his life. Cautious Tam, careful Tam, thoughtful Tam, perhaps not as wise as Granna Sofi, but then she was older, deeper in wisdom. Now he wondered if he knew Tam at all. And if he knew too little of Tam, what of his daughter Lin? If Tam could turn grasping, so late in life, would Lin draw back her hand from life-giving? Would she be a fist and not an open hand after all?

He wished his father had lived. He could not talk to his mother about this, not now. She had asked the ritual questions back before Lin sat in the square, and he had said yes, he was sure the Lady's blessing lay on Lin and on their union. He had been sure.

He was not sure now. He knew only that he woke each night in the darkest hours, after foul dreams, with strange music humming in his head.

He squeezed his eyes shut and sank below the surface. Cool water lifted the strands of his hair, washing away the sweat and grime. Cool water supported him everywhere. If he were a fish, he could live in this cool cleanliness always, in this silence. He opened his eyes underwater and watched tiny silver bubbles from his nose rise past his eyes. Air seeking air, its own kind. He was not waterkind or airkind, neither fish nor bird.

His lungs ached. He lifted slightly, rolling his head back to catch a breath, and blinked the water out of his eyes. Even as he heard a startled hiss, he saw them.

Two squat shapes, half the height of the men but not boys, stood in the shallows staring at him. One muttered at the other, no tongue he knew. Of course not: They were Elders, rockfolk Elders. He knew that from the tales, every detail of which came back to him in that instant. Squat, broad, long-haired, bearded, teeth like stone pegs, hands and feet overlarge for their height. Clothed in leather and metal. Armed with metal weapons. And angry. In the tales, the rockfolk were always angry, usually with a human who invaded their fastnesses or stole something from them.

He was aware of a chill from more than the water, and aware too of his own nakedness. His clothes . . . one of the rockfolk had them now, stretching and poking at his shirt with a finger he knew would tear it . . . yes. He heard it rip. That one sniffed at the shirt, and wrinkled a broad nose; it gave a harsh sound that might've been a laugh. The other answered in its language.

Then came the sound of someone else brushing through the bushes, crackling leaves underfoot, nearer and nearer. The two rockfolk looked at each other and vanished. His shirt fell to the water's surface, where the current took and folded it, then slid it downstream, slowly, rumpling over the shallows. Ker lurched forward out of the pool, back to the shallows, and made a grab for it. The wet mass resisted, and he yanked it up just as Tam broke through the bushes and stood on the bank scowling at him.

"Looking for another?" Tam asked.

"No, I was hot," Ker said. "I was in the pool . . ."

"You're not in the pool now. What have you got in that shirt?" Tam sounded almost as angry as the rockfolk had looked.

"Nothing," Ker said. He held it up, wrung out the water, and spread it. The rent was a hand long, a three-cornered tear.

"Something made that—" Tam came into the ford, looking around as if he expected to find another of the odd rocks, as if one might have fallen through that hole in Ker's shirt.

"It was the dwarf," Ker said. "Two rockfolk were on the

ford when I came up from the water. One of them had my shirt. Then I heard someone coming, and they were gone. My shirt fell into the water—"

Tam's eyebrows rose. "Gone? Where?" he asked. "I don't see any rockfolk." He looked around, then back at Ker.

"I don't know," Ker said. "They just . . . weren't there. Maybe it was magic."

"Maybe there weren't any rockfolk," Tam said, his voice hard. "Maybe that's why I didn't see them."

"I saw them," Ker said. "I came up from the water and they were there, in the ford, with my shirt—one of them poked a hole in it—"

"And you didn't say anything?"

"No. I couldn't think—"

"Mmm." Tam didn't say more, but Ker suspected he hadn't believed a word of it. He didn't know what to say, how to convince Tam that he had seen dwarves, and they had disappeared. "I think I need a soak too, lad," Tam said. "Best you get back to the village, now, and sit your time."

Ker nodded and fetched the rest of his clothes from the bush he'd laid them on. He put on the trews and draped his wet shirt on his head. He would have to put it on to enter the village, but it might be drier by the time he'd made it to the clearing. And he'd have to explain that rent to his mother. Would she believe him about the dwarves or would she be like Tam? Perhaps he could tell her simply that the shirt had gotten torn, and nothing more.

His mother turned the shirt in her hands, examining the ripped cloth, seeming to half-listen to his explanation. "I will fix it this evening," she said. "Don't worry about it." Ker felt guilty. Though he was almost sure that not telling everything was not the same as telling something untrue, that *almost* pricked him like a thorn.

He thought so hard about that, sitting in the square that evening, that he scarcely noticed what anyone said or did. The Elders said that lies ripped the fabric of the community, destroyed the trust between people on which community rested. Between him and his mother stood the not-telling about the rockfolk. Between him and Lin's family stood the lies Tam had told and Tam's grasping at what was not his. Like father like daughter, like mother like son. Did he want to be married forever to the daughter of someone like Tam . . . the daughter of Tam himself?

He stumbled home in the dark finally, more miserable than he had been since his father died, and lay down sure he would not sleep. At least he would not dream if he did not sleep.

Despite himself, he dozed off after a time, and woke to voices whispering in the dark, just out of clear hearing. His heart pounded; he lay still, trying to breathe quietly so that he could hear what they said. Dry voices, evoking the rustle of winter leaves crisped by frost and blown by wind, or the little streaked birds of open grassland in midsummer. The blurred edges of speech sharpened slowly; he could hear more and more . . . but he could not understand. He shook his head, blinked against the dark, but the voices still spoke words he did not know. Then he heard his own name, clear within the bird-sounds of the voices. Once, and then again, "Ker." And "Lin" and "Tam" as well.

Blood rushed in his ears; he lost the voices in its rhythmic noise. He shivered, suddenly drenched in sweat and cold. Voices that knew his name when he did not know their speech. That must be the Elders, but which race? The people of light were the Singer's children; they had singing voices. The people of darkness, once also of the Singer's tribe, had fallen away but retained their beauty, it was said. The rock-folk spoke loud and deep; the people of the law with almost mincing precision. None of these fit the sound he heard.

He sat up and peered through the dark at the hearthstone. It must be the pretty Tam had given him; that must be what caused this. He must get rid of it. He thought of throwing it in the creek, burying it in the woods.

"Fool!" came the voice, now in his own tongue. "Put it back."

Back? He tried to remember just where on the path Tam had picked it up—just this side of the waystone, yes—and the voice crackled like a fire as it said "No! Fool! Restore, restore . . ."

Restore what? How?

Above the hearthstone now, a blue flame danced where no fire had been laid. Behind it, the banked embers of last night's fire sighed and collapsed with soft puff of ash; the air chilled again, and the blue flame brightened. Ker could not take his eyes from it. Within it, a tiny shape he could not quite see clearly twisted and turned.

"Put it back together. Every piece. Make whole, make well. Else—" A blast of fear shook him, shattering his concentration, implying every disaster that could come to him and his family, his whole village.

Then it vanished, leaving only a blurry afterimage against the dark, and Ker lay back on his pallet, sweating and shivering, until the first dawnlight crept through the windows. He put the water on and started the porridge as usual. He would have to talk to Tam about this, and he had no idea how to say what he must say.

Tam came out looking even grumpier than the day before. "Guardians bless your rising," Ker said.

"Guardians should bless my sleep," Tam said, as he had before. That was not the ritual greeting. Was he also having bad dreams?

"Honored one," Ker began, then stopped as Tam rounded on him.

"Don't you start!" he said. "You're not my son-in-law yet." He strode off to Ker's mother's house before Ker could say anything more.

When Lin's little sister came out with his bowl of lumpy gruel and piece of bread, she shook her head at him. "Da's angry with you," she said. "What did you do wrong?"

"I don't know," Ker said. Did Tam still think he had taken that other rock from the brambleberry patch? The only wrong he knew of was keeping the pretty, but Tam had given it to him.

"Yes, you do," Lin's sister said, staring at him wide-eyed. "You have a liar's look. I'll tell Linnie."

That was all he needed now, for Lin to believe him untrue. If she didn't already, if her father had not convinced her.

"I do not know why your father is angry with me," he said. "That is the truth."

She shifted from foot to foot, staring at him. "It sounds true, but something is wrong. Da isn't sleeping well—we're all tossing and turning and when I asked him what was wrong, he said it was you. You are a thief, he said."

"A thief! Me?" That accusation bit like an ax blade. "I am no thief. I have taken nothing—" He almost said: It was your father, but stopped himself in time.

"That sounds true," she said. Now her face changed, crumpling into misery. "But Da—my Dad—he tells the truth."

Sometimes, Ker thought. Not always. He would not tell the child, though; a child's trust in a parent was too precious to risk.

"You must have done something wrong," the child persisted. "Or he wouldn't be angry with you."

"I will ask him," Ker said. "I will find out and make it right."

"Truly?"

"Truly. You will see."

"Lin is crying," the child said, then ducked back inside.

Ker took a long breath of morning air flavored with cooking smells, and struggled to finish his gruel and bread. It would be discourteous, an insult to Lin's entire family, if he did not finish the food. It lay in his belly like a stone. When he was done, he walked back to his own house and waited for Tam to emerge.

"We have to talk," Tam said when he came out. His eyes looked red as well as his face. His hard hand on Ker's arm felt hot as a cooking pot.

"Yes," Ker said. "We do." He didn't resist as Tam pushed him away from the house, toward the woods and then into them. Before Tam could say anything, Ker spoke. "It's wrong."

"What?"

"That . . . thing. That rock. With the pretties. It's wrong. You have to put it back together, fix it, put it back."

Tam snorted. "So you can just happen to find it and take it for yourself? Not likely, my lad. That's just the sort of sneaky lie I'd expect from someone like you."

"I had a dream," Ker said, ignoring the insult. "Three nights in a row, and last night I woke and heard voices, and saw a flame on the hearthstone . . ."

"You didn't bank the fire right, and it burned through. You're lazy as well as a liar, Ker. I've done my best by you, but you needed a father years ago to teach you right from wrong . . ."

The unfairness of this stopped Ker's tongue in his mouth. Tam went on. "It has to stop, Ker. I didn't say anything because I thought, it's not his fault, he's just a boy, he'll learn. But after that day on the trail . . . you sneaking back to find more . . ."

"I wasn't," Ker said. He could hear the tension in his own voice.

"Lying to me about your shirt . . . did you think I couldn't tell you were lying? Rockfolk tore it, you said, when there were no rockfolk to be seen. You had something in that shirt, something heavy, and when you heard me coming you threw it into deep water. I say it was the other rock. You found something, saw something . . ." Tam's voice carried complete conviction; he had convinced himself that it was all Ker's fault.

"I was hot," Ker said. He thought, but didn't say, that he'd been working a lot harder than Tam out in the sun. "I went to cool off in the creek. I saw the rockfolk and then they were gone. That's all." Even to himself that sounded sullen and secretive; he saw again in his mind the rockfolk in their leather, their great axes, their sudden disappearance.

"Last year I might've believed that, Ker. This year . . . this year I think you want my daughter and my pretties as well. Maybe my life."

"Your—Tam, what are you talking about?"

"Sitting outside my house putting a curse on my sleep, and then claiming you have bad dreams—"

"I didn't—"

"Whispering mean things, putting ugly pictures in my head. That's not what I want in a son-in-law, a witchy man, an ill-wisher, a doomsayer. I'm taking back my daughter's troth, and I want that pretty I gave you before I knew about you."

"But I didn't do what you think," Ker said. "It's the pretties—they send the bad dreams, I'm sure of it. That's why we need to put it back together, so it will stop doing that, so the village will be safe. That's what it told me."

"Pretty rocks don't give bad dreams," Tam said. "They don't talk in the night, or make a man see his children flayed and burning . . . bad things. Ill-wishers do that. You can't fool me, Ker, trying to blame all that on a rock. My Ila woke in the night and saw you sitting up by the window—easy enough for you to slide in and out, with your pallet right there." He made a chopping motion with his hand. "No daughter of mine will marry a man who sends evil dreams. Now—for the last time—give me that pretty I gave you, and understand the troth is broken. You have today to make your peace with your mother, for this evening I will tell the Elders why the troth is broken. It would be best for you if you were gone by then."

"Gone—?" Ker stared.

"Wake up, boy. Whatever dream of power you had is over. We will not tolerate an ill-wisher in this vill, not while I'm an Elder. If I were not a kind man, forbearing, I would kill you where you stand."

"But I didn't—"

"Enough. Come now, and return to me that which is mine." Tam's hot, hard hand closed again on Ker's arm, and dragged him back toward the village and his house. Ker stumbled along, his mind in a whirl of confusion.

The other men had gone out to the fields already, but two children and their mother stared as Tam strode along. Ker kept up now, but Tam still held his arm as if he might try to escape. At Ker's mother's house, he heard his mother inside chanting the baking rhyme.

"I can't go in now," Ker muttered. Men did not intrude when women were singing the dough up from the trough. Tam must know that. Tam merely grunted, glaring into the distance, and kept his hold on Ker's arm. Ker sneaked a glance at him. Tam's face, his ears, his neck, were all as red as if he'd worked all day in the hot sun. Was he fevered, was that the source of his wrong thinking?

When Ker's mother finished the chant, Tam cleared his throat loudly and called to her. "We men must enter."

"Come, then," she said. Tam gave Ker a shove, pushing him through the doorway first.

"What is it?" she asked. She covered the dough with a cloth, and wiped her hands.

"Get the pretty," Tam said to Ker, then turned to his mother. "I have broken the troth, Rahel," he said. "My daughter shall not marry your son."

"Why—what is it? What's wrong? Ker—?"

"It gives me pain to say this," Tam said, putting his fist over his heart. "Your son is an ill-wisher."

"No!" His mother gave him one frantic look, then turned back to Tam, her hands twisting in her skirt. "No, you're wrong. Not Ker. He's always been a sweet boy—"

"He lies," Tam said loudly. "He lied to me. He tried to steal. And he sneaks out at night to lay a curse on my sleep and give me bad dreams."

"I don't believe it," she said. "Not Ker."

"Three nights I've had of broken sleep, and voices whispering, and in the morning he is there to wish me well, with a look on his face that would curdle milk."

"Ker . . . ?" Again she looked at Ker, her face pale in the dimness.

"Get the pretty, damn you!" Tam roared. He seemed to fill the room.

Ker scrabbled at the stone and pried it up. The pretty looked smaller, dusty, in the room's dimmer light. He picked it up in bare fingers, and nearly dropped it again—it was so heavy and so very cold. He held it to the light for a moment; in the cloudy center he could almost see something, some tiny writhing shape. Did it really move, or did he imagine it?

"Give it to me," Tam said. Before Ker could comply, Tam

grabbed his hand and forced the fingers open. Tam's breath whooshed in, and back out on "Ahhhhh . . ." He took it and put it in his pocket.

"What is that?" asked his mother. "That thing—a rock?"

"Some rocks have pretties inside," Tam said. "They bring a good price at the fair, pretties do. I found such a rock when your son was with me. I broke it open, and gave him one of the pretties inside, because he was to be my son-in-law, and in token of the care I had for him. That was before I knew about him."

"I can't believe what you say," his mother said.

"It doesn't matter what you believe," Tam said. "I will tell the Elders tonight why the troth is broken. I told him, make peace with your family and then leave before that meeting. For I will not have an ill-wisher in this vill."

"But—surely Ker may tell his story . . ."

"If he is that foolish, he may. But who would believe a liar and a thief, someone who has put a curse on the sleep of my household? The Elders respect me."

"Ker, did you lie to Tam? About anything? At any time?" The look in her eyes expected *no* but though he had lied to Tam he could not lie to his mother.

"When he gave me the pretty, I did not want to touch it," Ker said. "I was afraid of bad luck. So that is one reason I wrapped it in my neck cloth, and I did not tell him that reason."

"That's not what I mean and you know it," Tam said. "I found you in the creek ford, hunting for more—"

"I was not," Ker said.

"Spinning that yarn about rockfolk," Tam said. "As if I couldn't see with my own eyes that you were alone, scrabbling in the rocks of the ford. No rockfolk upcreek or down, uptrail or down. Did they fly up into the air like birds?"

Ker's mother looked at him as if he should have the answer. "I don't know," he said to her; he knew Tam would not believe him. "They just—weren't there, after I heard Tam coming."

"Not a skilled liar," Tam said. "If you think to make your way as a storyteller, Ker, you must do better than that. But never mind—a self-confessed liar, a thief, an ill-wisher— I am going now, and you may tell your mother whatever ice-stories you wish before nightfall. They will melt by day, as all such do." He strode out of the house, and the heat of the day went with him.

"Ker, I don't understand," his mother said. In her face he saw lines he had never noticed before. "You know that lies are wrong . . ."

He could not bear it that she would think he was what Tam had said. "Please," he said. "I did not lie. Let me tell you about it."

She did not quite shrug, leaning on her work table. Ker told her all about that day—only a few days ago, it was. Finding the first stone, and the second and third, Tam's actions and his own feeling of dread, his unwillingness to touch the pretty. His nightmares, his awareness of Tam's unfounded suspicions, and finally—last night—his realization that someone—something—demanded that the broken rock be fitted together again, mended, and then restored to its former location. Tam's anger this morning, and his accusations, his refusal to believe the rock and its pretties were dangerous.

"It is like a tale out of legend," she said when he had fallen silent. "Strange rocks and frightening dreams and dwarves that say nothing but disappear when someone else comes. Tam is respected, as he said, a father and Elder, a man with knowledge beyond our fields. You are scarce old enough to wed, and you have admitted lying to him about your reason for not touching the pretty."

"It wasn't a lie," Ker said. "I just didn't tell him all. And I didn't steal anything, or curse his sleep. The rock did that."

"It was a kind of lie," his mother said. "Not telling the whole truth, and now see what comes of it. He can say truly that you were not always true. As for the rest, I believe you." She sighed, wiped her hands on her apron, and shook her head. "But will anyone else?"

His heart sank. "Surely they will. They have known me from my birth. They know I tell the truth. They know you. And even if they do not believe me—must I really go? Leave the village?"

"I think you must, Ker. Tam will not give you—nor any of us—peace until you're gone." She seemed calmly sure of this.

"They know me," Ker said again. It seemed impossible that this might make no difference. "Why do you think they will think I'm lying?"

"They know Tam better, or think they do." His mother picked up a hand-broom and swept the hearth where the ashes had spilled out onto it.

"I have to talk to them myself. It isn't fair . . ."

"Fairness is for the gods, Ker. We are not gods, to know for certain what is and is not fair."

"But if Tam doesn't put the rock back together, something bad will happen. Not just to him, to Lin and maybe the whole village. They should be warned." He was sure of it now, sure that his dream was right, that Tam was wrong about more than his own conduct.

His mother sighed. "It's you should be warned, Ker. You have never seen a shunning; you don't know . . . if you talk to them and they side with Tam we will both be shunned away."

"And if I don't, and the village burns or the rockfolk come

in anger? Will that not be my fault if I have not warned them?"

She sighed again, shaking her head. "It is the cleft stick, and we are fairly in the trap. For you are my son; what they judge you to be, they will judge I have made you. I tell you, Ker, it is never easy for a vill to choose a young man's story over that of a wise Elder. And it is a hard thing to be thrust out into the world alone at my age."

As he watched, she began to set in piles all their belongings, and Ker realized she meant to leave . . . for the smaller pile would fit in the packbasket his father had used to carry fleeces to market or in the basket she herself used to carry sticks or berries or nuts home from the wood.

Slowly at first he moved to help her, thinking ahead to what they would need if they were cast out. Food, clothes, cooking things, tools. Everything he touched brought memories of the one who had made it, and stabbed his heart with the possibility of loss. It must not happen. He must find the words to say, words to convince the others that he was right about the danger. He tried not to let himself think about Lin, about never seeing her again.

When the men came in from work that evening, Ker stood outside his house with his mother. Tam glared at him, even redder of face than in the morning. "I told you—" he began, but Ker interrupted.

"I ask the village Elders to meet," Ker said, as loudly as Tam. "Tam has a grievance against me, and I have my own words to say, a warning to give."

The other men looked at each other. For the first time Ker wondered if Tam had said anything to them during the day's work. How had he explained Ker's absence?

"After you sit your time?" Beryan asked, glancing at Tam. He was senior of the men in that group.

"No," Ker and Tam said together.

"I am not sitting my time," Ker said. "I abide the meeting."

"Not for long," Tam said, and strode away to his own house. The other men looked at Ker. He felt the force of their stares, but said nothing.

"At starshine, then," Beryan said. "Lady's grace on you, until." He turned away and the others followed.

Ker's mother set out a supper that Ker saw included most of the perishables in the larder. He tried to eat, but the food sat uneasily in his stomach. Outside the day waned, and he knew word of something unusual would have spread. He and his mother came out into the dusk and looked up, waiting until the first star appeared.

The oldest men and women in the village had gathered around the well, holding candles; others, he knew from murmurs and shufflings in the dark, hung back in the houses or between them. No one spoke to him. As Ker and his mother walked toward them, the Elders drew back into two wings on either side of the well.

"Guardians bless the hour," Granna Keth said. Her voice quavered.

"Guardians bless the air that gives breath," Granna Sofi said.

"Guardians bless the earth that gives grain," Othrin said. He was eldest of the men.

"Guardians bless the water that gives life," Ker's mother said.

"Guardians bless the fire that gives light," Ker said.

"Lady's grace," they all said together.

Then Othrin said, "Tam says he has a grievance against you, Ker, and you have acknowledged such a grievance. As he is elder, he will speak first."

Tam began at once in a voice thick with anger. His version of events now included a long-festering suspicion that

Ker had asked permission to court Lin only because he sought to rob her father . . . that Ker had always intended to go back and steal the special rocks, that Ker had learned sorcery while wandering in the woods and used it to harm anyone he disliked. A fatherless boy, Tam said, despite the care he and every other man had given him . . . such boys might easily find a way to learn evil things.

Ker could feel, as if it were a chill wind, the suspicion of the others as Tam blamed him for one mishap after another. Yes, he had been in the field that spring when Malo stepped on a rake, but no one then had blamed him. Malo had left his own rake tines-up and forgotten where he laid it. Yes, he had been at the well when two scuffling boys slipped and one cut his chin on the well-curbing, but their mother had scolded them, not Ker. Now she eyed Ker askance.

By the time his turn came to speak, he felt smothered under the weight of their dislike, their anger. Had they always disliked him? He was no longer sure.

He did his best to tell his own story, straight from first seeing the stones to the uneasy dreams, and his conviction that it was wrong to keep the stones, that they must be returned to their real owner.

"Wrong! Yes, wrong to have an ill-wisher—" Tam burst out. Othrin put out a hand.

"Let the lad say his say," he said.

Ker said it again, trying to make them understand, but Tam's obvious anger and certainty drew their attention.

"Liar!" Tam said finally. "I was there. I saw no rockfolk at the ford. The first rock I found was gone, and only you knew where it was."

"They were there," Ker said. "Two of them, this high." His hands sketched their size. "They had my shirt; one of them sniffed at it and poked it and it tore. It is all true, what

I told you then. I do not know how they disappeared—how would I know the ways of rockfolk?—but they did. You must believe me—you must put the rocks back, all the pieces together, or something bad will happen."

"Bad things will happen to a vill with a liar and an ill-wisher in it," Tam said. "A man who lies about one thing lies about all." Ker saw heads nodding. "A rock is a rock—look—" He showed the unbroken rock to the elders, who leaned closer; several touched it. A drop of hot wax fell on the rock, and Ker flinched. Tam went on. "It is easy for him to say that bad dreams woke him, but I tell you that he did not sleep because he was putting bad dreams into my sleep. Ill-wishing. There is the bad thing."

A low mutter of agreement, heads moving from side to side. At the back of the group several women turned their backs on his mother. His heart went cold.

"I did not . . ." he began, but Othrin held up his hand.

"It is not right that a young man not yet wed should tell the Elders what to do," he said. "You make threats as if you were a forest lord or city king, but you are a boy we knew from birth. Even if the rockfolk come here, I have no doubt Tam will restore to them their property, if indeed it is their property. They would have no complaint against us. As for the rock, it looks like a rock to me. It is shaped like an egg, but what of that? You all but accuse Tam of stealing and lying, when he is your elder and would have taken you into his family. It is not right." He looked around the circle of Elders, and they all nodded.

"Go out, Ker, and do not return. You are not of us any longer." He glanced again at the others, who nodded again. "And your mother as well. Like mother, like son; like son, like mother. Take her with you, liar and ill-wisher." He turned his back. The others turned their backs, until Ker faced a dark wall of backs. Only Tam still faced him, his red face almost glowing in the dark.

"Drive them out now!" Tam said. "They will ill-wish us all—"

"Not by night," Othrin said without turning around. "We are not people who would turn a widow and orphan out to face the perils of night, no matter what they did. But be gone by the time the sun's light strikes the well-cover, Ker. After that, it shall be as Tam wishes."

Ker and his mother walked back to their house in silence and darkness; the others had all gone inside and barred doors against them.

"Well," said his mother when they were inside, with their own door barred. She did not light a candle; Ker remembered that their few candles were in the packs already. "We must sleep, and rise early." Her voice was calm, empty of all emotion.

"Mother—" he began.

She put up her hand. "No. I do not want to talk. I want to remember my life here, before it ends forever."

That night Ker had no frightening dreams, but woke in the dark before dawn to hear his mother sobbing softly. "I'm sorry," he said into the darkness.

"It is not your fault," she said. "Not entirely. I could wish you had not lied even in so small a thing as leaving out one reason for an action. But if you are awake, let us go. I have heard the first bird in the woods, and I want to be long gone by daybreak."

They rose and felt their way to the bundles packed the day before, unbarred the door, and came out into the fresh smells of a summer night. Overhead the stars still burned, but less bright than in deep night. Ker could see the dark bulks of the other houses, the looming darkness of the wood, and the pale thread of path leading toward the fields. The dust was dew-damp under his feet.

He could not believe he was seeing his home for the last time, but even as he hesitated he heard a cry from Tam's house up the lane. Light blossomed behind the windows, around the door, and Tam's angry voice grew louder. Ker took a step back onto the path.

"Come," his mother said. "Come now."

Still he hesitated. And then Tam flung open the door of his house—outlined against the light inside—and yelled into the night. "Damned ill-wisher—he's still here, he's putting his evil on the village even now—burn him out! Burn him out, I say!"

Up and down the lane Ker saw light appear in windows and doors as men and women snatched up brands from their fires and waved them into bright flames.

"Come on," his mother said, tugging at his arm. Ker turned and stumbled after her as fast as he could under the load he carried. Behind, he could hear angry voices. As they reached the turn into the first field, he glanced back and saw that the twinkling brands were together in a mass near their house.

"We must go to the hills," his mother said. They had crossed the ford, stumbling on rocks that seemed to have grown all points in the darkness and now stood among the bushes that edged one of the grazing areas. "My mother's mother's people came that way; I will have kin-sibs somewhere in that direction."

"But it's the wrong way," Ker said. "That's the path the stones were on, that the rockfolk were on. We should stay far away from it and the curse they bore."

"If we see any stones, we won't touch them," his mother

said. "And we have none, so the rockfolk—if they were seeking the stones—should not bother us."

He was not so sure, but they had to go somewhere: They could not just stand here arguing. The smoke from their burning house trailed after them like an evil spirit. He could hear the villagers yelling in the distance; they might pursue. His mother started off and Ker followed, bending under the load as they climbed away from the creek and back onto the trail.

By afternoon they were beyond the vill's farthest cow pastures; taller hills loomed ahead. The well-trodden path had thinned to a track scarcely wide enough for one. When they came to a little dell with trees arching over a spring, Ker's mother left the trail and went down to it. She sat down in the shade with a sigh. Her face sagged with weariness. "We will sleep here," she said. "It has been too long since I walked the day away. Go and find us some firefuel, Ker, while I sing the water."

Ker shrugged out of the packbasket's straps and leaned it against a tree. He paused to take a drink from one of the waterskins they had filled the day before, then left everything with his mother and climbed back to the trail and looked around. Back down the trail, a narrow fringe of trees and shrubs they had passed a handspan of sun before. Far in the distance he could just see a smudge of smoke where the village lay. Ahead the woods in the dell widened up the slope to meet the trail ahead. That was closer, and he'd be coming downhill with the load.

He walked up the trail, light-footed now without the load on his back, and turned aside where the scrub met the trail. He found a rocky watercourse, now dry, though the trees overhead indicated water somewhere underground. Tiny ferns decorated cracks in the gray rock. One delicate-petaled pink flower hugged the ground just below that ledge. All the rocks were rough, gray, blocky; none were egg-shaped. Lodged against one of the rocks was a tangle of sticks, all sizes and all dry. He pulled a thong from his pocket and bound them together. Working his way down the dry creek-bed, he found here a branch that he could break over his knee, and there another flood-tangle.

As he neared the dell he heard his mother moving about, but no more singing.

"I'm coming," he called, just in case.

"Come, then," she said.

He worked his way slowly toward her, the bulky bundle catching on vines and undergrowth. Just above the spring a rock ledge jutted from the watercourse, flood-worn to smoothness. Here was another tangle of sticks—a quick flood, he thought, must have dropped it before the water could push it over the edge. It looked almost like a house of sticks. Perhaps some animal—? He bent over awkwardly and picked them up. Blackwood, yellowwood, blood oak, silver ash. Odd. He hadn't seen any blackwood or silver ash uphill. But they burned well; he carried them in one hand as he found a way down and around the ledge into the dell.

After a meager supper of bread wrapped on sticks and cooked over the fire, Ker sat watching the coals as the fire died down. No need to bank the fire; they would be moving on at dawn in the morning. His mother, tired out by the day's walk, had already fallen asleep, warded from the night's chill by their blanket. He was tired too, drained by all that had happened. His head dropped forward on his chest, and he dozed.

———

Pain shocked him awake, stinging blows to his face; he heard his mother cry out and struggled up from sleep to find himself facing a blazing fire and four rockfolk as angry as any in the tales. Two held his mother, and two more confronted him. His cheeks burned with the slaps that had wakened him.

"Where are they?" asked one. His voice could have been rocks grinding together.

Ker blinked sleep out of his eyes. "What?" he asked. Another slap.

"You stink of them," the dwarf said. "Do not lie. You have held what we seek: Where are they?"

He realized what they meant. "I don't have them," he said.

"Who does, then? Where are they?"

He hesitated, and the other one slapped him again. Again his mother cried out. "Don't hurt her!" Ker said, suddenly as much angry as scared. "She's my mother—"

"She is not hurt," the first one said. "She is scared."

"Ker . . ." came his mother's voice.

"Don't hurt her," he said again, surprised to hear his own voice deep and firm. "It's not right."

"It was not right of you to steal what was not yours," the dwarf said.

"I didn't," Ker said. *It was Tam* hovered behind his lips, but he stopped himself. Tam had been unjust to him, but he would not help that ill seed grow.

"But you know what we seek. How do you know, if it was not you who took them?"

Ker glanced at his mother. The whites of her eyes glinted; he could not read her expression as the light of leaping flames came and went across it. Which was worse, to betray Tam to the rockfolk, or see his mother frightened . . . hurt . . . dead?

Another slap rocked his head, more bruise than sting. "Who?" the dwarf demanded.

"What will you do to that one?" Ker asked. His mouth hurt; he tasted the salt that meant his mouth was bleeding.

"It is not for me to bring someone else into trouble."

"Ha!" The dwarf facing him straightened. Standing upright he was taller than Ker sitting down, but not by much. Firelight glinted on the metal in his harness; he looked strong as a tree. "You invade our lands, steal our patterans for firewood, despoil our spring, and you worry about getting someone else in trouble? You have enough trouble of your own."

"But the trail is open to all . . . I thought," Ker said. "And what is a patteran?"

The dwarf grunted. "The trail, yes. So the treaties ran, from the days the first men came here: The trail is for all, folk of the air and folk of the forest and folk of the rocks. This is not the trail. The trail is there—" a thick finger pointed upslope. "This is not the trail. You took our patterans— our trail markers—for firewood—"

Ker remembered the curious shape of the "flood drift" he'd found on the rock ledge; his face must have shown that memory because the dwarf nodded sharply. "Yes. Leaving aside the other, that is a thief's action. And you have polluted this spring—"

"We did not," Ker said. "My mother sang the blessing."

The dwarf cocked his head. "Did she now? And does human woman not know that such a blessing sung by a woman must not be heard by a man, and sung by a man must not be heard by a woman?" He looked across at Ker's mother, now sitting slumped between the other two rockfolk. She said nothing.

"I left so she could sing it—to gather firewood," Ker said. "I did not hear it."

"And you took our patteran."

"I didn't know it was a marker—a patteran," Ker said.

"What matters that? You took it. If not for your fire, and

your snores, which made you easy to find, we might have gone astray from the path our comrades left for us. But we found you, and you have knowledge we seek. So, human, let us come back to that; if indeed you did not take our treasure, why do you bear its smell? Who took it? Where can this person be found? For if we find it not, and quickly, great peril falls on all this land."

Ker believed that. Between his dreams and the rockfolk, he believed absolutely in the certainty of some dire fate.

"I will tell you," he said. "But you must not hurt my mother."

"That is our business, not yours. Yet I say that it is not our habit to harm human women. Or human men, if they do us no harm."

With a last glance at his mother, Ker told the story yet again. "I was coming back from the cow pasture with an older man, the father of my betrothed," Ker said. "I saw a strange rock in the path . . ." He told about the egg-shaped rocks, about Tam's reaction to the second and third rock. "He said it was like rocks from Blackbone Hill."

"Blackbone Hill! Your people travel so far?"

"Most do not, but he had, he said, when he was young. And he had found round rocks with pretty crystals inside, he said, and he wondered if this might be such a one. So he—he broke it on the waystone. It had pretty things inside; he gave me one."

The dwarf growled something Ker could not understand. Then: "Fool! Idiot! Stupid child of dirt and water! On the *way marker!* Tell me, is this person accounted a simpleton, one with scant mind?"

"No . . . he is an Elder."

The dwarf stared, busy brows raised high. "This man is what you call wise?" Then he scowled. "I do not believe it!

No one who has been to Blackbone Hill could fail to know the dangers of such things."

"He said they fetched a good price at the fair." Curiosity finally got past fear. "What are they, those rocks?"

"Rocks." The dwarf turned away and tipped out the packbasket. Pots clattered onto the ground. "Is it in here?"

"No! I gave it back to him," Ker said. "I told you—" The dwarf paid no attention, pawing through the pile . . . skeins of wool twisted on wooden knitting needles, his mother's spare skirt, two aprons, his spare shirt and trews, his winter shoes, last year's straw rosette from above the fireplace, the jar of bread starter, the jar of lard, the waterskins, the sack of beans. Those hard, stubby fingers probed through the pile, found the bracelet and tossed it aside, found the silver bits and paused.

"Where came these? Did you sell that piece of rock for them?"

"My father," Ker said. "He had many sheep and sold their fleece; over years, he saved that much."

"Where is he?"

"Dead," Ker said. The dwarf grunted.

"Tell me more. This person gave you a piece of the . . . the broken stone. And you did what with it?"

Ker told the rest, while the dwarf stared at him out of shiny black eyes.

"You put it under the hearthstone? Near a fire?!" From the tone, that had been the worst place to put the pretty. Ker nodded.

"And then?"

"I had dreams. Bad dreams." The dwarf nodded.

"Yes, yes. It is dangerous to put such near fire."

"But you said it was just a rock," Ker said. The dwarf grunted again; Ker saw his boots shift a little on the ground. "I don't understand," Ker said. "I mean, I understand that if it belongs to you—to the rockfolk—then you must have it back. But why is it dangerous to put it under a hearthstone?"

"You ask too much," the dwarf said. He looked at the others, and began talking in a language Ker had never heard before. Soon they were arguing—or so it sounded—waving their arms and stamping their feet. Ker wondered if he and his mother might escape unnoticed and glanced across at her, but she was sitting slumped, her head in her hands. The argument died down finally, and the dwarf who had been talking to him turned to him again.

"You have a problem," the dwarf said. "It is that you have the scent of . . . of what we seek about you. And you travel on the Way. And you have *nedross* words."

"*Nedross?*"

"Rock is *dross* or *nedross*. *Dross* does not crumble; it is rock to trust, grain pure throughout. *Nedross* rock cannot be trusted, even if it looks solid and pure in grain: It fails. It is—" he paused, searching, "not truth."

Ker felt this as another blow. "I am not lying," he said.

"The words you speak are not whole," the dwarf said. "You know more you do not say."

His mother shifted slightly; the dwarf holding her said something that sounded like rocks grinding and the one facing Ker nodded. Then he spoke again to Ker.

"This is who to you?"

"My mother," Ker said. Did the rockfolk have mothers? Would he understand at all what mothers were to humans?

"Mother is one who birthed you?"

"Yes." Much more than that, but that was the beginning.

The dwarf left Ker abruptly to the hold of the others and went to his mother. Ker started to move, but the ones holding him tightened their grip. It was like being held by rock.

"No smell of dragonspawn," the dwarf said, facing Ker's

mother. His hands were clasped behind his back, near the handle of the dagger thrust through his belt. His voice was slightly softer, speaking to her. "You never touched this thing . . . but you know something. What do you know?"

"I don't know what you speak of," Ker's mother said. "I saw a pretty piece of crystal that Tam said he had given Ker, and he wanted it back."

"Tam. Tam is this one who picked up the stone and broke it? Tam is where?"

"In the vill—the village you call it. Ravenfield, we say," Ker's mother said. Her face, across the fire, was patched with moving light and shadow. Ker could not read her expression. Her voice sounded tense, even angry. "He is an important man in the village, is Tam Gerisson. And he drove us out— drove us out for nothing. For nothing, I say!"

"Your son did not say that." The dwarf looked back at Ker, scowling. "I said you were not telling all you knew." Then again, to his mother, "Whose words are *nedross*, your words or those of your son?"

"Ker is a good boy," she said. "It is not for the young to condemn their elders or to bear tales of them."

The dwarf's clasped hands shifted, the fingers of one spreading and then folding again around the other. He spoke in his language, and a dwarf Ker had not noticed before moved into the firelight carrying wood, and put it on the fire. The fire leapt higher, giving more light. He turned back to Ker's mother.

"So this is why he told us not more of this person Tam? Because in your folk the young must respect the old?"

Ker's mother nodded. "The young are hasty; the young do not understand everything. So they could make trouble, not understanding, and they must not spread tales of wrongdoing, especially not to strangers. The Lady commands peace."

"But you?"

"I am a widow, a mother, and of the same age as Tam Gerisson. I can judge the rightness of my own words, and I can bear the load of shame or sorrow if I misspeak."

"And you say—" the dwarf prompted.

"I say that Tam planted falsely from the beginning. I say he tricked us, lured my son into plighting troth with his daughter, gave false gifts, lied and plotted to fashion an excuse to send me away."

Ker felt his jaw drop in shock. He had never imagined his mother saying anything like this. "No!" he said. His mother ignored him and went on.

"Ker does not know this, but years ago I turned aside Tam's offer of marriage. He was a lightfaring man, I thought, and I married Ker's father instead, for he had been steady in his affection since we were children. Tam must have held anger against me, though he pretended friendship . . ."

In the brighter light of the fire her face looked intent, determined.

"Was he selfish, this Tam?" the dwarf asked. "Hungry for power among your people?"

"Not in seeming. We do not esteem selfish men," his mother said.

Ker stirred. The dwarf whipped around as if he had seen that slight movement.

"What is it?"

"Granna Sofi said Tam became an Elder younger than others. He had the knowledge from his travels . . ." Ker said.

"So he did," Ker's mother said. "I had forgotten. His oldest children were scarce hip-high. It seemed reasonable, though, because he did know so much. He had often advised the Elders."

"And your husband?"

"He tended the sheep of our people," she said. "He died out on the hills in a storm. He fell and hit his head on a rock."

"Tam had just become an Elder," Ker said. If his mother was telling all about Tam, he had no reason not to tell what he remembered. "He came to tell us the news, and he offered friendship. He said I would be like a son to him, and he a father to me."

"He said he would not hold against me that earlier refusal," Ker's mother said. "He said he would care for me as for a sister. After that, he taught Ker as his own son in the lore of field and woods."

"Not sheep?" the dwarf asked.

"He was not good with animals," Ker's mother said. "He did not like them, nor they him. Barin Torisson took over the village sheep herd, and Ker learned the arts of planting and harvest. I gave his father's shepherd's crook to Barin for an extra share of wool."

"And for this Tam gave what?"

"We shared the village harvest. Tam never failed to bring our full measure of grain." Ker saw the sparkle of tears in his mother's eyes, and her head dropped suddenly. "He must have held that anger close, so long . . . I was afraid, at first, but then all seemed well, until Ker and Tam's daughter saw each other."

"Saw—?"

"As man and woman, not child and child, sister and brother," his mother explained. Ker had not thought about Lin for hours in the shock of leaving. Now he let his mind wander back to those first hours in which he had seen her truly, not as one of the gaggle of village girls, not as Tam's daughter, but as herself. An individual. A person someone might desire and marry and live with. Suddenly she had seemed wreathed in light, set apart from the others. And on that same day she had looked at him, recognized him as himself. While he still stood, staring, amazed at what was happening, she had spoken his name, *Ker*, and it had reverberated through his whole body.

Everyone knew marriage meant joining a family, a lineage, an inheritance of body and mind and soul. But beyond that was the delight of a pairing that worked—fit neatly in all respects as in body. Mere liking was never enough—for as the Elders said, in the spring of youth all maids liked all men and all men liked all maids—but desired in addition to the other criteria.

"The flower of love is the children thereof, but the fruit is peace, harmony, contentment in the whole village," his mother said to the dwarf, as she had told him often. A good marriage enriched everyone; a bad marriage impoverished everyone with the tensions it brought.

"Dwarflove is not like that." The dwarf grinned suddenly, showing those square yellowish pegs. "It is that we find grain match, and of gems those most desired. Dwarflove is blending of the rock, as when fire mountains melt rock into liquid fire."

Ker could not imagine that. The blending he understood was root into soil, or water into root: the growth of green things, flower and fruit.

"But no matter," the dwarf said. It was as if he had never grinned. "It is not the time to speak of love, but of judgment and justice. It is our saying that you go to this man, this Tam Gerisson, and bring back those things of which we spoke, with or without his consent. Bring him also if you can."

Ker felt a cold gripe in his belly. "I can't," he said. "We were banished. If I return, they will kill me. What good will that do?"

"If you do not return and fulfill this task," the dwarf said. "*We* will kill you." He fingered the ax handle in his belt.

"It is your rock," Ker said. "Why can you not get it for yourself now that you know where it is?"

The dwarf glowered, then shook his head. "You humans! You know nothing of the matter, and yet you will give orders. The Singers say we are hasty, and men say we are greedy, but in all the world none are so hasty and greedy as humans."

"I didn't say—"

"Be quiet." The dwarf's expression stopped the words in Ker's throat. He sat as still as he could, stone-still, and waited. Finally the dwarf heaved a gusty sigh, and shook his head. "It is not good for the Elders to mingle with humankind, so our wisest say. For where there is no mingling of blood in families, there comes mingling of blood in battle, and we would not begin a war without cause. For this reason, we ask humans to deal with humans, when needs must."

"But why? What is the need? And why didn't those other dwarves just come into the village and talk to Tam? Why did they vanish when he came near?"

"Were you not listening? Have you stones in your ears? You had seen them already: one human already, and I misdoubt they knew you were there until you rose from the water. We are not suited to seeing in water, we rockfolk. So one had seen, but there was no need for two to see. And you had the scent of dragonspawn on you—"

"Dragonspawn . . . you said that before, but you said rocks—"

The dwarf muttered what must have been a curse from the tone. "The scent of what we seek, I mean. Have you no words that mean different things—is there not a food you call dragoncake?

"Yes . . ." Ker remembered the village dragoncake, centerpiece of Midwinter Feast. "But—I was in the water. Water washes off scent—"

"Not this scent, not to our noses. Touch it but once, and you bear that scent to the end of your days. Faint, yes, if it is but once, and yet it marks the one who touches it forever."

Ker shuddered. The dwarf nodded.

"You see, now, why this matters. It is worse than that, for the one who handles such carelessly for long, and someone who desires many . . . they are ill luck for those who do not know how to master them."

"I thought at first," Ker said, "that it was some kind of egg. That it might hatch—" Even now he wouldn't mention Tam's comment about dwarfwives laying eggs.

"Men!" The dwarf spat into the fire and a green flame shot up. "Can you do nothing but think of that which should not be spoken and bellow it aloud? Be quiet, now."

Again Ker sat silently while the dwarf paced back and forth between him and the fire.

"It is ill, very ill, to speak of some things outside the fortresses of stone," the dwarf said finally. His voice was softer, still gruff but almost pleading. "It will be worse for you and your mother and every one of us, if the wrong ears hear certain things, or the wind carries the tale to certain lands I will not name. You must trust me in this. In time, perhaps, you will know of what I dare not speak. Now—now you must retrieve those stones, to the last splinter, and bring them to us, before . . . before trouble comes."

"They *were* eggs, weren't they?" Ker said, hardly above a breath in loudness.

The dwarf threw up his hands. "O powers of earth! Save me from this insanity!" He leaned close to Ker then, his strong-smelling breath hot on Ker's face, and murmured into his ear. "Yes, fool, they are eggs. Dragon's eggs. And full of dragonspawn, as your dreams tried to convey. Every crystal splinter holds one, and every unbroken splinter can transform into a dragon if nothing stops it. A hundred, two hundred, a thousand dragons from one egg, do you understand? Those eggs were a thousand and three years old, given into the care of my great-great-uncle straight from the mouth of the dragon himself—"

"Males lay eggs?" Ker asked in a normal voice, forgetting in his curiosity the need for quiet. Quick as a snake's tongue, the dwarf clouted him across the head. He had his dagger in his other hand; he had moved so quickly Ker had not seen him draw it.

"Fool! Idiot! Be quiet before you get us all killed." He sat back on his heels, then twisted to look at Ker's mother. "Madam, speak to your son! If you have any of the proper powers of a mother make him be silent—"

"Ker, please," his mother said. "Please just listen."

Ker nodded, and the dwarf heaved another sigh before going on. "We must be more careful," he said. In his own tongue he spoke to the others, and three of the dwarves trotted away from the fire, up toward the trail. Then he turned back to Ker. "Man, if you try to run I will kill you myself with great gladness and your mother's heart will be reft in twain."

"I will not run," Ker said. "I would not leave her."

"Thanks be for that," the dwarf said. The dwarves holding Ker let go his arms and walked away; he could not hear their footsteps, and once they passed beyond the bright firelight, they disappeared into the darkness. The remaining dwarf watched Ker, and ran his thumb along the side of his dagger with an unmistakable intent. For a time there was no sound but the crackle and hiss of the fire as it burnt lower, and then the dwarf spoke in a low voice.

"It is a trust, a trust between the firefolk of the mountains and my folk of the rocks. No land could sustain all the firefolk that might be born if they all came hatchlings from the egg, and nothing now in the world can prey upon the great ones, do you understand?"

Ker nodded without speaking. He did not understand what the dwarf meant by all this, but he did understand that the dwarf's patience had worn to nothing, and the dagger blade, naked in the dwarf's hand, glinted in the light that ran blood-red along it.

"For ages of ages, we rockfolk have had this trust, and for ages of ages the firefolk have not numbered more than the land could sustain. Some say of us—the Treesingers would say of us—that we and the firefolk are one in power-lust and greed, but this is not so. The hatchlings, aye: The Young of every race are hasty and quick to grab and snatch. Human younglings, I have no doubt, run about and take more than they can use." He turned back to Ker's mother. "Is it not so, mother of a man?"

"It is so," she said.

"Age brings long sight and steady thought," the dwarf said. "The firefolk live long—even longer than we rockfolk, as long as the windfolk perhaps—and the firefolk in their age hold mountains in their care, mountains and valleys and the lands around. They have no wish to despoil what they love."

Ker opened his mouth to say what he knew of drag-onkind, but the look on the dwarf's face stopped him. He wanted to say: But they are wicked, greedy, vicious; they are misers who heap up stolen treasure; they prey on travelers. Like dwarves. He did not say it.

"Long ago they made pacts with us rockfolk, for we know the ways of stone as they know the ways of fire, and between us great magics wrought protection for both their younglings and the world. Stone only can stand against such fire; only rockfolk can withstand the pressure of their desire to be free. They enter the bodies of those who touch them,

bringing the fire of their ancestors but no wisdom, for they
are young and full of foolish ambition. They grow, feeding
on their host's body and spirit, until the host is consumed
and all but dragonet itself: greedy for power and wealth,
proud and lustful."

"I had dreams," Ker said. "Something trapped in the
crystal. When I woke up I saw a blue flame, a shape, danc-
ing, and then the banked coals went cold."

"And you touched it with bare hands—"

"It felt cold."

"It found no host in you. Perhaps in truth you are
drossin, as the rockfolk are, for the spawn cannot take a
drossin host without its consent. Yet from what you say, one
or more found a host in this Tam. You say his face was red,
and his touch hot: This is indeed the way humankind reacts
when filled with dragonspawn."

"So it's . . . eating him?" Ker's gut twisted as he thought
of it. Would it be like maggots that sometimes infested the
sheep?

"Not exactly. Changing him. When it's grown as far as
that host permits, it moves to another. To another of the
same household, often. This man has many children?"

"It would go into *children?*"

"Indeed. For it takes time and more time to mature to its
next stage."

Lin. Whatever was in Tam would get into Lin, would consume her, change her. Ker forgot his earlier concern, that she
had inherited her father's clenched fist. It was not Tam; it was
the dragonspawn inside him, and Lin—he could think only of
Lin, his Lin, corrupted and consumed by dragonspawn.

"I have to go," he said abruptly, and stood. The dwarf
swung a massive fist and knocked him down with a blow to
the chest.

"Stay. I am not finished."

"You want me to go. I want to go." Ker could feel his heart pounding. "I have to save her—"

"Save who?"

"Lin. My—Tam's daughter—the girl I was to marry—"

"Ker, no!" That was his mother, across the fire. "She may already—"

"It doesn't matter. I have to—"

"You have to find and return the stones and fragments," the dwarf said. "That is what you must do. Anyone already harboring a dragonspawn is beyond your power. Only a dragon can deal with such a one."

"But if she isn't—" Ker could hear his voice rising like a girl's.

"Take her away, if you can. But I do not think you can." The dwarf shook his head.

"If they do not kill me first, I will," Ker said.

"If you rush in to save a girl, they will kill you," the dwarf said. His voice now held amusement. "By Sertig's hammer, I find myself where you were but an hour agone. You cannot go without being killed—not in this mood—so you must not go until you see sense."

"I won't rush in," Ker said. "I'll be careful."

"And why do you now think being careful will work, while before you did not?"

Ker could not answer that, but an idea came to him. "If you would show me how to do that—what the others did— to not be seen, then I could get in and out and no one would know."

"It is not something for humans to learn," the dwarf said. "It is born in us. But perhaps we can help without that." He pulled from his pocket a gray cloth about the size his mother draped over the dough trough. "This is not a way to be unseen, but a way to be unnoticed, if someone moves quietly and quickly. I do not know if it will work on you, but we shall see."

He draped it on Ker's head; for an instant the fire seemed to blur, then his vision cleared. The dwarf leaned close. "Get up and walk around the fire, very quietly, until you are near your mother. Say nothing. When you are beside her, speak to her."

Ker stood; he was stiff from sitting so long, but he moved as quietly as possible. When he looked at his mother, she was looking where he had been, not at him. He spoke, then, and her head turned sharply. "Ker! I didn't see you move! Are you leaving, then?"

"Yes—very soon, now." He looked back at the dwarf.

"It is only deception, and not as strong on you as on us; I could see you easily. But then, I knew about it. Stay close to hedges and thickets, cast no shadows into someone's eyes, and you may pass unseen." Or may not, the dwarf's expression said. "Rest a little," the dwarf said. "You will need your rest." That, as if he and his fellows had not broken Ker's sleep in the first place. But under that commanding gaze, Ker lay down. When the dwarf shook him awake, dawn was gray to the east. "You had better go now," the dwarf said. "Take this—" he handed Ker a flattened lump. "It is food, and will give you strength. And whatever you do, do not trust one who might have the dragonspawn already, no matter who it is."

⬥━━⬥━━⬥

The journey back went swiftly, for it was mostly downhill and Ker had no burden to carry. The dwarf's food brought him fully awake with the first bite and lent speed to his feet.

He moved cautiously as he came into the vill's pasturelands.

No one watched the cattle grazing in the upper pasture; Ker knew where the herdsmen rested, and no herdsmen lay there. No one watched the sheep in their meadow; half had strayed into the hedge where the rustvine grew, which no shepherd would allow, for the thorns that tangled the fleece. Ker wondered at that, for it meant the shepherd had been away for hours. He took the sheep's path to the stream, to the shelving bank where the sheep drank. Here the water swirled in, clean and clear, but there was no ford and no path on the far side.

The water cooled his feet, and he waded upstream to the women's bathing pool, alert for voices, half-hoping he would find Lin bathing alone and could speak to her. No voices. He came out into a little glade, the grass dry underfoot and followed the women's path back to the village. He saw no one, heard no one, until he was very close, close enough to see through the fringe of vines at the wood's edge. The blackened ruin of his mother's house, burnt to ash and scorched stone hearth, lay between him and the rest of the village. It still stank of the burning.

Now he could hear voices, many voices and one angry voice louder than them all. He could see Tam in the middle of the square, yelling, and the other adults talking. The men should have been in the fields at this time of day, and the women in houses and gardens, or at the well, but all the people seemed to be there milling about. Ker watched, trying to hear what they said, but he could not. He wondered what had happened.

"You have to!" Tam yelled louder than before. "I know more! I have power!" He raised a fist.

Ker edged around one house and then another, working his way toward Tam's. If they were all in the meeting arguing, perhaps he could get in and out with the eggs before someone saw him. At the corner of Granna Sofi's garden, he looked across at Tam's house. Its only door faced the square, but two windows looked out on this side. He had only to cross the garden with its clusters of pie plant and redroot, and climb in through the window. If no one was inside.

He dared not look to see if Tam's family were all in the square; he was too close. Even with the dwarf's cloth, someone might notice him. He could see safely out of Granna Sofi's windows though, and she had a back door. He eased through it, blinking as his eyes adjusted to the darker room, pulled off the cloth, and took two steps toward the front of the house before he realized that Granna Sofi was there staring at him, her mouth open. She lay on a narrow bed, propped on pillows.

"You . . ." she breathed in her quavery old woman's voice.

"Please," Ker said, not even sure what he was asking. Don't raise an alarm. Don't be afraid. Don't turn your back on me."

"You came back," she said. Her voice rasped.

"Yes. I have to do something."

"You said something was wrong with Tam," she said. He looked more closely at her, with the way she lay, with the shape of her legs and the color of her skin.

"Granna Sofi, what is it?"

"You were right," she said. "He has changed. He has become something else."

"I know. I have to stop it—"

"You cannot stop it. He will kill you. He killed me because I spoke against him."

"But—" *But you're alive,* he thought, even as her eyes sagged shut and her last breath rattled free of her ribs. He saw then that her legs were broken, that great bruises marred her arms. Ker made the signs to send her spirit away in peace, and looked around for the necessary herbs. There they were, wrapped in a twist of sourgrass, as if the old woman had known she was going to die that day. Perhaps she had. He shivered, and laid the herbs on her eyes and mouth, at her head and feet.

When he looked out her front window, he could see Tam clearly, the red sun-burnt face and arms, the fierce expression on his face. He could feel the waves of heat that came off the square. Tam's wife, Ila, stood beside him, and she too looked ruddy under the sun, her yellow hair blazing with light. Around them at a little distance stood the others of the town, children at the back, peering between the adults.

It must be now. He hurried out Granna Sofi's back door, and quickly stepped across the first row of plants, then the second, and then he was flattened against the wall of Tam's house. He listened a long moment, hearing nothing from within. Tam continued to harangue the villagers from the square. Ker tried not to listen, as he would have tried not to swallow filth, but some words leaked through his ears anyway.

He must do it. He must enter the house as a thief, and as a thief he must steal away Tam's treasure, both the dragon's eggs and the daughter. He turned and climbed in through the low window. As before, his eyes took a moment to adjust to the dimness. He reached for the cloth to take it off, and realized he'd left it in Granna Sofi's house. He moved aside from the window and stumbled against a bench, and then in an instant he was wrapped in someone's arms and a hot mouth pressed against his, and the voice he had long dreamed of said, "Oh . . . you came back . . ."

Lin. He freed his mouth and said, "Lin. I have to do something."

"Yes—you have to kiss me. Oh, Ker, I've been so unhappy—" She clung to him and he could feel every sweet curve of her body. They had never been this close; he had dreamed of being this close. "Take me away, Ker; take me away with you! I want you, I want you forever."

He had never imagined that she would choose him over her father's will. He had expected to have to argue with her, persuade her.

"I will," he said. "But first I have to do something. Help me, and then we'll go—"

"No, let's go now," she said, dragging him toward the window.

"No, Lin, it's important—" He pulled back far enough to see her clearly. Lin with her yellow hair inherited from her mother, her clear eyes, her creamy skin . . . now flushed with passion, with love for him.

"What, then?" she said, clearly impatient. "If Da finds you here, he'll kill you—maybe both of us. We have to go—"

"In a moment. Lin, where does he keep the rock eggs, the ones with the pretties—"

"You're going to steal his pretties?" Her voice rose, then hushed quickly, and she grinned at him. "What a sweet vengeance, Ker. I hardly dared think you could think of that—"

"Under the hearthstone?" he asked, turning toward it. The dragon had told him he would feel the pull of the dragonspawn, but all he felt now was Lin's nearness and his own body's response.

"Some of them," she said. "But not all—" And with a gesture very unlike the girl he'd known, she pulled open her bodice to show him the purplish crystal spike hung from a thong around her neck, nestling between her breasts. His heart faltered, then raced.

"Lin, no! Take it off! It will hurt you!"

"Take it off? I will not! Da gave it to me, to make up for sending you away. It's the one you had; I'll never take it off."

"But Lin, they're dangerous!"

"Ker, don't be silly. It's a rock, a pretty rock. How can it be dangerous? The only dangerous thing here is Da, if he finds us. Here—I'll show you the others—" And she lifted the massive hearthstone as easily as Ker would have lifted a hoe, and scooped up two whole egg-shaped rocks, and a handful of shards. "This should be enough."

"We have to get them all," Ker said, and his own voice sounded strange to him. Where had Tam found another egg? He looked around and took a cloth from a hook near the fireplace. "Here—put them in this. We shouldn't touch them."

"They don't burn," Lin said, but she gave him what she held, then reached down for the other shards. As she did, the banked fire went out with a last hiss, and Ker saw the glow of her skin against the dark hole, and all at once her hand seemed clawlike, the nails talons. When she looked up at him, his stomach clenched at the expression on her face . . . exultant, hungry, eager . . .

"Is that all?" Ker asked. "Are you sure?"

"My father was right," Lin said with a giggle that froze his heart. "You are a greedy thief, aren't you?"

He could say nothing. He was robbing her father, though it was not greed, and he had no way to explain it. Not to the girl whose skin shone in the dim room. He wanted to tell her everything, but the dwarf's final warning stopped his tongue. That and his fear.

"Come now," Lin said, moving to the window. "I don't mind if you're greedy. I'm used to that in a man. I know you'll provide for me—"

"Lin—" What could he say? What he had most feared had happened already; he could not prevent it; he had come too late. He could not go with her, wherever she was going; he could not stay here.

"Come *on*, Ker," she said, reaching back to grasp his arm and tug at him. "We need to leave now. We can find a place later, and—"

He moved, hardly aware of moving, following her out through the window, across the garden again, behind Granna Sofi's house toward the next garden, the next house. Behind them the crowd in the square gave a concerted gasp. Lin did not look around, but Ker did.

Above the square hung a shadow of light, light condensed into form, form overwhelming light. The shape writhed, growing until it filled the air above the square, brightening more and more. Ker paused, terrified but fascinated. What could it be? What was Tam doing? Beneath that light, Tam looked up, and the other villagers edged away, pushing at the children behind them.

"Ker!" Lin's voice, from the edge of the village, near the ashes of what had been his house. "Come quickly! Before Da sees us!"

Light squirmed in the air; shifting colors flowed over the crowd, then faded. Tam's face paled; his mouth opened; his hands spread as if to push the light away. Heat pressed down, heavy, inexorable. Something crackled; Ker looked across the crowd and saw a ribbon of flame leap up the thatch of Othrin's house and spread. Those nearest turned, opened their mouths to start a warning. With a roar two other houses burst into flame, then a third. People screamed; Ker could see their mouths open, but only the roar of the fires sounded in his ears.

Pain stung his hands. He looked down and saw the cloth wrapping of his burden browning like toast over coals.

He ran. He ran without thought, without plan, away from the heat, away from the light, straight into the woods on no path at all, blundering into trees and stumbling over briars until he fell headlong into the stream. Steam hissed away from his burden; the blackened cloth fell to pieces. His hands opened; water flowed between his fingers, cooling, soothing. Under the water he could see the stones: two whole, one broken, a heap of shards.

Behind him in the village fire raged; he could hear the roar, the crackling; he could hear screams. Acrid smoke spread through the trees. Overhead, thunder boomed in the cloudless sky; lighter light departed. Shaking, Ker got to his feet in the shallow water, took off his shirt, and wrapped his scorched hands, then fished the stones and pieces out of the slow current and waded downstream to look for a place to climb out.

When he came around a turn of the stream, Lin stood on the ford waiting for him. She looked flushed and lovely, her hair curling around her shoulders, her body the shape of every man's dream. She smiled at him.

"We don't have to worry about Da now," she said. "We can go back. You can be an Elder—"

"No," Ker said.

"Well, then, we can go somewhere else. With Da's pretties we'll have enough to start a new place—" A little breeze blew a lock of shining hair across her face; she tossed it back, the gesture he remembered from their childhood.

"No," Ker said.

"You're not running away," she said. The smile changed, reshaped into a mask of anger. "Don't think you can take what's mine and run away from me, leave me again!" Her hand reached for the crystal she wore, and he could see in her all that he had seen in her father. "Give them back then, thief!"

The words echoed, throbbing in air that once again thickened into light incarnate. He had a momentary image of Lin consumed in light, rising into its maw.

She was gone. The strange light was gone. On the ford stood a man dressed in such finery as Ker had never seen or

imagined: brilliant colors, glossy fabrics, feathers and lace . . .
he did not even have the words to say what he saw. The man
stood in a shaft of brilliant sunlight that pierced the over-
arching trees, and the smoke filtering through the trees
flowed around him.

"I believe," the man said, "you have something of mine."

Ker tightened his grip on his bundle. "It belongs to the
rockfolk," Ker said. "I do not know you."

"To the rockfolk." A dry chuckle, thornbush scraping on
stone. "I suppose that is one way of saying it. Are you then
returning it, or are you the thief she called you?"

"I am not a thief," Ker said. "I am taking it back to them."

The man stared at him until Ker coughed on the smoke
blowing through the trees, and then the man shrugged and
blew away, as if he had been smoke himself. Ker struggled
out of the water, and made his way up the trail, coughing
now and then as the smoke eddied past him.

Over the first rise, the same man stood by the path,
leaning on a tree. "You might fare better if you had a
horse," he said.

"I have never had a horse," Ker said.

"A walking stick, then," the man said, and held out a
trimmed length of wood with the bark still on. "You have a
long way to go."

"It is ill luck to take gifts of strangers," Ker said.

"It is ill luck to refuse gifts of dragons," the man said, and
as before he blew away . . . but this time into the thickening
of light, which condensed into a shape the size of a hill. Green
as the man's coat on the back, and yellow as the man's shirt
underneath, clothed in shining scales that shimmered from
one color to another. Ker gulped, swallowed, and stood still.

"Mortals," said the dragon. The dragon was not looking
at Ker, but up into the air as if talking to it.

Ker took a step forward up the trail, and the dragon's great eye rolled toward him. He stopped.

"You interest me," the dragon said. A long flame-colored tongue flicked out of its mouth and touched Ker on the forehead; he felt it as a bee sting, hot and then sore. "I taste my children on you, but not in you. I taste dwarf on you. Perhaps you tell the truth?"

"I—I am," Ker said. Sweat rolled down his face; heat came off the dragon as off a rock wall on which the sun has lain all day. "They sent me to bring these back—" He shifted the burden in his hands.

"It is . . . difficult," the dragon said. "They do belong . . . there." The dragon sighed, and the grass before it withered and turned brown at the edges. For a moment the dragon's eye looked down its snout, then it lifted its head. "Lowland life is so fragile," it said, as if to itself. Then to Ker: "Approach me."

With the dragon's eye on him, he could not disobey. He took one step after another, until the heat beat against his face and body.

"What do your people say of dragons?" the dragon asked.

It was impossible to lie. "My people say dragons are wise," Ker said. "And greedy, treacherous, and cruel."

"My people say humans are stupid," the dragon said. "And greedy, treacherous, and cruel. Which is better if one must be cruel: stupid and cruel, or wise and cruel?"

In the worst of the nightmares, Ker had never dreamt of holding a conversation with a dragon. "Wisdom is good," he said, trying for caution.

"Wisdom alone is useless," the dragon said. "Wisdom without power is wind without air . . . it can do nothing of itself." Ker said nothing; he could think of nothing to say. The dragon twitched his head. "And power without wisdom is fatal. Power without wisdom is a mad bull running through the house." The dragon focused both eyes on Ker. "A fool should have no power, lest he bring ruin with him, but a wise man must have power, lest his wisdom die without issue. So which are you, mortal: fool or wise man?"

Something more than his own life hung on his answer, Ker knew, but not what it was. "I try to be good," he said.

The dragon vented flame from its nostrils, over its head. "Good! Evil! Words for children to use. Can fools ever bring good, or true wisdom do evil? No, no, little man. You must choose: Are you fool or wise man?"

"Anyone would choose to be wise, but it is not possible to choose," Ker said. "Some are born unable to become wise."

Something rattled off to his right; Ker glanced that way and saw the tip of the dragon's tail slithering across its vast hind leg.

"You interest me again," the dragon said. "So you would choose to be wise if you could be wise?"

"Of course," Ker said.

"And of what does wisdom consist?" the dragon asked.

Ker could think of no answer for that. He knew he was not wise; how then could he know what wisdom was? Finally he said, "Only the wise know."

"Does beauty know what beauty is?" the dragon asked. "Does water know wetness, or stone hardness?" Its head tilted so that one great eye was higher than the other, and both looked cross-eyed down its snout at Ker. His mouth went even dryer than before. Scaled eyelids slid up over the dragon's eyes for a moment and dropped back down, leaving that penetrating gaze even clearer than before. Ker's stomach twisted; eyelids should not move like that. "Surely not," the dragon said, hissing slightly. "Nor the blue of the sky know its blueness, nor the green of grass its greenness."

A throbbing silence followed; Ker could find nothing to

say. He glanced around, trying to think of something, anything, that would free him from the dragon's gaze, and saw that its tail now lay between him and the trail back, a narrow but steep ridge. He was trapped in the dragon's circle.

"I will tell you," the dragon said finally, "what wisdom is, if you will promise to become wise."

"How can I promise that?" Ker blurted in a panic. Sweat ran down his ribs, and dried in the heat of the dragon's breath.

"Small beings can have small wisdom," the dragon said. "And small wise beings are better than small fools. Listen: Wisdom is caring for afterwards."

"Caring for afterwards . . . ?" Ker repeated this without understanding.

"After action, afterwards," the dragon said. "Choose the afterwards first, then the action. Fools choose action first."

Ker opened his mouth to say that only fortune-tellers could know what would happen, but fear stopped him: Would he really argue with a dragon while trapped in its circle?"

The dragon's snout edged closer, nudged him. He staggered back: A dragon's nudge was like a blow from a strong man. Or a dwarf.

"You see," the dragon murmured. "You do know."

He didn't know. He didn't know anything except that he was surrounded by large lumps and ridges of dragon and too afraid to shake or fall down. He closed his eyes, expecting searing flame or rending teeth, and tried to think of the village as it had been, before Tam found those terrible eggs . . . of Lin before she had been invaded . . . of his mother, who now waited out on the hills in a hollow with a spring and a handful of rockfolk.

Cool air swirled around him, rose to a gale of dust and leaves, then stilled. He opened his eyes. No dragon. No strange light in the air. He blinked. A streak of dead grass, scorched, where the dragon had breathed that tongue of fire . . . and new grass, growing quick as a flame, brilliant green against the charred ground. At his feet lay the walking stick he had refused before, now sprouting incongruous flowers and leaves.

Ker looked up and around and saw nothing of the dragon, but he had seen nothing of the dragon before. Cautiously, he picked up the stick in his free hand. At once, strength flowed back into his limbs. He felt rested, strong, as if he had just come from a full night's sleep and a full meal. The scent of those flowers filled his nose. He took a step and stared as the land blurred around him, reappearing when he put that foot down. A league, two leagues, had fled behind him. Already he could see the hill where his mother waited with the rockfolk.

One more step and he was there, standing above the dell and looking down into it with eyes that saw through leaves and wood to where his mother sat knitting, while the rock-folk snored. The ones who should have been watching the trail slumped near it, also snoring. The little camp looked orderly and peaceful; someone had put their scattered belongings back into the packs. Probably his mother; he could not imagine the dwarves being so helpful. Somewhere a bird called, and another answered. Ker looked at the walking stick. Flowers and leaves had disappeared, leaving it bark-covered once more.

Ker came carefully down the slope into camp; his mother looked up and her face brightened but she said nothing.

"I'm back," he said.

"What happened?"

He did not know how to tell her; he was not sure exactly what had happened.

"Why are they sleeping?" he asked instead. His mother shrugged.

"I know not. Only that at noon the light changed and

they all fell into sleep. I would have slept, but their snores were too loud and I was worried . . . did you bring Lin?"

"No." Ker leaned the walking stick against a tree; the tree's foliage thickened. His mother stared at him.

"What happened? What is that? How did you come so soon?"

"I don't understand," Ker said. "It was a dragon—" He could say no more; exhaustion fell on him like a sack of wet grain, and he slumped to the ground. In a moment, his mother was at his side. A long drink of water, a hunk of bread smeared with jam, and he struggled up again to sit with his back against a tree. She handed him his spare shirt, and he put it on. He tried to tell her everything, but how could he say what he did not understand?

The rockfolk roused suddenly, their snores cut off in an instant. Their eyes opened; they sat up and stared at him.

"Why are you here?" asked the leader. "Why did you come back before you had finished?"

"I brought you what you asked for," Ker said. He nudged the wrapped bundle with his foot.

"You could not have gone so far so fast—" the dwarf broke off, staring now at the bundle. He muttered in his own language, and two of the others approached, one drawing a thick leather bag from his pack and opening its mouth. The first unwrapped the bundle gingerly, and revealed the same egg-shaped rocks, the same shards. He reached out, touched them, turned them over. Then he glared at Ker. "How did you do this?"

"Do what?"

"They're dead. They're all dead. What did you do to them?"

"I did nothing," Ker said. He couldn't see any difference in the rocks and shards, but the dwarves clearly did.

"These can't be the same . . . you could not have traveled so fast . . ."

"It was the dragon," Ker said. They all stared at him now. "It—gave me a walking stick. It helped me."

Now they stared at the walking stick, and the thick growth of new leaves on the tree overhead.

"You talked to a dragon and it *helped* you? It brought you eggs to carry?"

"No." His head ached now, sudden as if someone had hit him again. "Let me tell you—"

"Go ahead."

He told it as well as he could and they listened without interruption, though some of them muttered softly in their own tongue. When he finished, with "And then you woke up," the questions began. What was the dragon's name, and how big, and what color, and what had it done with Tam and the villagers and Lin? Ker said "I don't know" over and over.

"You cannot know so little," the dwarf said. "You were there! You say you saw these things, and yet—"

"Don't bully him," his mother said. "You're as bad as Tam, you lot." She glowered at them, and to Ker's surprise they gave way. "What would he know of dragons? Do you think they give their names away to anyone?"

"Rarely," drawled a new voice. Ker twisted around to see the same elegant man lounging on the slope above, a stalk of sweetgrass in his mouth. The dwarves drew into a huddle, eyes wide. The man lifted one shapely eyebrow. "Frightened, stone-brethren? Lost something? It would have been wise, would it not, to have told me before I heard it from others? Before I had to reveal myself, to undo the harm that came from that loss?"

One of the dwarves burst into speech in their tongue, but the man held up a hand. "Be courteous; these human folk have not your language nor mine. Speak as they can hear."

"We weren't sure," the dwarf said. "Not at first. We thought—"

"You hoped you could retrieve what you lost before I learned of it, is that not true?"

"Yes." The dwarf scuffed one boot against another.

"So this human—this idiot, this fool, I believe you called him—has proved more wise than you, has he not? He, not you, retrieved the lost. You sent him to do it, knowing it was perilous—"

"It was his fault in the first place," muttered one of the dwarves.

"You accuse him of thievery?" the man said. "You think he slit the carrybag and filched the eggs in the first place?"

"Well . . . no. Probably not." The dwarf looked down, hunching his shoulders.

"You know they seek life," the man said. "My kind always do. Whoever carried them grew careless, I have no doubt: drank deep and slept, as you slept today, or set the carrybag on sharp rock, and so they fell free, to be found by something or someone they could use." He sighed. "I should remember that ages are long for you, stonebrethren, and a trust passed from generation to generation can be a trust weakened."

"We didn't mean—" began the first dwarf, but his voice trailed away as the man looked at him.

"Intentions . . ." the man said slowly. Then he looked at Ker's mother. "Madam, what does a mother say about intentions?"

"Meaning to never mended a wall," Ker's mother said. "Not meaning to drop it never patched a pitcher."

"So wise a lady," the man said. "This must be your son." Now he looked at Ker, and it seemed that behind his mild brown eyes red flames danced.

"He's a good boy," she said.

"He's an interesting man," the man said, in a tone of mild correction. "He may become wise one day. We shall see." Now he looked at Ker. "What of you? What do you see in all this?"

Ker's throat tightened, but he forced words past the tightness. "You are not a man," he said.

That elegant figure laughed. "True and true: what then, am I?"

"A dragon."

"Perhaps. Perhaps merely the shape a dragon sends to talk to those who cannot bear the sight of dragons. For if the shape be the thing, then this shape of man cannot be a dragon, nor—" The man was gone; words hung in the air as the light condensed once more and a very visible dragon sprawled on the trail above, its head lying aslant on the slope to the dell. "Nor can this be a man's shape. But if some essence, not the shape, be the thing, then either the man's shape or some other could be dragon."

"Lord dragon," one of the dwarves said, coming forward past Ker. Ker noticed that he was paler than usual. "If you permit us—"

"I do not," said the dragon. "Be still, rockbrethren; we will talk hereafter." There was in that a chill threat. Ker and the dwarf both shivered, but the dragon was looking at Ker. "You remember we talked of wisdom . . . what would a wise being say of these who lost somewhat of value held in trust and did not warn the owner that it was lost?"

"You ask me to judge them?" Ker said. He glanced at the dwarves, now standing motionless as if the command to be still had turned them to stone.

"I ask your opinion only," the dragon said. "I am capable of judgment; it is my gift."

"I do not know the ways of rockfolk," Ker began. The dragon's eye kindled, and he went on hastily. "But these had cause to hate and distrust us—me and my mother—and instead they listened and did not harm us."

"You bear their bruises on your face," the dragon commented.

Ker shrugged. "I bear them no malice for it," he said. "They were frightened; they thought I might have stolen those things they sought, and that danger would come of it."

"They sent you into danger," the dragon said.

"Yes, but—" The dwarves' reasons now seemed like excuses, as he'd first thought. Even so he wanted no part of vengeance. "They did not force me; when I thought of Lin I wanted to go."

"To save a friend."

More than a friend, but he did not think the dragon would care for a correction. "Yes. And these dwarves were trying to make right what had gone wrong. They wanted to restore what was lost. I think they are honest, but too frightened—of you, I suppose—"

"Oh, yes, I am frightening . . ." The dragon rolled its head and inspected its own length. A cloud of steam gushed from its mouth, warm and moist, smelling of baked apples. "And so fear is their excuse, is that what you would say? But you . . . you were not frightened enough to give me what you were not sure was mine. Are you then braver than the rockbrethren?"

"No," Ker said instantly. "I'm—I was scared. I am scared. But I had to do it anyway."

"Hmmmm." That vibrated in the rocks beneath their feet; the trees trembled. "So, you make no judgment against them for the harm they did to you, by loosing such dangers on you and your people, and then by striking you, and then by sending you into danger?"

"I am not the judge," Ker said. The dragon's eyelids flipped up and back down again, and again Ker felt sick at his stomach.

"You are more clever than you seemed at first. Remember what wisdom is?"

"Care for afterwards," Ker recited promptly.

"Yes . . . and have you a care for afterwards here? What about *their* afterwards?"

Ker looked at the dwarves. They all looked at him with an expression of resigned defeat.

"If I were the judge," Ker said, "I would do no more than has already happened. They have been afraid to the marrow of their bones; they have suffered enough."

"Would you trust them again?" the dragon asked, cocking its head to peer closely at Ker out of one eye.

"I would," Ker said. His back felt cold; he glanced around to see that the fire had died down to glowing embers.

"Why?"

Ker shrugged. "I don't know. They feel honest to me."

"So in *their* afterwards they prosper as the result of their carelessness . . . will this make them less careless?" The dragon had propped its chin on one vast front claw.

"I do not know," Ker said. "You asked what I thought."

"So." The dragon's head lifted a little, and the warmth of its breath touched Ker. "Hear my judgment, rockbrethren. For your carelessness in a sworn trust, you shall lose the gems in these—" A lance of flame, accurate as a pointing finger, touched the rocks and shards; Ker hardly felt warmth as it struck past him. When he turned to look, the rocks and shards had vanished. "Yet I will trust that you continue to guard the other well, and make no demands of reparation. So tell your king. I will watch more closely, but that is all. And I will also watch how you deal with this human, whom you have to thank for my inclination to mercy."

The dwarves threw themselves on the ground; the dragon withdrew into the fastnesses of air. They looked up when it had gone, and scrambled to their feet.

"We've you to thank," their leader said. His mouth twisted, then he smiled. "Well, that's fair, I suppose. And what do you want of us, then?"

"N-nothing," Ker said. His knees felt shaky again.

"That won't do," the dwarf said. "Sertig knows we're not as rulebound as our cousins of the Law, but no one can say the brothers are mean enough to take such a service as you did us and give no gifts in return. And it's not for the dragon's sake, either," he said, glaring up at the leaf canopy overhead. "I need no dragon to teach me generosity." A bubble of light rippled through the dell, and he paled but shook his head. "No, and again no. We're in your debt, a debt we can't pay, but we can gift you with what we have." He looked around at the others. "Come now, lads, let's get busy."

Before Ker quite realized what they were about, the dwarves had picked up the bundles he and his mother had carried from the village the day before.

"Where was it you were going, ma'am?" he asked Ker's mother.

"I—I have family in the hills west of here," she said. "Swallowbank . . ."

"Swallowbank, yes. A difficult road, ma'am, and a hard three days' journey, if you'll pardon me saying so. Would you consent to travel an easier one?"

"I—" she looked at Ker. "I—I suppose so. What road?"

"Ours," the dwarf said. He turned to Ker. "We will take you on our road, smooth and straight and safe underfoot and overhead, we will carry all your burdens, and we will set you down safe and rested in sight of Swallowbank with all that you desire," he said. "If you will accept our gift."

"I thought—maybe—with Tam gone, and the dragon-spawn—we could go back," Ker said. "Rebuild our village—" Surely they were not all dead, all the people he had known; surely the dragon would not have killed them all.

The dwarf shook his head. "No. I'm sorry, but what the dragon deals with cannot be changed. For all they are great healers in their way, they are also great destroyers. That land will not accept humans for a span of years; the dragon would have made sure of that. You must find a new place, and a new life."

"Then—I accept your offer with thanks." Ker picked up the walking stick, half-expecting to be dragged a league away with his first step, but it remained a bark-covered stick.

The dwarf led them back up the way Ker had come down with firewood, to a rock fence smoothed by falling water. The rock opened suddenly, like a door, and they passed into a dark tunnel, smooth all around. At once, the walking stick burst into cold flame, lighting the tunnel in blue radiance. Ker stared at it, but it did not burn his hand, so he held it firmly and walked on.

LOVE IN A TIME
OF DRAGONS

by Tanith Lee
From a Cluster of Ideas by John Kaiine

"Love in a Time of Dragons" is a fable set in vivid antiquity, with an engaging heroine, an offbeat plot, and a twist along the way. Tanith Lee's numerous fantasies include *The Birthgrave, Don't Bite the Sun, The Storm Lord,* and her collection of unforgettable feminist versions of Grimms' fairy tales, *Red as Blood.* Her earlier stories about dragons include "Draco, Draco," in *Beyond Lands of Never;* "After I Killed Her," published by *Isaac Asimov's Science Fiction Magazine;* "The Champion," in *Xanadu 3;* "Age," in the anthology *The Ultimate Dragon;* "The Children of His Old Age," in *Realms of Fantasy,* and a children's book, *The Dragon Hoard.* "They have also been featured in quite a lot of my novels," says Lee, who is the winner of the August Derleth Award, the Nebula, and the World Fantasy Award. "Love in a Time of Dragons" is based on a cluster of ideas by the author's writer-artist husband, John Kaiine. The couple resides on the seacoast of southern England.

Part One—Of Love

I

The woods were hot fire-yellow, yet full of rain and mist. Leaves floated thick on the pool where she was gathering black sloes and wineberries. That was when Graynne saw him, the first time.

To begin with, just the gleam and shadow of a moving reflection on the water, through the interrupting leaves. Not knowing what it could be—then *seeing*, and knowing not only who but what he was. Turning her head so slowly it hurt her. Staring up the slope between the poles of the great trees.

Leaves were falling endless in the rain, and mist closed all the distances, but even so, she could not miss him, not now. The sable of his burnished armor, the way he moved—powerful, graceful, as only something so surely dangerous could be. A practiced and accomplished killer. She thought (did she?) he flicked her half a glance under his long arched brow, passing by on his way. She shivered and held her breath, and out of the depths of her valueless life some unknown dream welled up through her like blood.

It was that immediate, that savage and absolute. It was insane—but then, hadn't she always heard so, in the tales, the song of bards? A madness that had no laws: that was Love.

At the hamesheld they were bringing in behind the stockade the cattle from the evening fields. Goats and cows pushed through last light and the street, knocking Graynne aside. Men also knocked her aside, slightly less rough and much less kind. "Out the way, uman." And those that had been *known* to her—they were more jollily unkind than the rest. "Think we want custom so early?"

Long dusk shadows fell, as if the horizoned sun itself cast a shadow from its own broad disc, deadly red with mist and night and the village's condensing smokes.

In the in-house they were already drinking deeply, thirsty. Graynne, having left her gatherings in the kitchen (sworn at because she had not gathered more), went about with the ale.

She was, she found, waiting. It was like the moment before the tongue of the swung bell strikes—only, that moment went on and on. She thought it would go on perhaps forever. The rest of her life.

Then *he* walked into the in.

At once a hush, a graveyard silence.

"Do I have the favor to help you, lord?" This, the in-keeper, intent on fawning placation. For the man who had come into the house was a man of power.

Graynne stood, as the others stood or sat, watching him. Of course, she knew what he was. (She had nearly dropped the pitcher.) Did *they* after this long while? Yet how, even if you were a fool, could you *not* know?

He wore a cloak of lynx-fur, and the black-washed mail of a kingsman, a sweord. His long hair, braided around strips of soft gold no one had been clever enough to take from him, was also black. The long black brows and dark wicked eyes of him, like a bird of prey. There were sharp weapons too in his belt, and over his back. Handsome? Oh, yes. But it wasn't that. It was his *power* that sat on him, both worldly and of the spirit. He would always get what he wanted. He believed it too, and so must they.

So far he hadn't answered the in-keeper, who, lurching and swerving round him, was filling a beaker—gratis—and giving it to him.

Then the sweord did speak.

"Not what you can do for me. I think, what *I* can do for yourselves."

The room sighed, muttered.

It took one of the old men to chirp out, "You've come for it, then."

"May-it-be, granddad. I've come for it, I have come for it, I have. It and I shall have dealings."

"Aah," they said, as if drinking down great quaffs of his presence, the words, the promise.

"You like that?" he asked, teasing, one arch of his brows going up.

"We like it!" they cried. "May-it-be!"

They stood up, all of them now, to toast the sweord.

The in-keeper approached and shoved Graynne back toward the kitchen. "Take down the flitch of pig. Get the fire up. And the soup—put in more flour and vegetables. You slut—why are you holking about there? Move yourself. Here he is, the One."

Graynne whispered, "To kill the draakor?"

"What else? Who but? Could *you* do it, you sloven-slop?"

"Not I," she said.

He kicked her as she ran kitchenwards, but not hard. He wanted her able at her duties.

She easily heard them, all that noise, in the ale-room.

At first, she had been shaking all over. As if pieces of herself might shake off and fall on the ground. Then she took some ale, secretly, where no one could see. She'd had to do that in the past, after the master beat her, or the in-wyfe. Or other things. The drink steadied her.

She saw to the cooking and the serving.

He never glanced her way, the man who was the One. The sweord-knight.

Why would he? She was the kitchen drab.

When everyone was drunk (Graynne too a little, unknown to them), the room full of smoke and fumes and sottish songs, she watched the sweord conducted ceremoniously up the ladder-stair to the best, and only, bedchamber, under the thatch.

Of everyone, he was the least drunk. Not because he

hadn't drunk more than any of them, but because, plainly, he was used to better and more virile stuff.

"G'night, may-it-be. Allgod bless you, lord," groveled the in-keeper.

He swung, the sweord, into the room and the door thudded shut, and Graynne slunk back to cleaning the pots before any of them saw her, getting round the rooms by means of the shadows, like a cat.

She knew his name now, the champion who would kill the draakor. It was Beolrost.

The in slept. Graynne bathed herself in the fresh water she had drawn from the well, which she hid and kept for herself under the stair. She rubbed herbs she had plucked—rosemary, starkiss, lavender—into her long hair.

Graynne was still quite young. Aside from the bruises, and scars of beatings, breakages, and knives, her body was white, and if not as firm as a girl's, still slip-sleek skinned and with a narrow waist from starving.

She took the little pot of best ale the master also kept where he thought no one knew. She drank a mouthful herself. It was bitter and good. Then she climbed the ladder-stair in the dark, accustomed to the way.

Going up, she passed the cubby where they slept, master and mistress, behind a curtain but acrobatically straight off the stair. She had been taken there once or twice, by the old man, for a friendly rape when she wasn't at the service of in customers. But that was only when the wyfe was from home, for he feared the wyfe, who was quite likely to tip boiling water on him or punch him in the guts.

Above was darker yet. A slit let in the seamless overcast of blank, black night. She leaned a second there in the window, smelling the fragrance of the leaf-ebbing trees, the outer smokes and animal odors nicer than the shut-in stink of mankind.

Then she opened the door to the underthatch room.

Graynne knew better than to creep up on a trained fighter. Even under the circumstances that he was a savior, Beolrost would no doubt keep some guard against thieves in this allgod-forsook place.

She was right, of course. One step in the room and something he had set there dropped down with a clatter.

In the black she saw him surging up on the bed. And the flash of an iron knife against the night, like a trick of the eyes.

"It's none but myself," said Graynne. "They sent the best ale for your night-cup."

At that he grunted. The grunt was not unwelcoming. Below, no one had stirred—blind drunk, blind *deaf*, the lot of them.

His candle was lit next moment.

Graynne straightened up in the spray of light. She was not much, she knew, but she was here. And from the look that moved across his face, she thought perhaps that even if he didn't see *her*, he saw what she *was*, female, handily available.

"Come here. Bring it over."

She carried him the best ale.

———◆———◆———◆———

Dragons had been in those parts for a century or more. Those of Graynne's age could always remember talk of them, but so could the oldest people in this hamesheld, and the surrounding country. Far inland, along a river, lay a large town, with a king. Even there they had heard of the dragons. And for a fact, kingsmen had left the town from time to time, to fight and kill them. Or to be killed.

They were rife, dragons. Everywhere, always possible. Sometimes they slept for decades. Sometimes only for a year. Sometimes when men thought that dragon which haunted their particular region was dead at last, it would only wake up and become active once more.

If there was enough game for them in the land, they might be content with that. But sometimes anyway they would go after more. They would go after men. There were stories of some beasts that could fly vast distances, and that, as they flew over, vomited out columns of fire, destroying everything beneath. Both these tales were true, aerobility and arson, but even so the acts of dragons varied. The hamesheld here, for example, where Graynne was born, had never been burnt except by the clumsiness of its own occupants. Yet there *was* a dragon, one specific dragon. It had been in the area for one hundred and ten years, according to the reckoning of the priests. These had a richly adorned drawing of it in a huge book, with the date of its coming—and although this book was kept some miles away at the priestery, one or two in the villages around had been shown it.

Where dragons were, there was always an aroma, generally faint, yet often turning pungent and excessive. For those who lived with it, it was rarely especially noticeable. They grew up with it in their noses, like the smells of the countryside and their own kind.

When had Graynne first heard of the local dragon?

Oh, when she was five or six.

She had been sitting playing with a bit of rag in the muck where she usually sat, and back in the hut she heard her mother talking to the man. And he said, "Best enjoy ourselves while we shall. Draakor's up and about again."

She hadn't known what *draakor* meant, that it meant

dragon. Graynne was slow at learning most things.

Now presently her mother emerged from the hut, pushing down her skirt as she came. "Up, you kid-bitch, and fetch some drink." So then Graynne had to run to the backdoor of the in, and beg some of the leas, as she often did, shouted at and cursed by everyone, and with vicious chickens pecking at her legs.

After that time, she was always hearing of the draakor. How it flew only a short way, but some had seen it, passing through the twilight sky like a great hornet. How it had taken goats. How they must send again to the river town, asking for someone to come and see to it.

She had been twelve or so when she saw her first champion—she had never, herself, seen the dragon. The man came strutting into the village, his sword bouncing in a leather sheath across his back, his belt full of knives. He wasn't a sweord, no king's house had trained him. But he was tough and ready, and had gold earrings.

Graynne had thought, if he fought it, what would happen? And she'd imagined the furious draakor flying over and enflaming the hamesheld from rage.

That night something did occur.

She woke to cries and shouts all through the village. Her mother wasn't home, but off with men, so Graynne alone ran out into the street in terror.

There was a towering light, coming and going out of utter darkness. And the light, which was red, and appeared to be setting the sky on fire, rumbled. It seemed so near she thought it was at the end of the street, but not so.

"It's the mountain going off—" the hameshelders called to each other over and over.

The mountain was a high cliffy hill just visible above the trees in fine weather. At the top was a bare and rocky vent, and from here it belched flame, but only if a dragon roused in its hollows.

All night long, shuddering with fear, Graynne, with the rest, kept watch.

When dawn came, the fire of the mountain was diluting. Soon after the sun rose, all the red sank.

"It's sleeping, bale-fucking thing."

They believed too the champion had slept right through the fire, brave and full of drink. But no, he was gone. Gone to fight? It seemed not, in the end. He'd run away.

All that summer, the mountain intermittently let off fire. Sometimes dense ashes fell on the village. The air smelled solely of that omnipresent conflagration—metallic, tasting in the mouth, and everything always extra dirty. But eventually the fire seemed to grow stale, and crumbled out.

"It's dead, the draakor fucker."

But it wasn't dead. It had soon been seen again, sliding through the fall leaves, long as three horses, sinuous as a serpent, belly low, its folded wings breaking boughs.

All the green hill-mountain was blackened too. And the woods and lower hills round about, for a span judged to be many miles.

Out of this black, however, things quickly grew, even as winter came on, new plants and weeds, high crimson thorns that looked thick in blood. On nearby trees and bushes that should have borne fruit but had been scorched, the fruit came back, but in strange shapes and shades—apples big as a dog's head, hard yellow as honey; berries dark blue as hyacinths. Animals and birds normally avoided the spot.

That winter, wolves instead howled round the stockade, got in through a weak place and stole chickens, and were witnessed snuffling at the doors and garbage tips in the predawn, like foxes. When the wolves vanished, the village said the draakor had eaten them. Men had come across heaps of wolf-skulls and scraps of fur.

During the next years, Graynne beheld three other champions stalk into the village. Only one was a sweord, a short, fair-haired man with a necklace of gold and copper, who smiled and gave her a penny, and wanted nothing for it. By then, *used to* what men wanted of fourteen-year-old women like herself, and even of hags like her mother, Graynne was surprised.

This sweord, without doubt, went to seek the dragon. He never returned. Unlike the other two, who hadn't returned either, his body was finally found—or parts of it, enough to know. The dragon had not eaten all his mail, though it had the necklace.

The following winter a fourth champion set off toward the mountain, which was erupting again. He *did* come back. He said he'd well and truly seen to the beast, and he had brought in a black claw-case, the kind of thing a cat might shed, but half a forearm long. There was blood on it, and the man looked singed and had deep scratches down his arms. Besides, the fire had gone out. The village loaded him with food and drink, and gave him money, too, a lot of the coins kept under the old sacred stones. Some wanted to go and see the corpse of the draakor. "Best leave it lie awhile," said the successful champion. "Poison comes off those creatures in death for some time. Can blind you, or worse."

So they left it lie. And a month after the champion was gone, a goatherd saw the dragon walking along over the hills around the mountain, brushing careless through the crimson thorns that could scratch a lying man's skin.

Yet this new champion now, all these years after, tonight, this sweord—he wasn't like the others. For Graynne it seemed everything had altered, the world had changed.

Drinking the ale, he looked at her. She let him, smiling slightly, lowering her eyes. She acted shy but was not, not even
now with this fateful man, all shyness long ago dredged out
of her.

Even so, she had experienced male power at last, out in
the wood. It was magnetic, electric, like lightning or certain
metals.

She showed Beolrost her reaction to male power, quivering before him, her shiny hair blown in a curtain, the dress
off one shoulder.

Presently the sweord reached out and rubbed his hand,
hard and barbed with callouses, over that shoulder, and
down over her breast and straight down to her sex.

"You're skinny," he said. "But you've got a bonny wild
look. Are you?"

"May-it-be."

"Get in with me, then. Take your dazzled finery off first."

She cast the scavenger gown on the floor. As she glided
into his bed (the only bed at the in, and one of only three in
all this hamesheld), both the harsh scaly hands roped round
her waist. She abandoned herself to them, to his mouth and
the grazing stubble already hedgepig-bristled about his lips,
cheeks, and jaw. He had good teeth, well-nourished in the
town.

Maybe pleased, or aroused by the idea, "Do you like
me?" he said.

She moaned and clung to him. She said, into his scalding
mouth, "I love only you. Do your wants to me, lord. I your
slave, yourself are king."

"You say so." He was big, thrusting into her. She could
feel him filling her, even though she had been so used. They
rolled and humped together and away and together, until she
felt his banging up in the height of her brain.

He caught his breath. Convulsion burst inside her. She kicked and groaned. Then he collapsed on her, all his weight. He cried out twice, louder than she did.

"A wonder this flea-feast of a bed stays whole at such knocking," he commented.

Humble, she lay at Beolrost's side.

"Shall I go?" she murmured. "Let me stay."

"May-it-be, stay. You've earned a share of the mattress."

"Not for that," she said. "To be near you."

He laughed. He had appropriated the fancy of women before. But something in this drab must have tickled him, more than lust's itch-scratching. He had perhaps liked her response—violent and swift. Liked the texture of her skin and hair. He'd take her again in the night. No need to rush to meet the draak. Have his satiety.

The sweord began to snore, then his breathing calmed, and he lay sleeping in silence and Graynne lay against his back. She thought of her mother, who had been stabbed dead by accident in a drunk brawl over a game with small stones. Then she thought of love. Only of love. She grasped its dark and marvelous beauty, its danger and despair. She'd never had anything of her own before.

2

Graynne had her plan, most of it. The plan was tenuous but not unlikely.

When he woke in the morning she had the relief-pot ready for him. Before that she'd slipped away and come back with bread warm off the kitchen fire, four baked eggs, a slab of cold pork, a broth with cream.

He ate, sharp and fierce as a knife, cutting, biting

through. He gave her also generous morsels to eat, more than she ever got. When that was over, he pulled her atop his loins and she danced for his joy.

"You're a crazy lass," he said.

She gazed at him. He smiled: "May-it-be, all melt-eyed for me you are, uman."

"Truly."

"And creamy there, like the sweet-curd off the soup."

"I love you."

"Is it that you do?"

Then she knelt to him, naked, sealed by current bruises and old scars, and by the action of his body, hands, teeth, starting beard, bold forward tail.

"Take me with you. I'll perish if you go. I know you won't want me long. But while you do. Just till it's done, the killing up there. I can care for you. I can find food, and cook on an open fire, on a hot stone. I can salve wounds." She glanced, and saw his pools of eyes, thinking about it all, under the two black bridges of his brows. "If the draakor comes—" she said, low as a prayer, "you can give me to it. I'll go, if it will help you. By allgod, I swear it."

To her surprise then, he sat back and he said, "Why all this?"

"Love," she said. She stared him in the face. "*Love*."

"You think me a simpleton not to know you love."

"You think you know, only not how much. How could you?"

"Disdain, now? May-it-be. What a one you are."

"You," said Graynne, "are the One."

He pointed at his risen self. "Do this now. Let's see."

She closed the upright tail of him in her mouth, perfect as a rose. He saw.

Roses have thorns. They were inside her, piercing up through her skin as she waited.

She could hear him, talking arrogant to the master.

The master (unexpectedly?) talking back.

"But how can I spare the girl? She serves here. She's myself's."

"So what's *that?*"

"Is a big coin you gave me—"

"So it is. That's for my hire of her."

"Na, lord—all that, the night, the food—was for free—"

"Hire of her up on the hills. You've had your say. What?" said the sweord, "would you rather it be you with me, up there? Come you up then, do my cooking for me. I won't want you for the other thing."

"But—"

"You say?"

"The—*draakor*—"

"*She's* not fearful of it. Not with me by. Why are you feared? I thought you wanted to come with me. Come on, get yourself together. I'll take *you.*"

"Na—na—lord, let me alone—I've the in-house to run. I've the wyfe. Na, lord, pray-you let go. Take her, take the slop-slut. Welcome you are. Take her."

She might have gone on her own, years before, but where would she have gone to? Who would have wanted her? Besides, though they sent her out to roam the woods and gather roots and fruits for their table, she'd been warned long since she was the master's property, for debts of her mother's. And warned also, if she failed to come in at evening, some of them would go after her, with the village dogs, and that would be bad for her, once they caught her. Which was if the wolves or boar or a hungry bear didn't chance on her first.

But really it was inertia. She couldn't think of escaping them, for all places must be alike to one of her sort. What could she hope for anywhere? And then—then this. Love was sent, from some magical realm. Not the creation of men, but given to them. She had heard a priest say this. Now she knew it to be true.

Yet also, obviously, going off with the champion she would be clear of pursuit, nothing to hamper her, and with all this help now, Beolrost's guidance, however briefly it lasted, in finding her way. What had, for a moment (when, stunned, she was still deciding what she should or could do), seemed to be an impassable obstacle, an end to all, had now become her friend. He *wanted* her with him. Even if only for another day: she would try her best to make it last longer than that. And if she died? Oh, she had *been* dead. This was life, this now, a sudden flood of it, bright as the gush the hearth gives, just before it goes out.

Leaving the hamesheld, Graynne saw they pushed the gate close in the stockade, as normally only at dusk. A precaution. She turned her back on the village. For always?

It was a steepish climb beyond the fields, up into the woodlands.

Beolrost strode before her.

From the back he was also impressive, the lynx-fur cloak, the sword in its leather scabbard hanging from a sling of embroidered waxcloth studded by silver. And over the rest the rivulets of shining, raven-black hair.

She walked behind, and on her own she carried his bundle now, light enough, and a collection of things he'd wanted brought from the kitchen, doubting, it seemed, her skills in the open.

Acorn-colored, the spectral pillars of the trees, which

soon closed round. And then came too the runneled black boles of the pines, spined hawthorns, and the rowan clumps bloody with berries. There was still a deep green in the woods, but it was only a backcloth now, the stitchwork was all of amber and yellow, darkest red. Berries were there on the bushes too, in crowds, raspberries and blackberries, juniper and savory. Graynne plucked them swiftly as they passed, tearing her hands on the briars, dropping everything—bloody berries and her blood—in the bag at her waist. Where she saw herbs, she pulled them up or ripped off their heads. She was merciless. Had had to learn to be. This was nothing. Now and then she had been put to slaughtering. Even the pig the in-keeper always kept, killed at intervals, replaced by another. He had said to her, "You'll like that, you've fed and made he fat while you've gone without. Get your revenge on it." But she had made herself iron, and killed the pig cleanly. She was merciless, yes, but not cruel, and wherever she could, had paid first, in whatever kind, for anything she had.

The sweord and she traveled by other paths and, ironically, at no point went by the so-significant pool, where yesterday the arrow had entered Graynne's heart. (Had he *seen* her then? Might he remember?)

At midday, they stopped. Beolrost told her to make a fire, and fashion him some food. "Let's find what you can do, other than the other."

While she was at work he moved about, examining the undergrowth and trees. He was looking for signs of the draakor. Perhaps they were there, in places. Even though the hamesheld had assured him the dragon never came down this far, at least on its feet, preferring the open land of the hills and mountainside. As for flight, no one had recently seen it fly. It wasn't, they said, so young now.

But of course that made no difference. Dragons lived for centuries. What was ancient to a man was infancy to the draakor.

He sat to eat, his back to a beech tree

"Well, you're no liaress. 'S good."

As he was content with the stores he'd made her bring, so far Graynne didn't trouble to look out for rabbits or birds. She had thought anyway they would be scarce hereabouts.

Having eaten, Beolrost leant back. "See the shadow there? Wake me when it reaches that hazel tree."

Graynne sat watching the sun move behind the autumn-rent veil of leaves, the shadow turning on the ground. Fifteen minutes worth of sleep.

Once he was again awake (she sensed he could wake himself, it had been a skittish test of her vigilance), he put her against the earth and had her.

Then they shook themselves. She packed away the cooking utensils while Beolrost drew out his knives, and then the long sword, rubbing them over with cloth, touching them. "See this blade," he said to her. "I've shaved my own face many a time, looking in the metal." He moved the weapons possessively, settling them back in their sheaths with a practiced deftness. But it seemed he had liked the contact. Then he stood up and urinated on the fire to quench it. They went on.

Soon the way grew vertical and the trees partly horizontal, leaning off from the slope and hanging their heads downhill. It had been sunny and still, but now panes of mist began to show themselves along the tilted avenues, like ghosts.

At a spring she filled the metal flask he had given her to carry. On the flask was a little pattern—done in gold, worn and polished by use, the shapes blurring as the afternoon light now did.

She had never come up so high. Nor he. Beolrost had come down through the woods, but from the west, he said. He'd been looking for marks of the draakor, but, besides that, he knew their smell. He wasn't from the river town, either. He journeyed, he had told the in last night, from a northern country.

The bag of berries bled on Graynne's ragged skirt.

During the next three hours, the steep path—which was no path at all, untrodden save by them—leveled. Oak trees spread up in crowns, frayed and golden. The mist lay down the slope now. The sun westered over.

They came out on a wide bare stony place, a terrace of rock with a few ferns growing, the woods falling back. There was a valley below, also wooded. Graynne hadn't known of a valley. Mist patchily wrapped its trees, which were mostly dark, evergreens of bay and pine and fir. Across the divide, struck by the sinking sun, the hills lifted like grave-mounds of bronze. And behind them, above them, the brazen cone that was the top of the mountain.

"We'll go back a step, under the trees here," he said. "Tonight there may be something."

"Will—it come over?" she asked.

"Maybe. It's been down in those last woods, further back a way. There were its shitful tords. I never showed you, in case you took fright. Like giant owl pellets they are, full of bones and such. Does it fly? Perhaps it flies. But it's walked about, scraping its scales along the bark of the trees. You took that for marks of boar tusks likely. No fire for us tonight. Eat cold, keep each other warm. Tomorrow there's the wood down there, then up. You're no sorry feebling. You've kept up along of me."

"I said."

"May-it-be, proud lady. Look, there goes the sun over

world's edge. Get us some fodder, my lass. And you, you sun, be off. Let's have some night."

Even the sun obeyed Beolrost. It split between the bottom of the sky and the rim of the earth, ran like an egg, was gone.

In the night, he sleeping by her, his arm and some of the lynx-fur to keep her snug, she lay listening for the dragon. Tense for it as the string of a bow.

Nothing moved. There was no mobile life in the woods—only the mobile death of shedding leaves. Sometimes leaves fell on them where they lay. She lifted them from his hair, not waking him. He must trust her now, somewhat. Anything else, anything more than a leaf or her hand, he would have woken instantly, and with him his friends the sword and the knives. Yes, she could trust that for sure. But too he did not mind her either, lying up against all his weaponry. Her slight movements did not make him uneasy even if, without design, she touched the sword on its sling.

The mist came creeping closer up the slope, and up from the dividing valley, a noiseless cauldron boiling over.

The stars burned only in the sky's liquid indigo center, at the edges hung mist and cloud, and no moon.

Sometimes priests arrived and talked to the hameshelds, and had done so in Graynne's village too. They said the dragons were the curse of the allgod on the earth for its wickedness. This was for some sin long ago. But the draak-ors were also cursed. A draakor, and the first woman, had plotted together in another land, at the world's dawn, and so brought the first man to ruin. For this act the draakor was worse-cursed, the woman second-worse. For the man there were other penalties.

You would know Something Else was hereabouts. From the silence and no-sound, you would know it. From the mist that rose and left the sky empty in the center but for sparkling dragon-eyes. From the unheard loud quick beating of Graynne's heart.

Beolrost had said she might light the fire, tomorrow after sun-up. So she would make him a hot bread-porridge, with all the sumptuous berries mixed in, garnished with wild apples. She would slice the pork thin and put the white rich cheese between all the slices, with the herbs. She would comb and braid the sweord's hair, and shave him herself—she was well able—if he wished (he would wish), and suck him to his agony of pleasure. She curled against him to keep him warm, pushing the fur off her body and tucking it about his as though he were her child.

No. The dragon would not go by this night.

They woke early, but—due to her ministrations—started late down toward the valley wood, picking among the rocks. He took the bundle off her here, and the cooking gear, saying to her she must have a care where she trod.

Once in the wood below, the mist was gone again but vast shadows fell, gloomy and scented as the priestery with its incense of balsam.

Here, directly below the fortress of the draakor, after all she saw a coney. She had already found, on the chance, a sharp stone and instantly flung it. It snapped the rabbit's neck at once.

Beolrost stared and nodded, impressed.

She put the rabbit, poor soft tender shattered thing, into the waist-bag where the fruit had been.

After a time, the trees grew tattered as the wings of old black crows. Through these openings Graynne beheld the rock hillsides going up. Now, against the flanks of them, she saw their size and awkwardness, at which she had already guessed.

He led her under an overhang. They sat down and ate some bread. She dug in the earth and made a smokeless fire hidden beneath heaped stones, and cooked him the rabbit.

"Listen now, uman. I have a thought. You'll stay here, and come up no further."

Graynne turned her face to him and fixed her eyes on his.

"May-it-be, lass. Eye me all you want. You're a bonny kind, and you know this and that. You've made me comfortable as a king in his kingshame. But *it* is up there for sure. You may think, if you never saw it yet, it isn't there. And you've lived all your days in the stench of it. But here, I can hardly taste the air off the trees for the filthy bane of draakor. And it smells of fire too. And so does this wood. Look there. You see that, where the vine grows, that's no usual plant, and the fruits on it white as childer's bones . . . That is a spot the draakor has burnt, and spent its shitten tords on. I'll go up the hill. And you'll bide."

Graynne said, "Let me go with you." She kept her voice low, as he did now.

"I will not."

"I've said, give me to it," she said, "as they do in the tales. I've no fear—do you think so? While it comes for me, you have your better luck of killing it."

"So you say. Tie you up and offer you. May-it-be, so they do it, here and there. And the girl may even live, it's true, if the man who ties her is swift at his swordwork. But she mayn't neither."

"I don't care. I will do it. I've said."

"Not if I tell you not."

Graynne said, "Leave me, I'll follow anyway. I'll be your shadow."

"By the ungod, uman. I'm to fight it, not you."

"What is my life to me?" she said. "Take me up. Without

you I can't make my way on these hills."

"Then you can't be following me."

No doubt he saw the dismay, almost terror, in her eyes. Was he flattered? Then she frowned. She said, "Had you no other ever that loved, that you saw?"

He said, soberly, "Once I did."

"I will make my way under your guidance, or alone. I will go up."

"Blood and stars, girl."

"I will go up."

"Come here then. This may be the last time."

"I will come there to you, if I'm to come up the mountain next."

"How can I stop you, eh? You're more terrible than the draakor, so you are."

3

Next day, they climbed up. They came soon to burned parts, again and again, where weird things flourished, hawthorns covered with hard russet fruit, a leafless pear tree, slanted and thin from clinging on the hill, with shining black pears.

The mountain hadn't hollered its fire for twelve years, more. So then this must be from the directly proximitous flame of the draakor's mouth.

And the day was overcast—not the high sky, which was a flimsy blue, powdered with cirrus, but from low, colorless, earthbound clouds, which floated slowly about the hills.

The air smelled like an angry forge. No, more like a burning-yard for the dead.

They climbed all day. Sometimes he looked back, returned, and helped haul her roughly up. Graynne saw that truly she would have had some difficulty alone. He told her often how to walk and where to put her feet. *Could* she have managed such a climb? (Of a descent she had no thoughts.)

When night came down from the sky and up from the snorl of lower clouds, there was a tiny cave leant above a sudden total drop, and into this they went, after he had paced the nook through. It had a granite back not far behind the entrance. Nothing lived there, or could come in there from out of the hill's inner vents and tunnels.

"No sight of it," said Beolrost. He hadn't allowed fire. The night was close as wool.

He began to speak to her of dragons again. How the armor of them might turn even an iron sword, but still there were places to hit. Of the bat-like wings. The teeth. He told her how the scales, if ever found shed, which was rarely, made a wonderful dye that showed green within doors during the daylight, deep azure in the gleam of fire or candle, but which flared up scarlet under full sun. Bands of obscure, half-mad women wandered the isles and uplands, he said, searching for these scales that made the dye. But that was long ago, when kings required it for their robes of state. He said the pictures of dragons in priest-books from that time, these too were colored from a draakor scale. It would be worth something to take a few off the hide of a beast you slew. Not too many though, they stank.

They lay to sleep. He didn't take her, or want her attentions. He muttered on in his slumber, now talking to someone else from long ago, maybe, far away.

Was he, the sweord, finally afraid?

Graynne lay tight as a bean to its pod against his body. When he was still and in his deepest sleep, she turned and watched the blue-white stars that came and went in the drifting overcast, like daggers pointing through.

Then she reached her hand over him, and slipped the smaller knife out of his belt. (He was used to her hands, the caress of them, the way gently she'd picked the fall leaves from his hair.)

With his knife she cut the sling that crossed his back. She grasped the sword in its scabbard as it came loose. Then she drew the other, bigger knife also out of his belt.

Sometimes in the night she got up and left him briefly, restless, or needing to make water. He was, sleeping, accustomed to that too.

First light, and the champion woke. He sat straight up. His eyes were crazy and his arm knocked her away, not noticing.

"In ungod's name—where is the blade? Where's my knives—"

He was on his feet, whirling this way, that.

"Where? Where? Godfuck—" he shouted in a whisper, still recalling so well what was near. "Fuck and bale—where do they lie, uman? Did you do this? Some other— Get up, you cow, and look—by all stars and the shitten earth—"

Graynne stood. She did not pretend to search. She shrank back.

She trembled.

"Where did they go?" he ranted. "What took my blades? Didn't you see? Was it sorcery? Useless bitch you are—" all the while turning over stones and heaps of dirt.

She did not tell him she had thrown the weapons, each of them, spinning off the hills, down the drop, and into the wooded valley a day below.

At last he grew motionless, standing at the cave entrance, rooted staring at the ground like a child that forgot the errand it was sent on.

"Go down to the wood," said Graynne. "How can you

fight it, without your sword?"

"I must," he said, woodenly.

"Na, it can never be. Go down to the wood. It won't come till darkness, or till afternoon. Leave me here for it. Take yourself away."

"Shut yourself up."

She waited, dumb.

He said, "Let me think."

Beolrost stumbled out of the cave. Early morning lit the valley in long pale embers. He stood now on the lip of the hill, gazing over.

Graynne went out to him softly.

She touched his arm. He flinched. Weapons gone, he was, as they said, unmanned.

"Leave me here," she said. "That'll content it. I want you should be safe."

"Shut your mouth, you bitch."

"Who'll know?"

He rounded on her. He hit her across the face so she staggered. His eyes were full of tears. "*I* will know it. *I*. Stopper your noise, you pigwyfe. Let me think what I must do. There's a way yet. I can make a sling for stones. There are pebbles. Blind the eye of it. Come to it that way. I'll do that. May-it-be, I'll tie you for it, then. That'll do well. What do you say?"

She put out her hand, loving and quiet, and set it on his breast, where the prow of breastbone was above the ribcage. "Whatever," she said.

Her arms were strong from carrying and labors. She had slaughtered swine, goats, rabbits. She pushed him hard and all at once, and he was still puzzling over it all, where the sword had gone, how he could best secure her, how to make his sling and choose the shards for throwing, as he rocked back. Only then he turned his head, and glanced, casual, over one shoulder at the abyss underneath. Just as he began to topple into it.

His eyes slewed back, enlarged, on her face he'd struck, like fifty others. He made a sound. Not a yell. It was much less than the outcry he summoned during the deed of sex. But he was falling by then, and he vanished. Graynne didn't hurry to the edge of the drop to watch him go down, or to see him, as he presently did, strike the roof of the wood a day below.

Part Two—Of Dragons

I

The last part of the way up the mountain was not so difficult. Graynne had thought this would be so. The slopes were gradual, and jumbled with fixed boulders. In places, the stone of the hills came through, providing steep natural steps. Springs welled out of the mountainsides, but they carried a strong aroma of strangeness. Graynne drank from them, a sip or two. They tasted salty, bitter.

Above, the cone showed like a castle built up out of the last shaggy shoulder of ground.

Most of the hill was blackened, or stained sulphurously. Things grew here but were seldom encountered—a few leaning trees, shorter than she, with long yellow filaments like hair, bracken that was blood-red.

The earth-clouds sank away and hung below.

Miles off in the clear pond of sky, a single bird flew over. Later she saw it again, or another, still solitary, still only a bird.

There was nothing to see of any existing dragon.

Yet she knew he lived, was here, or somewhere nearby.

She had seen him, hadn't she, that late-of-day by the woods pool. Had seen him pass like a dark ripple through the water of the fall-weeping wood, and how it had seemed he flicked his gaze at her from under the architecture of his brows.

What had happened? She had never loved her own species, had no cause. The other creatures about her, wild or domestic, she had been trained to treat as food or slaves. But this—neither man nor beast—was a god.

She had formed, after she saw him that day, some half-plan for escaping the in, avoiding pursuit. She knew he would have gone back up to his mountain. (Why had he come down so *far*? As if—seeking for something . . .) She had been asking herself over and over if she herself could get up the tall hills alone—and then the sword walked into the in.

Of all the champions she had ever seen, he looked to Graynne as if he might manage to harm, perhaps to kill, a draakor. She was used to making up to men, had had to, like everything else.

And she was merciless, remember. And smitten to her bones with love, if not love of anything human.

Graynne sat on a boulder. She had climbed all day, and now the sun was low in the sky. The cone of the mountain seemed very near, perhaps a scramble of only one halved hour.

For a moment, sitting, she slept. There was a dream in her sleep. Waking, she glimpsed it, already turning from her, elusive and fading. She never recalled her dreams.

When she opened her eyes, staring up the dark turfy slope, the faintest whisper of smoke went floating across it.

That was all. Like a trick of the sight—but not.

Why had he come down that day so far into the woods?

She thought of him, his long, lean body in its armor of scales, sliding through the shadows and the leaves and the trees, returning up and up. Not flying, not needing to do that.

And then, around the shoulder by the cone, around that hub of land (where a vivid saffron stain was), simply, merely around and out into the leveling sunshine—the dragon came.

Graynne stood up.

About a hundred paces above her on the tumbled mountainside, she saw his immaculate body, like dully polished ancient bronze, between jet-black and nut-brown. The sun snagged on the mathematical outline of each scale. His head pointed, dog-like, the ears set back, the mouth closed. The deep arches that held his eyes gave him a brooding, intelligent frown. The eyes themselves were grey in this light. They were like gigantic human eyes that had no white to them, save at the very rims, now and then a glimmer, as the pewter balls of the irises rolled. And the sun fell also into these dragon eyes, amber-red.

He had seen her. She saw he had. He poised there, the long sinuous coil of him, and the serpent of his tail that was almost another being of itself.

His wings were folded on to his spine, darker than the rest of him. His tongue too would be black—Beolrost had told her.

Graynne began to clamber up the last of the slope.

The draakor stood waiting.

Now, climbing, she had also to help her feet with her hands, clutching the higher ground, pulling herself by a grip on stone or roots, or the clumps of matted wiry grass. He observed while she did this.

He might blast out fire any instant and kill her. If she thought, she thought this wouldn't happen, any more than lightning would strike the mountain from the clear sky.

But then she was so close to him, she could truly *see* his size, and the glow of his patterned skin. She could smell him, separately, metallic still, but also *animal*. It was a hot smell, yet he would be cool to touch.

The sun was right on the lip of the world, about to topple off at a push, as the champion had. Power was nothing. Not that sort of power.

She'd reached the shoulder. On the turf and rock, dry lakes of what looked like tar, sticky under her feet. She straightened.

The draakor was twice the length of her own body from her.

She became motionless looking at him, watching the reflected sun sink in his eyes.

In the interval after the sun set, and before night came, the draakor turned round. He walked, swaggering a little, back up about the shoulder, and Graynne followed him.

There was an entrance to the mountain, around the slope. It was a cave-mouth, huge, lightless now, though high in the vault of it inside she could see a vent-hole, open to the sky, which was now itself just the color of his eyes.

Graynne followed the draakor into the cave.

She walked a few steps after the slithering sweep of the long tail. The second they were in the cave, he and she, there was no light for her to see by. His darkness blended at once with the dark in the stone.

So then she followed sightlessly by listening to the rustling of his tail along the floor of the cave, all she could hear, that and the occasional subtle scrape of one of his sides against the wall.

They had left the entrance behind.

She smelled only dragons. She rested her hand on the wall to her left so she shouldn't quite lose her balance.

And then in front of her, he stopped. Before she could herself stop, her foot made contact with the tail's end. It flipped, sulky as a cat, and slunk away from her. But she had felt its arid smoothness, unlike all other things. After a minute, it twitched back again, rasping over her feet, playfully harsh.

Then he spoke. Oh, not in words. In his own language, if he had one. A sort of murmur, like thunder over a hill. And then he—*sighed*—and a gush of golden liquid—no, not liquid, it was *flame*—rushed out and undid the world. She saw him again suddenly, black and huge in front of her, and beyond, a great open cavern that itself took fire from his breath.

Lighted, the space was enormous, in width, in height. Far, far above, a tiny *absence* (night) showed another opening in the rock—one of the upper vents of the cone itself. She did not notice it at first. She could see nothing but the cavern.

The soaring walls were faced with deep reds and shrills of vermilion, pourings of cobalt and violet, detonations of yellow that mixed to a searing green. And over all this crowding of color, spread starbursts of bright silver, copper, gold. The fires that the draakor had lit, to show her, it seemed, burned in a chain of black waters on the cavern's floor—where things must grow that were only slowly flammable. Fluttering, the light, coming and going. At first, in the shock of the colors, she did not see them. The others. Against the brilliance of the walls, these dull black shades depending downwards, their long narrow heads pointed to the floor, their upper bodies melting into shadow. Dim stars ignited on their skins. Wings stirred a little. The eyes, half-open, looked at her through tidal firelight. They had fixed themselves into the rock, their bodies pressed firm, anchored by claws like huge nails of iron. But they were yet like bats, bats hanging from the roof of a cave. Dragons. She counted eight of them before the water-fire muddied and went out.

Then in the second dark she stood, unable to make out her way, or anything, knowing she must not move or she would fall, or stumble into the untold depths of the water. She heard him leave her there, heard just the soft rasping of the tail as it left her.

Later, in the pure blackness, she saw a star blaze in the vent high above. But also by then she believed she had begun again to see the draakors as they lay stretched downward on the walls, among the unseen colors made there: the now-and-then glimmer of their sleepless, sleeping eyes.

━━━◆━━━ ━━◆━━ ━━◆━━

Always she'd been alone, among her own kind. She was used to being alone among indifferent others.

She pushed back against the wall by the entrance, and curled herself up. Graynne too slept.

She dreamed, on and on. Waking, would never know what she had dreamed, only that she had.

Morning came and sent down a shaft of smoky blue through the upper vent. The scene was phantasmal in this dusk of dawn, the stasis of the dragons, the massing of shadows and contrary bleaching away of any color. She couldn't count them anymore, or be sure there weren't more of them, or less. The chain of pools that crossed the floor had kept black night in them. Groups of strange reeds grew everywhere in the water, the things that had caught fire last night and then gone out. Only the metal splashes on the rock burned now.

Graynne got up. She walked down to the first pool. She took up water from it in her hand. In her hand after all, it was quite clear. It tasted bitter, as the outer springs had on the mountainside.

The strange reeds were blackened, but not brittle. On some, a flaxy white head remained. Others were renewing their plumage from tufted buds. Every so often, a new one would open and unfurl. Still others lazed just below the surface, emerging when ready with the glint of a bird's turning wing.

The cavern was dizzy with sleep.

Graynne looked along the pools, into the deep farthest shadow, and saw he lay there, on the cavern floor alone, not lengthways down as did the others. His eyes were open. She found them, or course, more easily than last night's star. Now they were so large and pale, she made out shapes and secret inner lights, moving independently about on and in them, or thought she did.

She stayed by the pool, where she was. She sat looking at him. In the end his eyes shut, and he put out the world.

Men were easy to woo, she had learned. One way, they were.

She didn't want the draakor for that. Had never wanted that, only taken it when she had, from men, because she must—her mother's men, the in-keeper, his customers. Beolrost.

When she woke again, the daylight was stronger, through the vent. Graynne took two of the reed-heads, snapping them off two-hands-length down, with two sharp cracks. (And heard them stir, along the walls.) Then she drew out a pair of sticks she had kept in the bag at her waist, retained for the next fire-making.

What would he think of her, doing this?

Would she surprise him, her glorious, uncaring lover, lying there sublime, and immune to her?

They must know, surely, men too could make fire.

Graynne irritated the sticks together. The rasp, the little

sparks that began to jump up, reminded her of the sound of his spinal-tail snaking along the rock. When the flame came she put it to one of the flax-heads. As she thought it must, the head burned, the stem not.

She got to her feet, holding up her own flower of fire.

Graynne was proud. She wanted the draakor to see what she had done, and what she was. She had never wanted any human thing to see any of that. Allgod forfend.

He did see. The slight fire jeweled in his eyes.

She walked about the cavern. She looked at it. She held the taper high to examine the extraordinary conflagration of the walls, and wondered at how such color had been produced. And gradually she started to believe it came from the outbreathing of their fires, these colors. If the scales of their bodies could offer famously curious dyes and inks, perhaps the action even of their ordinary nonincendiary breath had formed *this*.

But the blasts of metals—for metal they were; she knew to recognize, from the occasional wealth of others, all three—from what had *they* come?

After her inspection, she passed along by the down-hung shapes of the dragons. She asked in her head why they slept. They seemed lulled but leaden, as if drugged, and by this new, individual light, it appeared to Graynne their hides were not so perfect, so burnished and *living* as his, her lover's. Were they dying then? Was this old age and sickness that kept them here, bat-like, hanging down with their iron claws locked into the stone of the mountain?

They still looked at her, eyes half-lidded over, actually now more closed to slits. Their wings shivered faintly, like the vanes of colossal moths.

Graynne bowed to them, each one, as she had seen the hameshelders do, once or twice, before some visiting official from a lesser king, or the higher ranks of the priests.

Then the first flax-head began to perish. From its end she lit the second one she had snapped off.

The second flame spurted up, more energetic than the first. And it seemed that might trouble them, these sleeping or dying priestly kings, in their robes of fading scalery. Graynne moved away.

She walked along the sides of the water-pools, to the cavern's end, where he lay. As she approached, Graynne started to speak quietly to him.

"Let me near. Let me come up to you. You let me follow you. Let me near."

When she was very close, she halted. Graynne said, "Speak to me, lord."

Then the draakor she loved rose up and up. But his head was lowered toward her. She stayed immobile, and his dog-snake's face came close. He snuffed at her, a curious rushing of sound, and his nostrils winked. Then he opened his mouth and she saw the rows of gleaming flawless teeth, all pointed, save for some at the very back of his long, long jaw. His tongue wasn't black, as the sweord had said. The tongue of the draakor was translucent, like grey amber, the shade the sun had been yesterday, mixed sinking in his eyes. His breath smelled metallically, and distantly of meat, but it was clean. He at least was healthy, vital, and whole.

Having shown her these further things about himself, the draakor turned his back on her. He threw himself down, heavy and graceful, like a great cat on the rock, resting his head against the curling of his own tail.

It was marvelous to her, everything he did.

But she crept through the shadows as the second flax expired. She crept up to him. If all he would do was sleep, then she would do as he did. She put her hand on him.

He was cool, as she'd anticipated. Cool and fine, like metalwork—which was alive. She felt the motion as he breathed. Then, only then, he spoke. His thunder sounded lower than before. She considered, also without words, in images, if she could ever come to understand his language, or his song. By then she too had lain down, against him. She pressed her cheek and forehead to the smooth impossibility of his scales.

She had told Beolrost often that she loved him. That was a lie. She didn't confess love to the draakor, since it was true.

2

Five further days the eight dragons lay suspended. Graynne watched a terrible thing happening to them. Gradually their carapaces ceased to be even sentient, became opaque and deadly black, like coffins. Their eyes too were completely closed away within this grave opacity. They were blind, fossilized. Their wings had stopped moving. They might have been carved from the rock to which they were fixed.

During this season, Graynne waited on the dragons, trying to serve them. She went out of the cave, having learnt the way, confident she would be allowed to return, and gathered running water, rather than the standing water of the cavern, in a hollow stone. This she brought to them, holding it up to each of the long mouths in turn. Only one put out a coated tongue, and lapped the water, but after this initial response, would or could not repeat the process.

From the slope, on the second morning, she had seen rabbits on the hills below. She went down and took three. These carcasses she carried back to the cavern, skinned and peeled them before the encoffined dragons, trying to tempt them.

As for himself, her lover, he did come at last and sample the rabbits. He ate one in a single gulp, bones and all. The other two he left, disdaining them.

Mostly he lay at the cavern's other end. He too, if not sick, was yet not prepared to do very much.

She thought he grieved for the eight draakors who died, so relentlessly, in front of him.

Graynne cooked and ate the other rabbits.

Additionally she brought in berries and peculiar fruits from the outside. She placed these also before each dragon, and before him. They lay like offerings, untouched.

But he let her lie beside him. When he stirred, his great bulk, which might have crushed her, would have done so if he had been careless, was maneuvered delicately away and back again. He knew she was there. He *let* her be there.

Graynne didn't mind remaining much in the cavern. Sometimes she lit all the oily flaxes in the pool for light (their rate of being consumed varied; while the buds grew again always, sometimes within an hour of their being burnt), and studied the metals and colors on the wall. She reasoned how the metal had come there. It was from when the draakors had devoured, along with flesh and bone, mail and swords, knives and jewelry. Rather than digest and pass this matter, they must spew it out in gusts of flame, adorning the cavern further with exquisite vomit.

In the night, Graynne embraced her dragon-lover. She moved her hands over his vast body, thrilled to emotional pain by the texture of the perfect scales covering a being breathing and living, and asleep beside her. She went out every day to the slope, and washed herself, drying her hair in the ending sunlight. So she shouldn't offend him, since he was a god.

But for the other draakors, she herself commenced to

grieve. She wept for the first time in all her life she could remember, staring, on the fifth day, up at their blinded masks, their silent wings.

On the sixth morning, Graynne started awake to a fearful sight and sound.

The eight slanted draakors had taken on an awful life, thrashing and screaming, a noise indescribable that changed her blood to water. She thought they were in their final death-throes. She got up and ran toward them, not knowing what she could do, instinctive, holding out her hands.

And as she did so, one of the black-dead coffins split apart, and Graynne herself screamed in terror.

But out of the breaking carapace, a *second* head unsheathed itself, a lean smooth head that shone with health and two clear and burning eyes.

Graynne saw how it was. Her panic turned to delight. Now another carapace exploded open, and another. All eight dragons were emerging together.

She ran against them then and helped them tear their way out of the half-resistant, half-friable wreckage of their old shed skins.

He too was there, assisting them.

Together he and she acted as the midwives of this mythic rebirth.

And when all the slough lay on the ground, they stood there, the eight, bronzy and flawless, as he was, their eyes like smoky pastel suns.

Presently they roared, shooting fire into the water, at the walls, upward to the vent in the mountain, which would let it out to appall the hameshelds of men round about.

Graynne thought they would kill her then. Mutely she gave herself to them, standing in the midst of them as they loosed their flames. They did not kill her.

They stood aside and let only him come up to her.

Now they were all alike, yet she saw their differences to one another. (She grasped most humans had not done this, mistaking them when seen singly for each other, so thinking there was only one.) And she saw that, though each was a miracle of splendor, he, the one she loved, was the more beautiful.

The draakor lowered his head. His jaws opened. He took her up in the door of his mouth, positioning her, cushioning her with his tongue that was like wet velvet. She lay against his teeth, which, being of such size, did not hurt her, though they were as sharp as swords. Had he bitten down upon her, they would have cut her cleanly in two. She thought he would bite down on her.

He didn't do that. He carried her away, gentle, into the back of the cavern. There he put her on the ground. He licked her over, all her body, discarding her garments incidentally, so eventually she was naked under the action of the silvery tongue.

Graynne did not know what this was, nor did she care. She abandoned herself to it. And when the orgasmic convulsion surged through her, wave on wave, she did not even for a second compare it to the convulsions of others who had had her, those secondhand upheavals rocking her flesh so she knew she must then pretend, as her mother had taught her she must. But this—was hers. It was all her own. And he had given it to her, instead of anguish and death.

He seemed amused, she thought. He curled one paw about her, possessive, pleased with her. She lay naked and relaxed in the obsidian cage of his claws.

When night arrived, the nine draakors left the cavern. They stalked about the mountainside, gazing up into the star-kindled sky, which they might have lit from their own fires.

Then they lifted up, great engines of iron and bronze, powered by the vanes of their moth-bat wings, through which the starlight faintly glowed, luminous.

Graynne watched them dart like hawks across the night sky.

When they were gone, she sat on the side of the mountain. The night was cold, the stars frosty in the last of autumn-fall. Graynne hadn't put on her clothes. They were rags anyway; his tongue had shredded them. She did not feel the cold as anything to distress her.

She was changed. Even in the starlight, she could see her skin was altered, already colored over by her time among them, soaking up their painterly breath. A dusk color, her skin, like the bloom on a wineberry. And her hair, that had a sheen of altered color too, red or gold—like a leaf.

When they returned, they brought the carcasses of deer with them. On this they fed. Graynne fed with them. Like her, she found, they preferred to broil or char their meat first. It was easier for them—she would have needed the two sticks, and they only to breathe in the correct fire-making way.

Autumn ended as the draakors flew, hunted, and feasted. Sometimes they played, savage as lynxes, aiming scything blows across each other's impervious hides, eyes slammed shut against the rake of claws.

Now and then they descended the mountain on foot. On these excursions, as on the flights, Graynne did not accompany them. She'd sit in the winter sun on the hill, turning herself over to it, as they often did. She copied very much of their behavior, all that was possible to her. She wanted nothing else, nothing at *all* from the world of humankind.

Sometimes in their mouths they brought back fruits from the wood. They let her open these so the ripened hearts were exposed, mingling their juices, pear liquor over apple, plums squeezing out red syrup. One or other of the draakors would then come and breathe across the waiting dish, the thinnest most transient flame. Meeting the fruit, it burned a glassy blue, changing the juices to tart sweetness like that of the alcohol said to be given to kings.

Graynne began to menstruate. It surprised her at first. Her menses had been rare and meager, malnourished as she'd been. The regular feeding upon meat and fruit now accessible to her, seemed to have brought her on.

Graynne had no means, here, of concealing or stoppering her blood. The dragons noted it—definitely noted, they sniffed at her, and where the blood sometimes fell. But her lover directly reacted to her blood. He cleaned her, as she cleaned herself, but with his tongue. Then he stood away from her, and out of the depths of him evolved his sexual tail. It was long and fiery as it extruded from its case, and barbed, Graynne saw, like a cat's. Yet, though erect, it made no demand either on her or on him. Instead, at once, it sprayed a fountain of pearls across the little spaced droplets of her fallen blood.

Graynne looked in wonder. Despite the volume of this spurt of semen, it hardened at once. Even this was beautiful. It became a patch of sheerest nacre, containing within it the scarlet flowering of her blood, ruby under pearl.

She sat between his forefeet. Above her, his head, nearly the length of her body, swaying a little, like a tree.

How long since she had spoken? She didn't speak, but sang to him, and now he sang back to her, that muted thunder under the hill of himself.

This went on and on, this singing, in turn and together. (The others listened stilly and respectfully.) Graynne didn't know what the songs meant, neither his nor hers. They were songs of content and approval, of satisfaction and mad joy, needing neither language nor interpretation.

Soon after this the winter began to shut down the world. The mountain was sheathed in ice, the bar woods below turned bleakly through wanness to near-transparency, their evergreen dark only a shadow. Snow scattered, and the winds swung like vast sails between heaven and earth.

This was the time when animals slept. When men too kept much indoors, cleaving to their firesides. It was also the time when the dragons disbanded. His eight companions opened their wings and flew away.

He too. He showed her he would go. She stood in the cavern, knowing he would leave her. She no longer felt the cold, it wasn't the weather that chilled Graynne.

What could she say to him? *Don't leave me.* Must she explain that she could never, now, return among mankind. Or explain that she would die of loneliness. How would he understand?

What would she miss the most?

Leave me something at least.

These were the things that women said to their lovers who left them.

Leave me something.

Don't leave me.

But what had she been for him? A moment. A fragment of time so tiny that, once he was gone, he would no longer see it, nor carry the shimmer-image in his eyes.

The flight of his going left a chasm in her, and a hole in the sky—through more snow sluiced over the mountain.

Graynne sat out on the slope, and the snow fell over her as over everything.

Later she got up and went into the cavern. She lit the flax, her own poor way, and by its light gazed at the walls of purple and magenta and carmine and primrose, at the lovely sick of metals.

Climbing up a little way, only a little (she'd never been of great height), she hung herself down along the slope of the rock, somehow fixing herself there, firm as an iron blade, a woman who became a sword, there being nothing else for her to do.

She said aloud (it was so quiet there now): "It was never himself I saw, that day in the woods. Not me. It was my own reflection I saw, in the water through the leaves. And when I turned my head, nor was that he. It was a trick of my fancy, that shadow-shape, the way he glanced at me under his brows. He never came down so far. It was my dream of him I saw, the dream I never, wakened up, remember. But I knew him, how he was, from my dream. May-it-be, so I did."

Beyond the cavern mouth the snow fell thick as the whitest leaves, to cover everything.

3

It was spring.

Green spangled through the woods, over hills, across orchards and yards of hops, as if the rain had dropped it there. There was apple-blossom. The brown streams ran like busy beer.

That evening, as the village was closing its gate, he came striding along the track, planting his booted feet undaunted in the cowpats. Cloak of bear-fur. Metal plates on him, a sword across his back, and a horn bow. Necklet of thick hammered gold.

He was let in.

"There's work for you, hereabouts."

"So I hear tell," he said.

"Thank God," they said, shaking hands and heads. "Yes, a swordsman. He'll see to it."

When he reached the inn it was a big place, turf-roofed and with many windows. A chimney let out smoke, one of hundreds. The village was about its supper. That seen to, a mob of them would be along to the inn, to gawk at the new champion, the kingsman.

Even the priest came out of his house by the church, in the twilight, and took himself over to the inn, where his own cup was kept, and he got his wine, always gratis, naturally.

— ❖ — ❖ — ❖ —

Loud, the inn, that night (always). But tonight the swordsman was its pivot. They served him roasted pork with dumplings, pan-fried bread and savory, a fat pink trout set round with baked sloes soaked all winter in white whisky-bae. Also they put down a black bottle of the same whiskybae with a few sloes still in it, beside the guest-cup (rather better than the priest's?) of swarthy silver, filled up again and again with wine.

People came to watch the champion eat and drink. He was a champion eater and drinker, too.

The innkeeper's own daughter, a pretty girl, had put on her best gown and combed her hair, and waited on him directly.

He seemed sober yet, despite all the food, the drinks and sloes and what-not, and the daughter. He said very little.

Then the priest came over, clean and tidy in his wool

robe, and blessed the swordsman, who had to get up and then kneel down to acknowledge this—and then stand and sit again.

"Well, my son. And did the king send you to assist us here?"

"I sent myself. I heard of it, father, along the river."

"The dragon."

"Yes. Some years now," said the champion, chatty with the priest after all, this more important person. "Some tens of years since I heard of a dragon in these parts. To the north now, there are still a handful. But they're old."

"This one isn't old. Of the dragonkind, young, I would say."

"What's been done?"

"By the villages? Nothing, neither side of the mountain. It is the ramp of the Great demon, that hill. No one goes up there."

"I heard a tale," said the champion, pouring out a measure of the sloe-whisky for the priest, "that some of these dragons can send a shadow of themselves down to the valleys and plains, to enchant any that has the propensity to see it. They catch young girls that way, lure them," the champion glanced at the daughter, who quaked flirtatiously, "and devour the poor maids when once they reach its lair."

"I've heard this too," said the priest. He drank the whiskybae. "There have been plagues of dragons here, and the world over. Sometimes we think them gone, but, due to the sins of mankind, their wicked transgressions, God only sends the beasts back on us."

"I trust I'll not inconvenience God, by slaying the thing."

The priest scowled, wondering if he was being mocked. But the champion seemed serious, questioning.

"If God wills we be delivered, you will deliver us, my son

Cnori," said the priest. "Come to the church prior to departure. I'll shrive you, before your battle."

Upstairs, a couple of hours later, as the swordsman and the inndaughter romped in the inn's best bed, she too told him a story.

"I heard of a woman wed a dragon."

She told him how there had been a girl in one of the old villages, here perhaps, or the other side of the infested mountain. She was rich and sought-after, but wanted none of the local men, none could please her or were good enough for her ideas. And so one day she set out in her finest dress, and all her jewels of silver and gold, and sought the dragon's cave under the hill.

"Had it sent a sending on her, to make her go?"

Like the priest, the daughter wasn't sure whether Cnori was mocking her or deadly earnest and agog.

"No. It was, she saw her own reflection in a pool of water, and thought she was a dragon herself."

"Well *that's* a tale I never heard, for sure. Why did she think that, was she ugly?"

"Comely as the day she was," said the daughter, thinking of herself. "But when she looked in the pool, it wasn't as when she'd looked in all her silver mirrors. In the pool she saw she was, though human in appearance, in reality a dragon."

The champion Cnori digested this, and belched, but that may have been more the pork than the story.

He and the inndaughter danced loin to loin again awhile, and the bed groaned like a ship in a gale.

When they were done, she continued her narrative.

She told him the girl who was a dragon reached the dragon mountain. And the dragon came out. He, it seemed, also thought she was a dragon. Rather than kill and consume her, he led her in, and she laid down her embroidered dress and her jewelry on the heap of his hoard, where were already collected quantities of gems, silvered armor, iron and steel swords, copper and gold. The monster accepted these gifts of hers as her dowry, and made her a bed of flax and feathers, which he warmed by a magical fire he could produce that didn't scorch, only fondled. There he took her, and there she let him, and the days and nights rang bell-like to their cries of bliss.

"How could she accommodate him?" asked Cnori. He seemed genuinely curious. "They're large in size, and in all particulars, dragons."

"I told you, my hero, she was a dragon too."

"But you said not in her body."

"It didn't matter."

"Did she survive it?" he asked. "Or did the old feller split her in twain?"

"Never he did. She was his dragonwife. They lived together in harmony for hundreds of years, but to the places round about they were both a bane and horror all that time."

"And then?"

"Then he left her."

"For shame," said the champion uneasily. "A scoundrel, even if he was a dragon."

The daughter said softly, "I love you, my lord. Take me with you when you go."

"Maybe. But first I must fight the fellow on the hill. You won't be wanting to be about for any of that. I'll fetch you after."

"You liar," she said. But then she made herself laugh, as if she joked, and meant no disrespect.

"An alchemist," said the swordsman as if he thought she had and hadn't been either, "will pay gold for one scale of a dragon. But for the skin of a woman such as you describe, this *dragonwife*—he'd pay gold by the bucket. What they'd prize, these scientific men, is just such a combinement, human with dragon. That's a rare sorcery. What must she have been! What became of her, then?"

"Oh," said the girl, petulant at last, "it's only a story. Let it alone."

When she slept the inndaughter had a dream. She always dreamed, and usually remembered what each dream had concerned, on waking.

However, this time when she woke up, she knew she had been dreaming, but at once she couldn't remember a moment of it.

In the dream though, it had been two or more centuries ago. And though the girl saw everything, it was like another tale told her, she had no part in it, none at all. She was dreaming of the dragonwife.

There in the cave the woman was, lying down along the wall in some weird way, her hair hanging round her to the floor. It was winter, but outside the ice was noisily shifting and cracking on the hill.

The cave was painted in a thousand colors, and flowers burned on the pools at its middle.

Across from where the woman lay downward, near the back of the cavern, was a wonderful great oval pearl, the size of a cartwheel. It was just lying there, this jewel, and the watcher took it for a piece of the dragon's hoard. Inside it was a ghostly scarlet pulse that came then went away, then came back again, so for a while the watchful sleeper had taken it for a trick of the firelight.

Then there sounded a huge crack, nor was it the ice beyond the cave. It was the pearl cracking open.

If she'd been there herself, and *as* herself, the watcher would have shrieked and fled a mile. But in the dream she didn't mind it, not the loss of the matchless pearl, nor the little creature that was crawling out, sticky with the ichors of the egg, which was what the pearl had been all that while.

Its claws scrabbled in miniature on the rock. It made a little snorting, mewing sound, so feeble and faint no one would hear it. But the woman lying down on the rock, she heard. She raised only her head where she lay, like a snake. The watcher saw then she was not like other women, for her skin resembled a storm-rinsed dusk, and her hair was full of fiery colors, like the walls.

Graynne ran across the cavern to where the new-made dragon, formed from her shed wombal blood and her lover's sperm, had grown of itself, inside a shell, in the way of dragons' eggs.

Watching her, the sleeper thought this mother, whose skin, though odd, was soft and mortal, would be sorely bitten (already it had teeth, like bone needles) or scored by its talons—like needles of steel. But then she saw too this mother wouldn't mind that, had no caution of that. She had no fear.

Even so, the meeting between mother and son surprised the watcher very much. This was because, alas, in the watcher's life (admittedly not yet long, but nevertheless eventful), she had never seen displayed such total love on both sides. Not that the love was so *physically* evinced, though it was, physically, clearly to be seen—in embraces, nuzzlings, murmurs. It showed itself in some other way mostly, which the watcher, again maybe because she had no knowledge of such love, found impossible to determine or recognize—yet all the while, it stood up huge as the cavern itself, or more likely, high as the sky beyond.

After this greeting meeting, Graynne surprised the watcher even more than more. She'd wondered, the inndaughter, although asleep and calm, how such a child was to be fed in the manner of newborn things. But next she saw how Graynne took up a piece of meat, already cooked and lying by. She put it in her mouth and chewed it down to a pulp, which then she spat gently through into the baby's ready jaws.

Oh, no astonishment she forgot all this when she woke, the innkeeper's daughter. Nor that she forgot the dragonwife's name, which in the dream was known to her.

Leave me something at least, she'd said that night to *her* lover, the swordsman Cnori. But he'd left her nothing at all, only a coin under her pillow. Which had made her rage, for she wasn't a slut, was she, she'd gone with him out of liking, and because her father wished her available for the better class of customer.

But for Graynne something had been left.

All through the winter's ending, she was with her child, the dragonson. On the hillside, as the sun returned, they were out, playing. Inside seven days he knew how not to hurt her, something mankind had never learned. Sometimes she played more roughly than he, biting at his impenetrable brazen hide, swiping her long hard nails toward his pewter eyes, teaching him the proper gambits.

Through that spring and summer, he grew and then was grown, body long as three horses, and taller than a man's, and standing far higher, too, once his canine's serpent's head was raised. He had stopped kicking at his tail by then, or chasing it. He became grave and courteous and terrible. He and she hunted the hills. At dawn, they lay down and she sang to him. Her voice was strange, not like the voice of a woman—had it never been? Like a sweet-keening wind. Sometimes he answered, mild and experimental (no hurry), in a song that was like distant thunder.

Even asleep then, even after the passing of so much time, which to dragonkind was less than the blink of an eye, the dreamer began to withdraw, or rather to want and prepare to go away. She knew she was dreaming it. Even asleep then, too, perhaps she wished she would, on waking, forget it all, for once. And so she did.

The morning church was small and poorly lit; the swordsman Cnori had seen better often. But the priest heard Cnori's confession sternly, and set a stiff penance, nevertheless allowing it might be undertaken *after* the fight with the dragon.

Then the priest drew Cnori into a side chamber, and took out of a cupboard a huge slab of a dusty book, held together by woven rope. This he undid and opened the book with difficulty on a table. It was so old, the pages were yellow and stuck together, save in one place where they came open with no trouble.

"Look here," said the priest.

Cnori looked. The script was in the priestly tongue, which Cnori, for all his sophistication, couldn't read, though he saw, amongst the curlicues, the antique name *Draakor* written boldly. Above, there was a picture of the beast.

"Now see this," said the priest, and he lit a candle and held it near the picture.

The dull green of the dragon's body gradually changed to blue. Then the priest dragged the book, unwisely perhaps, it was very fragile, to where a single spot of sunlight fell through the narrow window. And then the green and blue dragon burned up red as a fire.

"I've heard of this," said the champion. "Ink from a scale?"

"Exactly. The book came to me out of the old priestery. Not many have looked at this. I've shown you, to strengthen you. Now go to victory with God's good will."

Alone, Cnori traveled swiftly. Before sunset he had got up all the distance past the fields and village woods, then over and down to the forest in the valley under the dragon hills. The valley trees were thick and fierce in the forest, gigantic pines and firs and bristling cedars, just putting on their fresh sprays of somber green. In the forest he noted dragon turds, as he had expected. Also, when the grudging light began to retreat entirely and the trunks seemed doubled, he found the bones of a man.

By then, Cnori was right up against the base of the hills, with the cone of the mountain standing aloft like a stone castle. The trees had thinned but not ended here. They too marched up the hillsides now for quite a way.

Cnori investigated the bones. They weren't young. *Historic* bones, but all broken, and the skull had come off, or something had run off *with* it. There was a metal flask, dented, with some gold, and a sword too, red with rust, and two or three soft golden strips wound with colorless hair.

The champion, though he'd been with a priest only that morning, made an offering to these bones of a warrior, in the ancient manner, pouring wine out to him, giving him a share of the dried meat from the inn. Foxes would thieve that during the night. Or maybe not. He had smelled no foxes. Probably they kept away. The smell of dragon he did have in his nostrils. Even at the inn there had been that. (Dragon— and here, something else, he thought. Something more uncanny.)

He didn't make a fire. He sat for a long while, his back to the bole of a massive pine. It had mated eccentrically with a hawthorn, and was all frothy white with blossoms up among the needles. He thought the dragon might nocturnally fly over. They said, in the last village, they thought it flew. But the other villages had said it flew less often than it walked.

He wasn't afraid. He never was. But during the night he must have dozed, and then the bones of the dead man got up and came and sat across from him, like the polite stranger they were.

"You'll be after it, then," said the bones. Having neither head nor lips seemed not to be an obstacle to their ease with speech.

"Yes," said Cnori, inside his doze.

"So was I, once. But oh, she pushed me down, that fuck-bitch, and down I went. All down the fuckcliff."

"I'm sorry for you."

"Well, no matter. We all come to it, so we do."

At daybreak, when the light flowed back, Cnori went to look at the headless skeleton, and it was a little disturbed. As if a fox had come and tried to seize the offered meat—which was still there, however. Or as if the bones really had got themselves up and about during the night.

That day, Cnori climbed the slopes with the trees, came out above them, climbed on toward the mountaintop.

The sun went across, then down and down like a king's sinking golden ship. It was colder here, and now nothing grew but the odd twisted tree thin as a worm, with snaky ocher hair.

By the time the sun reached the world's brink, the champion was up on the mountain's upper flank. It was simpler walking than it had once been, weathered, broken in. And here he found an apple tree with white blossoms big as rose-heads, and already in fruit. Lilac apples hung in tight clusters, like berries.

Under the tree, as he came up to it through the last of the day, sat a woman. She was wrapped in a cloak of some kind, made, he thought, of threaded grasses, such as the impoverished fashioned. It covered most of her, but for her hidden face and a few escaping locks of hair. *They* all had the color and burnish of the dying sun.

"Good evening," said the champion. (His sword and knives stayed in sling and belt. He had required his hands for some of the climb, despite the easing of the slope.) "Are you the one I've been hearing of?"

Then she turned and looked at him through the shadow cast from under her hood. Her eyes glittered brilliantly as spilled drops of the light, but only for an instant.

It seemed to take her a long while to think she would or could reply to him. When she did, she sang her words.

She said, or sang, "My son is from hame. He isn't here today. Tomorrow then."

"Your son. Ah. He's the one I want. Not you, woman. Just your son."

"He won't mind it," she sang, the woman to Cnori, "if I make you welcome on my own. There's enough," said the woman, "for two."

And then he stood there astounded by it—by her, and everything, at last by dragons—maybe even abruptly by his own life, which had been riotous and too brief. But mostly by the dim-bright sudden awareness of how he would, at sunrise, be over and done, all black cinders. And she came out from her cloak, which was only some down-trailing stuff of the tree after all. Yet that was, he thought, anyway as if she came out from her *cave*. From dark cover to the final flare of ending day. And there she poised. Blue as the approaching twilight, with coursing hair all bronze and gold, copper and silver. He didn't know her name to speak it. If he had he might have done: *Graynne, Graynne Dragonwife*. He put his hand over-shoulder against the hilt of his sword, sluggishly. Believing it, he didn't believe. (The secret of his previous success?) He beheld her open her mouth again, but not to sing. She sighed. And the last thing then he saw in that world, was her opening her mouth to sigh, and how, out of the sigh, and out of her mouth came

    Fire.

JOUST

by Mercedes Lackey

Mercedes Lackey is an awesomely prolific fantasy writer whose novels and short stories include several multivolume series: *Bardic Voices, Bard's Tale, Diana Tregarde, Knight of Ghosts and Shadows, Serrated Edge, Valdemar,* and others, some of them solo performances, others collaborative efforts with such acclaimed authors as Marion Zimmer Bradley, Andre Norton, C. J. Cherryh, Anne McCaffrey, and Josepha Sherman. A native of Chicago and graduate of Purdue University, Lackey is a former artist's model, computer programmer, and employee of American Airlines. She also writes song lyrics for Centaur, a recording company that specializes in fantasy and science fiction songs. "Joust" is the powerful story of a slave boy whose quest for independence is accelerated when he gets to know a dragon's ways and manners. When writing "Joust" for *The Dragon Quintet,* the author was so taken by the history of young Vetch that she went on to expand his adventures into a new novel with the same title as this story.

Vetch hunched his shoulders against the pitiless glare of the sun above him, and heaved at the heavy leather water-bucket that had been tossed at him by his master this morning. It was far too big and heavy when full for someone as small as he was to carry—a weedy little boy as he was, named for a weedy little plant not even fit for fodder—but an Altan serf had to do what he was told, with what he was given. Just now, Vetch's task was to fill the drip-cistern that fed the tiny copper tubes that in turn watered his Tian master's tala plants, droplet by droplet, so that the precious water wasn't wasted, evaporating into the air. Tala could only be grown during the dry season, after the Great Mother River had shrunk to a mere trickle and the sun-baked fields of corn and barley were riddled with cracks as wide as a man's hand. But tala-fruits were worth their weight in electrum, for tala-fruits gave the Jousters their ability to control the great dragons that had allowed Tia to conquer fully a third of what had once been Altan lands. Vetch's master made a great deal of money from his little tala field, more than enough to pay for many jars of fine date-wine, and melons, honey-cakes, and roast duck on his table on a regular basis.

Sweat prickled Vetch's scalp, and a drop of sweat trickled down his temple. But the hot, dry air swiftly dried it before he could free a hand to wipe it away. His stomach ached with hunger, and he was tired, so tired—even the anger that never left him was not enough to overcome how tired he was. A few steps more, and he made it to the side of the aboveground stone cistern. With a sigh of relief, he eased the bucket to the ground, and went up the two steps that allowed a little fellow like him to reach the cistern-lid. He slid the wooden cover aside, pausing for just a second to savor the momentary breath of cool damp that escaped, then groped behind him for the bucket-handle again.

It wasn't there.

Vetch whirled, expecting to find that one of the Tian boys who apprenticed with his master had tilted the bucket on its side, allowing it to spill its precious burden into the thirsty, hard-packed earth. Or worse, had stolen the bucket—

Someone had taken the bucket, all right, but it wasn't an apprentice.

Behind him, a tall, muscular Tian—a warrior, by his muscles, and one of the elite Jousters, by the linen kilt, the wide leather belt, and the empty lance-socket hanging from it—held the heavy bucket to his lips, gulping down the master's well-water with the fervor of one who was perishing of thirst. Vetch stared at him, the surge of anger he'd felt at having his bucket stolen by yet another Tian overcome with sheer astonishment at seeing one of the Jousters *here*. He had never seen a Jouster so close before.

Where there was a Jouster, could his dragon be far away? Vetch looked wildly about, then a snort made him look *up*, to the roof of the threshing-shed, and there was the great dragon itself, looking down at him with an aloof gaze remarkably like that of one of the pampered cats that swarmed the Temple of Pashet.

Vetch gaped; the dragon was a thing of multicolored, jeweled beauty, slim and supple, and quite as large as the shed it perched upon. A narrow, golden large-eyed head oddly reminiscent of a well-bred horse's, with the same slim muzzle, dished nose, and broad forehead, surmounted by a pair of pointed emerald ears as delicate and translucent as alabaster, rose on a long, flexible neck that shaded from emerald to blue. The wings, of blue shading into purple, rising from muscular shoulders twice the bulk of the hindquarters, were spread to catch the sun. The long, whip-like tail, which reversed the shading of the neck, going from green into gold curled around the cruel talons of the forefeet, as the dragon lounged comfortably on the flat roof of the shed. The eyes, though, that was what caught you and held you—slit-pupiled and the deep crimson of the finest rubies—

Not that Vetch had ever seen the finest rubies, or indeed, any rubies. But that was what people said, and certainly the colors were every bit as gorgeous as the magnificent wall-paintings in Tian temples depicting the jewels worn by gods and kings.

The Jouster finished his drink and dumped the rest of the bucket of water over his head. Vetch made an involuntary whimper of suppressed rage in the back of his throat as the man tossed the bucket aside; he scrambled after it, just as his master appeared in the door of his house. Khefti was huge, and terrifying; his size alone was intimidating as his gut bulged over his kilt, his fat hands were quick with a blow, and his doughy face wore a perpetual scowl beneath his striped headdress. He was the very last person that Vetch wanted to see at this moment.

Khefti the Fat was about as bad a master as any Vetch had ever had; technically, a serf was not a slave, but you couldn't have told that from the way that Khefti used and abused *his* serfs. Technically, serfs were not property; they could not be bought or sold individually the way that slaves could. They were bound to the land, land that had, in Vetch's case, been taken from his Altan family of farmers by the Tian conquerors. But Vetch was the only one of his family left, now; the Tian who had taken control of their land along with that of their neighbors, had sold it in turn to another Tian noble, who in his turn broke it up into smaller portions and sold them. Each time it was sold, Vetch's family got a new master, until at last it came to Khefti. By this time, the farm itself had been divided and divided again, until little more was left than the house and vegetable garden.

Khefti used this as an excuse to dispose of all of the remaining members of Vetch's family—his three sisters, mother, and grandmother—back to those who had purchased the rest of the land. What happened then, Vetch had no idea; Khefti had taken him to his house in Nefis. *Taken*

was perhaps too mild a word; Vetch had been dragged away
from his family, literally kicking and screaming, as the girls
were led away weeping by their new masters, Grandmother
shuffled off, head bowed, with every fiber of her registering
defeat, and the last Vetch saw of his mother was a final
glimpse of her collapsing to the earth. Then Khefti had begun
beating him to make him stop screaming, which was the last
thing that Vetch remembered.

Why Khefti had kept Vetch, the boy had no idea. Perhaps
it had only been for the sake of the records; certainly a man
from the capitol came every so often and Vetch was trotted
out for his inspection, perhaps in order to hold the land, you
had to have at least one of the serfs that came with it. At least
until the point where they were all dead . . .

One thing only was certain; Khefti intended to get as
much work out of Vetch for as little expense as was physically possible. A master was responsible for the feeding,
housing, and clothing of his serfs as well as his slaves, but
there was nothing in the law to make him do so adequately.
Vetch was *always* hungry; as the savory aromas from Khefti's
kitchen tantalized his nose, he would be making a scanty
breakfast of a palm-sized loaf of yesterday's bread (he could
have eaten half a dozen), or supper of a tiny bowl of pottage
his family wouldn't have fed to a pig and another little loaf
of stale bread. Sometimes the fare was varied by the addition
of an onion beginning to go bad. Lunch was whatever *he*
could find, in the hour when Khefti slept—a handful of wild
lettuce, latal-roots grubbed out of the riverbank and eaten
raw, wild onions so strong they made the eyes water.
Sometimes he found duck-eggs in season; sometimes there
were berries or palm-fruits. Mostly, he got only what Khefti
gave him. He hadn't seen cheese or meat or honey-cakes
since the farm was taken. He dreamed about food all the

time, and there was never a moment when his stomach wasn't empty.

And he was angry all the time. He woke angry, and went to sleep angry. Not that he could *do* anything about his anger, but at least when he was angry, he wasn't crying. Crying would make him a greater target for torment than he already was; tears were a sign of weakness he couldn't afford.

He slept on a pile of reeds *he* had cut, under the same awning that sheltered the wood for the bread-oven from rain, in the outer back-court, beyond the kitchen-court. Thus Khefti gave lip service to the provision of "food and shelter" for his serf . . .

Khefti had not seen the Jouster; he certainly hadn't seen the dragon. All he saw was Vetch, standing on the steps of the cistern with empty hands and no bucket in sight.

With an inarticulate roar, Khefti snatched up the little whip that never left his side, and descended on Vetch. For all his bulk, Khefti the Fat moved surprisingly fast; Vetch only had time enough to crouch down and cover his head with his hands when the quirt descended on his shoulders, leaving a strip of fire across his back that made him gasp with pain.

Once. Twice. Vetch squeezed his eyes shut, stuffed both hands in his mouth and bit his knuckles, strangling his cries with his hands. Khefti never delivered fewer than a dozen blows even at the best of times, but sooner or later he *had* to see the Jouster, and then he would stop. If Vetch could just hold on without fainting until his master realized they were not alone—

But the third blow never came.

Vetch risked a glance backward, and saw, with astonishment, that the Jouster had caught the wrist of Khefti's whip-hand and was holding it effortlessly at shoulder-height. Never quick-witted, Khefti's expression was caught between

the moment of rage when his hand had been caught and the
dawning realization of just *who* had stopped him from beating his property.

"The boy is not at fault," the Jouster said, in a mild voice.
"I took his bucket to quench my thirst. He could hardly take
it away from me."

Khefti went red-faced and spluttering, but what could he
say? Nothing, of course. Nor would he dare do anything further to Vetch while the Jouster was there.

Once he was gone, however, he would certainly extract a
double dose of punishment out of Vetch, for having looked a
fool in front of a Jouster. Unless Vetch could slip away, get
the bucket, and go back to his task again while Khefti was
talking to the Jouster. If he saw that, he might feel the beating he'd already given Vetch was enough. Vetch eased one
foot down the stair.

The dragon snorted again, and the Jouster looked up at
it, then down at Khefti. "From the look of things," he continued, in that same mild voice, "you've been abusing the
King's property. You do remember, don't you, that serfs are
the *King's* property, and not yours?"

Khefti went from red to white, all the blood draining from
his skin until he looked like an enormous damp, white grub.

The Jouster turned his gaze from Khefti to Vetch. "I need
a boy," he said absently. "And if you're getting *any* amount
of work from one that starved, he must be a good worker. I'll
have him."

He let go of Khefti's wrist, and Khefti dropped to the
ground, to lie there like a quivering, misshapen, unbaked
loaf. "But—" Khefti burbled. "B-b-b-but—"

The Jouster ignored him. Instead, he looked up at his
dragon again, which uncoiled itself and stepped carefully
down into the yard, then bent its forequarters so that its

shoulders were even with the Jouster's chest. The Jouster grabbed the back of Vetch's loincloth as if he was a parcel, and heaved him up over the dragon's shoulder.

Vetch landed stomach-down on the dragon's neck, but the Jouster had not thrown him hard, and his breath was not driven out of him, although the band of his loincloth had cut painfully into his stomach when the Jouster had seized it. He'd landed on a sort of carry-pad in front of the Jouster's saddle, and he clung to it like a lizard on a ceiling as the Jouster leapt into the saddle itself.

Then the dragon tensed himself all over, stretched his wings wide, and with a leap and a tremendous beat of those wings, took to the sky. The sudden upward movement pressed Vetch into the carry-pad, and he felt the Jouster seize the band of his loincloth again. A second wingbeat drove them higher—through a storm of dust kicked up by the wind of those wings, Vetch watched Khefti's striped canvas awnings over the woodpile, the kitchen-court, and the summer pavilion on the roof go rippling loose and flying off. A third wingbeat, a third tremendous gust, and half the thatch of the threshing-shed tore loose as well, and the furnishings from the rooftop tumbled over the edge into the street, light wickerwork chairs and tables, mats and pillows; passersby scrambled and carried off everything they could seize. Khefti was not well-beloved . . .

A fourth wingbeat, and Vetch could no longer see the house of his former master, only hear his thin wailing from below as he lamented his losses and called upon the gods to witness his ruin.

The ground whirled away as the dragon wheeled, and Vetch closed his eyes and hung on with all his might.

He had no illusion that this was rescue; he had merely traded one master for another. But this one, at least, had chided Khefti for starving and mistreating him. So perhaps this master would be better than Khefti.

At least he would be different.

Aside from the sheer terror of the flight, there were two things that branded themselves in Vetch's mind; one was the extraordinary *heat* of the dragon's body, hot as the hottest sand at midday during the dry season. The other was the feeling of the Jouster's hard, strong hand in the small of his back, once again holding to the belt of his loincloth. At least the Jouster wasn't going to let him fall.

The flight wasn't a long one. Just about the time when Vetch's muscles were starting to cramp and hurt from the strain of holding on, he felt the dragon dropping. He cracked open one eye, to see the ground rushing up at them, and squeezed them shut again.

With a *thud*, the flight was over. The Jouster's hand loosened on Vetch's belt, and without being prompted, he let go and slid down the dragon's hot, smooth shoulder to the ground. His legs buckled under him, but he scrambled to his feet quickly, his eyes never leaving his new master. The Jouster tossed his leg over the saddle and jumped lightly down, and gave his dragon a hearty slap on the shoulder.

"Now what've you brought back, Ari?" asked a gruff voice.

The Jouster spoke to whoever was behind Vetch; Vetch didn't dare turn to look. "New dragon-boy. Serf."

"Not some street-trash?" the voice replied dubiously. "He's got fresh stripes—"

"I was there when he got them, for 'letting' me take his bucket and quench my thirst," Ari replied, turning to unbuckle the throat-strap of the saddle, and laughed. "No, he's a serf. Now the fat slug that was beating him is going to have to find another in his bloodline if he wants to hold his land."

So *that* was why Khefti had never sold him!

"But a serf—why not a free boy?" the voice complained. "There must be dozens of free boys you could have from their parents for the asking!"

"Because I'm tired of replacing free boys when they get airs and decide they ought to be something better than a dragon-boy!" Ari snapped, and unbuckled the last strap. He pulled the saddle off the dragon's back and turned with it in his hands.

He dropped it in Vetch's arms; Vetch had been expecting this from the moment he'd heard what he was to become.

The saddle was heavy, and he staggered for a moment beneath its weight. It had an additional scent besides that of leather—a hot, metallic scent, with an overtone of spice. The scent of the dragon?

"There, boy—" the Jouster said, in a tone of dismissal. "You go with Haraket; he'll teach you your business."

Ari stalked off, and Vetch turned, the saddle in his arms, to face the person he had not yet seen.

The man wore a simple white linen kilt, augmented by a multicolored sash around his waist and a second that ran from his right shoulder to the opposite hip. His square head was shaven, and he wore a hawk-eye amulet of glazed pottery around his neck. He gazed down on Vetch with resignation.

"Come on, you," he said. Vetch ducked his head obediently, and followed as the man strode off. But he stopped dead at the sound of something large and heavy following *him*.

He turned. The dragon stared down at him; it had been right on his heels.

"Come *on*, serf-boy!" the man snarled, when *he* turned to discover that Vetch was not behind him anymore. "Kashet isn't like other dragons; Ari doesn't need tala to control him. You're damned lucky to be Ari's boy; Kashet is a *shapti* to handle compared with the others."

He turned and Vetch hurried to catch up with him, the dragon following along like a hound. For the moment, the ever-present anger had retreated before his feeling of complete astonishment.

The dragon had landed in a huge courtyard with enormously high walls around it, "paved" with dirt pounded hard and as flat as a smooth mud-brick. There were four entrances to this courtyard, one in the middle of each wall. All were tall enough to allow a dragon to pass through them, and broad enough for three. The man marched straight through one; Vetch followed, and the dragon followed him.

On the other side of the wall were more walls; the area was also open to the sky. These walls were not as tall as the ones around the courtyard, and dragon heads peeked over the top of them. Already Vetch could tell there was a profound difference between these dragons and Kashet. Ari's dragon had some interest in his eyes when he looked at Vetch—these dragons had the eyes of a feral cat, wary and wild.

He expected noise; there was very little. The dragons hissed and snorted, but there was no bellowing, no growling. The bald man turned a corner down another corridor, then another—and Vetch found they were inside another courtyard, this one, as he soon found, knee-deep in soft sand. He floundered into it, and the man reached out a long arm and hauled him back to the verge.

"Stay on the walkway around the edge, boy," the man said, but not unkindly. "That sand will burn you, else, until you're used to it. You'll need to toughen your skin to it." And indeed, the sand radiated heat upwards; as hot as the sun overhead. "Put the saddle over there," he continued, pointing to a wooden rack mounted on the wall nearest Vetch. "Kashet doesn't need to be chained the way the others do, so you leave him free—"

The dragon, ignoring both of them, plunged into the center of the room to wallow into the hot sand. Vetch put the saddle on the rack, and so began his first day as a dragon-boy.

It was not an easy life, but it was a paradise compared with his life with Khefti as his master.

"Kashet will be your sole concern from morning to night," Haraket told him. "And the first thing you must do now is to feed him so that he knows you. Only a dragon-boy, or at need, the overseer or the Jouster, will feed a dragon."

Haraket was leading him at a trot down the corridors; Vetch was hard put to keep up with the overseer's long legs. But those words worried him.

"Sir?" he panted, literally the first words he had spoken to anyone since the Jouster arrived at the cistern. "Sir, who is Kashet's dragon-boy?"

The overseer looked down at him, his lips tightening. "Imbecile," he muttered, and answered more loudly. "You are, haven't you been listening?"

He almost dared to hope. "Sir—I meant—who is Kashet's *other* dragon-boy?" In his heart was the dread that he was displacing someone else—or worse, would have to face a rival. Some of that must have shown in his expression, as the overseer's face cleared, and he grunted.

"There is no other dragon-boy for Kashet. Jouster Ari and I have been caring for him."

Now all that business about serfs and free boys made sense . . .

"Here—down this way is where the servants from all of the Temples bring the sacrifices," Haraket said, making another abrupt turn, and led him in through a closed door.

On the other side—

Vetch *almost* broke and ran. He was no stranger to the killing of farm-stock but never on a scale like this, and never anything bigger than a goat. There were carcasses of enormous cattle, goats, sheep, stacked up everywhere, being hacked up by a dozen butchers into hand-sized chunks, and the sight made him feel sick and dizzy for a moment.

And for a moment, all he could think of was the last sight of his father, covered with his own blood—and the anger surged, but the fear buried it, and he had to clutch the wall to keep from fainting.

But curiously, there was no blood, or very little. "This is all fresh from the Temple's butchers," Haraket was saying, as the nearest of the butchers tossed chunks of meat, bone-in, skin-on, into a barrow beside him. "It's a nice piece of economy when you think about it. Every day, hundreds of animals are sacrificed to the gods or cut up for divination ceremonies, but there's no use for the bodies when the blood and spirit had drained away."

Of course; the Tians believed that the gods required only the blood and the *mana* of the creatures sacrificed on the altars. There were so many gods, and so many people who needed their favor—

"There aren't enough priests in the world to consume all that flesh." Haraket continued, "Even if they were as fat as houses. So it comes to us. That's why they built the Jouster's compound on the Temple-road. So—he's filled that barrow, now you take it."

The barrow was heavy and hard to push, but Vetch was accustomed to being ordered to do things that were just short of being too much for his strength. He grabbed the handles and started shoving, following Haraket back to Kashet's pen at a much slower pace.

Kashet was waiting for them; he saw the now-familiar head peering over the walls long before they got to the opening of the pen. Kashet didn't wait for him at all; no sooner had he gotten to the part of the corridor outside the entrance than the dragon snaked his neck around the corner and snatched a chunk of meat from the barrow, startling him so that he jumped and squeaked.

But he kept pushing the barrow forward, telling himself that if Kashet had wanted to eat *him,* he'd have gone down that long throat while he was still struggling with the saddle.

Kashet plucked chunks from the barrow three more times before Vetch parked it where Haraket pointed. He ate neatly, if voraciously; snatching up a chunk of meat, tossing back his head, and swallowing it whole. Vetch could even see it traveling down his long neck by the bulge it caused.

When the barrow was empty, Kashet heaved an enormous sigh, and returned to the hot sand. Within moments, he was, to Vetch's astonishment, asleep.

"He'll sleep like that until it's time to go out again," Haraket said. "Ari was back early—so we've just enough time to get you kitted up and clean and fed before I show you the afternoon jobs."

With that, they left Kashet wallowing in the sand, sleeping off his meal in the noontime heat. Haraket hustled Vetch off again, this time to a room full of jars of water, with a drain in the center, where he ordered Vetch to strip off the filthy loincloth and saw to it that he scrubbed every inch of himself twice over. Then, skin tingling and arrayed in a real linen kilt of his own, Haraket led him to paradise . . .

Or if not *quite* paradise, it was as near as Vetch had ever been to it. "Paradise" was a kitchen courtyard full of benches and tables set with baskets heaped with bread, jars of beer, platters of cheese, baked latal roots, and sweet onions.

He stared at it, not daring to go near, hoping beyond hope that he would be allowed the remains whenever Haraket and the other masters were finished eating.

And then his stomach growled, and hurt so much it brought tears to his eyes for a moment. And the anger returned, anger at these arrogant Tians for making him stand in the presence of plenty that *he* wasn't to touch—

"Well, what are you waiting for, boy?" Haraket said impatiently. "Sit down! Eat! You do me no good by fainting from hunger!"

Vetch stumbled toward the table and took a seat on the end of the nearest bench, hardly daring to believe what he'd heard. He managed, somehow, to eat like a civilized thing and not cram his mouth full with both his hands. He took one of the little loaves, tore it neatly in half, and began eating; the taste of fresh breads nearly made him faint with pleasure. When he'd finished half the bread, he reached for cheese and onions, and about that point, the other dragon-boys started coming in.

He made himself as small as he could on the bench.

"Who's that?" one asked.

"Kashet's boy," said another, with a knowing glance. "I heard Jouster Ari brought in a serf over his saddle-bow."

"Huh," the first replied, and looked down his long nose at Vetch. "Mind your manners, Kashet's boy," he said loftily to Vetch. "We're all free here but you."

Vetch ducked his head. "Yes, sir," he murmured, and that seemed to satisfy the other, for he crowded onto the bench near his friend and paid no more heed to Vetch.

Vetch felt his anger churn inside him, but he hastened to make himself even smaller and watched the others when he went for more food, always snatching his hand back empty if it looked as if one of the free boys was interested in the platter or basket that he was reaching for.

But even so, for the first time in a very, very long time, he was able to eat as much as he wanted. Kitchen-girls kept coming out of the kitchen with more food, more beer; no matter how much the boys ate, there was always more.

Haraket came for him long before the other boys finished—but then, he'd had a head start on them, and *they* were lingering over their food.

The boys hushed their chatter when Haraket appeared in the doorway, and watched as Vetch scrambled to his feet in response to the beckoning hand. The chatter began again as soon as Vetch cleared the doorframe, following Haraket, and his ears burned, imagining what they were saying about him.

"Now you come saddle Kashet again," Haraket told him, as they entered the pen. Kashet was already easing himself up out of the hot sand, reluctantly. "Go over to the saddle-stand and call him. Say, 'Kashet, stand,' and make it sound like you mean it."

Vetch took his place beside the rack holding the saddle and harness. He imagined how he would feel if *he* was the master, and it was one of those boys back at the kitchen who was the serf. "Kashet!" he called. "Stand!"

Kashet snorted; the snort sounded amused. But the dragon came readily enough, and stood towering over him.

Now, how was he going to get the saddle on the beast when Kashet's shoulder was higher than Haraket's head?

Haraket watched him, eyes narrowed, waiting—for what?

For him to deduce how to handle the dragon from the clues he'd been given?

"Kashet!" he shouted, hearing his voice squeak a little at the end. "Down!"

With a grunt, the dragon knelt at the side of the sandpit,

putting his back just low enough for Vetch to reach. He heaved the saddle over Kashet's neck and took a quick glance at Haraket.

The overseer looked satisfied. Or at least, he wasn't frowning as much.

Vetch took the opportunity to buckle the highest neck-strap, then ordered, this time with more confidence, "Kashet! Up!"

The dragon stood, and Vetch puzzled out the remainder of the harness with a little prompting from Haraket.

When he'd finished, Haraket came over and double-checked the fit of each strap. Some he tightened, but the ones across the neck he loosened. Vetch watched him closely, making mental notes. What he *wanted* was to be free of masters—but that wasn't going to happen, short of a miracle. Failing that, this was the best place he'd ever been in, and he *did not* want to be sent away.

Jouster Ari reappeared at that point, and Haraket stepped back abruptly. Vetch scrambled back out of the way, certain that the Jouster would find something wrong, and all of this would come tumbling down and with a word the Jouster would send him back to Khefti—

But after an inspection of the harness, Ari gave a brief nod to Haraket. Without a command, Kashet extended his foreleg; Ari used it as a step, and with its aid, vaulted into the saddle.

Warned now by his own experience, Vetch shielded his eyes; Kashet spread his wings and leapt, and in a storm of sand and wind, vaulted into the clear blue of the heavens. They wheeled above the pen for a moment as Kashet gained height, and then they were gone.

"Don't just stand there gawking, get that shovel!" Haraket barked, and Vetch hastily looked back down and saw where the overseer was pointing. "Once Kashet's out of the pen, you clean it, each and every time!"

At Haraket's direction, Vetch got the shovel and the barrow he'd used to bring the meat, and began the cleaning. Kashet used a second pit, smaller than the first and unheated, for a privy. The droppings themselves, hard as stones and round, were dangerous to touch. Something about them burned the skin, even though they were actually cooler than the nesting-sands. They were very valuable, though.

"This stuff is worth its weight in silver," Haraket said warningly, as Vetch pushed the barrow at his direction. "You account for every dropping to me, and *I* account for it to the priests."

Vetch didn't ask what dragon-dung was good for; if it was priestly business, it was just as well not to know, and that was doubly true when the priests were Tian.

"Now you clean and mend harness," said Haraket, but this time, it was to be under someone else's supervision, a dour old man who had charge over a cool and shaded room that smelled like leather-oil and was full of other dragon-boys who were laboring to his direction. As the newest and most ignorant, Vetch got the dirtiest job, that of cleaning the saddles.

Eventually the man dismissed them all, and yet another overseer led him to Jouster Ari's personal quarters.

This haughty fellow looked down at him as if expecting him to stand there like an idiot—but Khefti had been too miserly to hire many servants or purchase slaves, so Vetch had done just about every task in the household that didn't require special training. Without being prompted, he began picking up discarded clothing, tidying away scrolls and rolls of reed-paper, capping a bottle of ink—

Satisfied, the overseer left him to clean the rooms; luxurious in some ways, curiously spare in others.

Ari had two rooms and a bathing-room shared with another set of rooms. The plastered walls were ornamented with beautiful paintings; in the outer room, scenes from court life—dancers on one wall, musicians on the second, acrobats on the third, and a group of men with the hawk-eye amulets lounging at a feast on the fourth. In the sleeping-chamber, scenes of nature; the river, with blossoming reeds and latal, horses racing across the desert, birds flying above a field—and on the wall visible to the bed, a great dragon, wings spread.

These were paintings that, if Vetch was any judge, were worthy of a palace. Yet there were few furnishings to the chambers. In the other, a scribe's desk (meant to be used on the lap of one seated on the floor), a chest of scrolls, a rack of writing materials, a few cushions, a lamp. In the bed-chamber, only the bed, a chest of clothing, and another lamp.

It seemed strange to Vetch that one as exalted in rank as a Jouster should live in quarters that were furnished more simply than Khefti's—but at least that made it easier to clean them.

He was standing in the middle of the now-clean outer room with a bundle of soiled linen in his hands when Haraket came for him again. "Put those there—" the overseer said, pointing to a basket just outside the door. "Kashet will be returning shortly, and that is when you will give him his evening sand-bath and his supper."

A "sand-bath" meant taking Kashet out of the compound to yet another place called a "buffing-pen," where Vetch burnished him with sand, then soft, oil-soaked cloths, until he gleamed. All the other dragons were in the buffing-pens as well.

"Only Kashet is safe to handle without chains," Haraket

observed, as another dragon-boy brought his charge into the pen, but not as Haraket had, with only a hand on his shoulder. This dragon wore a chain around his neck, high up, so that a tug on it would choke him for an instant. The other boy chained his charge to a post. "Parkisha is sated by the tala on her food, but he's wise to chain her. Fights between dragons are impossible for anyone but the Jousters to break up, and—" he fixed Vetch with a knife-sharp glance "—remember this, boy—fights are generally fatal to handlers caught in the middle."

Vetch nodded, and gulped.

But Kashet was nothing like the half-wild thing chained to the post next to him; once in the pen, he turned into a complete sybarite, leaning into each buffing stroke with his eyes half-closed.

Finally Haraket deemed the task done even to *his* exacting standards, and allowed Vetch to lead the dragon back to his pen for the last time that day. Leaving Kashet to bask in the sun while his hide absorbed the oil—which imparted that spicy scent to him—Vetch got another barrow-full of meat.

By now, drowsy and relaxed and more certain of his new dragon-boy, Kashet was not so impatient to be fed. He ate in a leisurely fashion, while Haraket and Vetch watched.

"The other dragons all get tala mixed with their meat at every meal; make sure you never get one of those barrows," Haraket cautioned. "Kashet is *never* to have tala. Not even at morning feed—and believe me, when you see the others snapping at their boys, you'll be grateful that you've got Kashet, and not mind the extra work he makes for you."

With Kashet fed and digging himself a hollow in the sand in which to sleep, Haraket gave Vetch a grudging smile.

"All right, serf-boy," he said gruffly. "You've done as well as anyone else his first day. You're finished until morning. Go back to the kitchen and get your supper, and you're free to do whatever you wish until dawn. You'll sleep on a pallet in here with Kashet, though, and not with the other boys. Ari's particular about Kashet."

"Yes, sir," Vetch said, feeling that for once he'd encountered Tians who deserved being called "sir."

"You're how old, boy? And what the Tophet is your name?" Haraket demanded suddenly.

"Ten or eleven, sir, Vetch, sir," Vetch stammered, surprised by the abrupt demand. Masters did not, in his experience, give a toss about how old you were, or what your name was.

"Not too old, not too young. Good." Haraket nodded. "Right. Off with you. I'll have the pallet brought here for you; it will be waiting for you when you're ready to sleep." With that, he turned on his heel, and left. Vetch gathered his courage, and looked for the kitchen.

He was not the first there, this time. Kashet took a lot of tending, and his sand-bath had taken *much* longer than the others. The room was roughly half-full, and Vetch once again took a seat on the very end of a bench, at the least-crowded table.

Supper was a generous bowl of pottage and lots of bread with pots of honey, with greens and boiled latal-roots. There was meat in the pottage, which so astonished Vetch that he stopped eating for a moment.

Not for long, though—and once again, he was able to eat until he was stuffed. He *was* the last of the boys to leave, and did so feeling so sleepy and sated that he hardly recognized himself.

The sun was setting, and he could hear the sounds of the other boys chattering together somewhere. And for a moment, he felt a strange emptiness inside of him that no amount of bread could touch—

But when he turned the corner into Kashet's pen, and saw the pallet waiting for him beneath the awning that protected the saddle and harness, all he could think of was sleep.

Tian was a desert land, and the desert was as cold by night as it was hot by day. Now the hot sands where Kashet rested were a source of comfort, not discomfort. Vetch was happy enough to spread out his pallet and sleep beside the lightly snoring dragon.

And for once, he did not dream.

———— ◆ ————

Haraket roused him in the morning, as Nofet, the Goddess of Night, was just pulling in her skirts to make way for Kere, the Sungod. Kashet still slumbered, torpid; Vetch went to fetch his breakfast of meat along with nineteen other dragon-boys. This time he had to line up for a barrow, but Haraket hustled him past a station where the other boys were scooping powder atop the meat and mixing it in. Morning chores were a repetition of the afternoon; Kashet was restive and a little snappish after the long night without food, but in the other pens, Vetch heard hisses and whines, and the curses of the dragon-boys. He knew then that he was very lucky to have Kashet as his dragon.

He saddled the now-sated dragon, and the Jouster arrived; he cleaned the pen after Kashet and Ari left, and at last, with the sun now well above the walls of the compound, got his breakfast of hot bread and barley-broth with the others.

He was the only serf; the rest were all freeborn Tian boys, mostly from large, poor families no better off than a serf—

But they were free and Tian, not serf and Altan, and he knew from that morning for certain that they would never

let him forget his inferior race and status. Not that he had
expected anything else . . . but once again, he got that hollow feeling as he watched them chatting and laughing with
each other, and pointedly closing *him* out of their circle; he
filled the hollow with anger, but it was a slim bulwark
against the loneliness.

After breakfast, he trailed behind the others, having gathered from what he overheard that it was time to get a bath
and a new kilt. He debated loitering until the others were
done, then decided to edge inside and hope they ignored him.

They did; and despite some horseplay and a little shoving, the presence of another adult who was handing out
clean kilts and inspecting the boys for cleanliness must have
kept them on good behavior. He *did* loiter just long enough
for them to clear out, taking the opportunity to scrub himself really well, much to the evident satisfaction of the
watching adult.

Hair damp, freshly kilted, around his neck was the same
glazed talisman of a hawk-eye that Haraket wore, which the
servant handed him with his kilt. This marked him as a servant to the Jousters, and meant that no one outside the
compound was permitted to interfere with him.

Until lunch, he learned that it was time to see to the
lances all the Jousters used, to spread fresh tala-fruits to dry
in the sun in yet another courtyard, to pound the dried ones
to powder with the rest of the dragon-boys. With them—but
not *of* them; they shut him out of their company by the
simple expedient of ignoring him completely. *He* was not
about to force the issue; they left him alone now, and that
was better than being beaten.

He discovered by careful listening that after supper the
free boys often went down to the river to hunt or fish; those
who had a copper or two talked about going into Mefis to

spend it. Their quarters became quiet as the dragons settled into their nighttime torpor and the boys themselves went out.

He walked about the dragon-compound until dusk, familiarizing himself with the place. The dragon-pens were ranged about the landing-courtyard, with storerooms between each pen so that the dragons couldn't reach each other over the walls. There were far more pens than there were dragons. On the west side were the Jousters' quarters and the kitchens, on the north and south, those of their servants and slaves and the dragon-boys, and on the east, the armory, the saddlery, and the butchery where the sacrifices were cut up, treated, and distributed. It was quite easy to figure out once you understood the pattern. Vetch didn't venture into the Jousters' quarters, which were a series of apartments like Ari's built around courtyard-gardens centered with pools, some overflowing with blue and white latal. There was a great deal of talk and laughter going on in there.

Vetch settled into his corner on his pallet, but he wasn't sleepy yet. As the gloom of dusk settled over the pen, he looked up at the robe of Nofet, spangled with the gold beads that were the stars.

He heard a hum of muted voices from the other parts of the compound, occasionally someone laughing loudly—both male and female voices. Well, the Jousters were the Tians' great weapon, the reason why they had conquered as much as they had. When they swooped down on an Altan village, carrying fire-pots to drop on the granaries and straw-sacks, when they descended on the chariots of the Altan army, terrifying the horses and sending them back through their own lines, there to wreak sheer havoc as they careened through the packed fighters. But worst of all was the tactic that struck true fear into the heart of every Altan officer—when the dragons plunged out of the sky, seized an officer or commander in their talons, lifted him into the air—and dropped him. Vetch had never seen this himself, of course, but everyone had heard the stories. He couldn't imagine how the Altan leaders were keeping officers in the field, when at any moment they might find themselves dragged into the air, then plunging to their deaths . . .

Not that he had seen any of that; only heard the tales. His father's farm had been only that, a farm, and not some enemy stronghold to warrant the attentions of a dragon.

The sound of footsteps just outside the pen broke into his thoughts.

He had no lights here, but it was easy enough to recognize Ari's profile against the stars.

"Kashet—" the Jouster called softly. There was a sibilant noise as the dragon shifted in his sand-wallow, and the dark wedge of Kashet's head loomed above the Jouster's.

The dragon lowered his head, and Ari began rubbing the hide between his eyes. "I raised him," Ari said aloud, making Vetch jump. "That's why he's different; that's why *we* are different. The rest were all taken from their nests, but I found an egg, I buried it in the hot nest-sands, I turned it and I talked to him every day. I was there when he hatched, and fed him, and when he made his first flight, we flew together. I suppose you could say that we're friends; I understand him, and he understands me. Oh, not in *words*, of course, and it isn't as if we hear what the other is thinking, though some people believe that is what we do. We just know one another very well." He paused. "I'm pleased that you are getting along with him."

"Why doesn't everyone do that?" Vetch asked, after a while. "Get eggs, I mean. If it makes that big a difference?"

Ari sighed; it sounded weary. "Because it isn't the tradition, I suppose. Or because it is a great deal less heroic to take an egg than a fighting, hissing nestling that is a few days from flight. Or, most likely, because tending an egg and the nestling that hatches is a great deal of work that *must* be done by the man who intends to ride the dragon. Why go to all that work when the tala keeps the dragons tame enough to ride?"

Vetch held his peace; the Jouster didn't seem to expect an answer. He continued to scratch Kashet, who was making burbling sounds in the bottom of his throat. "I am somewhat out-of-place among our mighty warriors, I fear," Ari said after another, much longer interval. "I was trained as a scribe; it is only by virtue of the fact that I ride Kashet that I am a Jouster. The others—well, they are fighters, always intended to be, and think as little as possible. Haraket says that I think too much, and I probably do."

Vetch sensed something that he couldn't quite put into words; he strained after it, but it eluded him. "It's important to think before you say or do something," he said finally. "That was what my father said—"

"Your father, the farmer? Did he own his land, before we came and took it away from him? Or was he only a serf to an Altan master?"

Strange questions. But the darkness made Vetch feel bold, and the calm and curious sadness in Ari's voice cooled his ever-present anger, and he answered them. "We—our family—held our land for five hundred years," he said, with painful pride.

"Five hundred years." A sigh in the darkness. "And did your father take arms against us? Or your brother? Or were they tilling the soil in peace until the day someone came and told him that his land was no longer his?"

"My father—my father didn't know anything about fighting," he said, his throat growing tight. "It was planting season. Father wouldn't leave the farm at planting season. And I never had any brothers, only sisters." Vetch didn't want to think about it; didn't want to remember the day that the strangers came, with their bronze swords and leather shields, their long spears—how they spoke to his father as if he were a slave. How he cursed them, and picked up a sickle—

He stuffed his hand in his mouth, to stifle his sobs, and the anger threatened to overwhelm him. One moment, and his tall, strong father had been standing; the next, he was on the ground, and his mother was screaming, and there was red everywhere, and the Tian soldiers grabbing her, grabbing him, grabbing his sisters. Throwing them down beside the road, in the dust. He remembered the taste of dirt and tears, remembered how his youngest sister wouldn't stop screaming and the soldiers kicked her in the head until they knocked her unconscious. She was never right after that . . .

He remembered how he shook all over, how he was afraid even to look up, while the sun baked down on his back, and flies buzzed in his father's blood. The soldiers made them lie there in the dirt beside the road as another stranger arrived, this one with a family and a wagonload of furnishings.

Then the soldiers dragged them off on their faces, all but Dershela, who lay on her side, her face black and blue. The soldiers made them all watch as the strangers invaded their house, and went through the house, pulling out everything. And it was all smashed, torn up, reduced to trash, then tossed onto the dustheap, atop his father's body. And the Tian family took possession of the house that had been home to his father's line, unbroken, for five hundred years. Only then was Vetch's family hauled to their feet while the officer explained to them what all this meant—that they had been punished for harboring enemies of the Tians, that their land was confiscated, and they were graciously being allowed to live. And what the word "serf" meant. Then, after seeing their husband and father murdered for nothing, lying without food or water in the hot sun for hours, they were permitted to make their beds in what had been the cattle-shed, to work their own land without profit or payment.

He didn't want to remember. But he could never forget.

"Five hundred years ago, boy," Ari said softly. "Five hundred years ago, a people called the Hekysin came to Tia. And they destroyed our army, killed our nobles, and sent their people to take the farms and livelihoods of Tians who had lived in their little mud-brick houses for hundreds of years. And the Tians who had called those places home now served the newcomers as slaves. That was what was happening to us, five hundred years ago, when your grandfather's grandfather's grandfather was settling his little farm beside the Great Mother River. Then we Tians learned to ride dragons, to drive chariots, and to make bronze swords and spearheads, and we rose up and drove the Hekysin out. And then—then we came, and did to you what the Hekysin did to us."

Once more Vetch had the sense of something very important that was just out of his grasp. But the grief and rage, the terrible emotion that Ari had roused in him—it was too raw, too painful to permit him to think about anything else. Tears cut down his cheeks, hot and bitter, his gut was a mass of knots, and his throat was swollen with grief. But he had learned since that terrible day how to cry without a sound, not even a sniffle, though his eyes burned and ached and his throat closed up completely and his gut was cramped with holding in the sobs he dared not release. Not even in front of this man, who had been absently kind, who spoke as if he might understand.

Ari shook his head, and reached up to pat Kashet's neck. "And none of that matters to you, I suppose," he sighed. "It certainly doesn't matter to the other Jousters. It doesn't seem to matter to anyone but me that Tians are doing to Altans precisely what we claimed were the most heinous of crimes when the Hekysin inflicted them upon us. Haraket is right. I think too much."

He patted Kashet again, and the dragon nuzzled him, then pulled away, settling back into the sand. And without another word, Ari turned and left the pen. Vetch was alone in the darkness, with a slumbering dragon, a sorrow too deep and wide to leave room for anything else, and his memories. And an anger that built walls as high as his sorrow was deep.

———◆———◆———◆———

Jousters were called by that name because they were not utterly unopposed in the air. The Altans had dragon-riders as well—in fact it was said that it was the Altans who had taught the trick of capturing and taming dragons to ride to the Tians—though the number of Jousters that the Altans could field was much fewer than the Tians, and their training didn't seem as good. When two Jousters met in the air above a battle, they dueled for supremacy with short lances, blunt, made to knock the rider from his saddle, or at least to knock him unconscious. One day, when Vetch had been serving Ari and Kashet for a month, Haraket sent him to the training grounds with a message, and Vetch got to see precisely what Jousting meant—and how very dangerous it could be.

He'd never been to the practice-grounds before; he'd always been kept busy at his assigned tasks when the Jousters were practicing. He'd never even seen the empty grounds.

It was not what he'd expected. The practice-grounds

were outside the final wall of the Jousters' compound. Fishing-nets were strung between strong poles, so that they hung parallel to the ground and well above it. Ari and Kashet were hovering in place high in the air above the middle of one of these nets, as Ari shouted directions to two more Jousters who were sparring above another net with the blunted lances. To Vetch's surprise, there were a lot of onlookers, and many of them seemed to be wealthy or of noble birth.

He hadn't expected that. The world of the Jousters within the compound was as isolated as that of any Temple—*he* had never seen anyone who wasn't associated with the Jousters, and although he had overheard some things from the other boys about feasts and gatherings at which there were outsiders, he hadn't seen any himself.

But here were spectators who were clearly of the elite of the Tians of Mefis. They glittered in the sun, all of them sporting armbands and wrist cuffs of gold, and collars of gemstone-beads, fine wigs or elaborate headcloths, and linen kilts of the best fabric with sashes and belts richly embroidered. There was even a woman there, dressed in a tightly pleated, transparent linen dress with a sheath made of turquoise beads over it, holding the folds of the linen close to her body.

The practice-session didn't look very dangerous, and even Vetch could tell that these two weren't very good at the Jousting. They made very clumsy passes at each other, all the while flailing at the air yards away from one another. He knew all the dragons by sight now, and it wasn't hard to tell which the two Jousters rode, even if he didn't know the men themselves; one was Seftu, a handsome, if irritable crimson male, and the other was Coresan, a female of a deeper hue and notoriously whippy tail. Coresan was usually very placid in nature, excepting only that she was known to leave her dragon-boy with black-and-blue calves and thighs with that unpredictable tail, but something had her on edge the last week; her dragon-boy was half-afraid to go in her pen of a morning, and kept her chained as short as he dared.

Their Jousters were the newest of the group, and certainly were nothing like the masters of either their weapons or their dragons. They made several passes without either of them getting close enough to strike anywhere near each other; both seemed to be fighting their mounts, which were circling each other in a way that reminded Vetch of something . . .

And just when he realized what it reminded him *of*, Seftu's rider finally got close enough to deliver a sideswipe with his lance to Coresan's Jouster. The latter wasn't paying any attention, since Coresan chose that moment to curvet sideways in the air, toward Seftu.

The lance connected—*hard*—hitting the Jouster across the back of his head.

With a terrible *crack*, it snapped in half. And as if a god had waved his hand to slow time itself, everything froze for a horrible moment.

In painfully slow motion, Coresan's Jouster went tumbling out of his saddle, and plunged toward the net below. But he wasn't falling right, there was something horribly wrong—he was limp, limbs flailing, and Vetch felt his stomach lurch as he realized that not only was he not conscious, but that he was going to miss the net.

The Jouster was Tian; the enemy. Vetch didn't even know his name. Vetch should have been silently cheering the demise of one of the people who was responsible for all the horrible things that had happened to his family.

Should have, perhaps—but couldn't. All he could see was the hands clutching at the air; all he could hear was the cry from above, thin and filled with utter terror.

Everyone else watching seemed to realize the same thing at the same moment; there were gasps and cries of horror, and the sharp scream of a woman cut across the heat-shimmering air.

Vetch's stomach lurched again—he wanted to look away, but he couldn't. He seemed to be paralyzed as the body hurtled toward the earth, unchecked. In a moment, there would be a spreading stain of red on the pale, baked earth, and the smell of death, and the buzzing of flies coming for the blood—

Then a flash of blue-green swept across the sky, and with it came the sound of dragon-wings, a thunder and a wind that shivered across the ground, driving the dust before it—

It all happened so quickly that it was over before Vetch registered *what* had happened. But the Jouster was no longer in the air, nor was he lying in a smashed heap on the ground.

The Jouster was lying across Ari's saddle, draped over Kashet's neck, and Ari and Kashet were coming slowly in to land. He dropped down with a thunder of wings that drove up so much dust that the onlookers had to shield their faces and look away, and they were on the ground. Ari didn't look at them; his attention was on the servants who were taking the unconscious Jouster from Kashet's saddle.

Then the crowd erupted in cheers and surged forward.

Vetch surged with it, and somehow Ari saw him in the crush, and roared an order to let him through. After a moment of confusion in which he tried desperately to get past the spectators—wealthy, powerful, dangerous—they realized who Ari was shouting for and parted for him.

"Haraket says—" Vetch panted, staring up at his Jouster with mingled awe and disbelief. "Haraket says—"

"Never mind what Haraket says—this isn't over yet." Ari

looked up with a scowl, and Vetch followed his gaze.

The two dragons were whirling together now, in the mating-dance that Vetch had instinctively recognized, and Seftu's rider, a tiny dot at this distance, was clinging on for dear life. Not only was he no longer in control of his dragon, he was going to be lucky to stay in the saddle.

"Idiots!" Ari snarled. "If they paid *half* as much attention to their dragons as they did to the vintage of the date-wine they drank last night, they'd have *known* this was coming on and ordered extra tala. Vetch!"

Vetch snapped to attention.

"Run and tell Haraket what just happened. Kashet and I will bring Coresan in when the mating's over; she'll be tractable then, and there's no point in losing a dragon because her Jouster was an imbecile. I think her Jouster got a crack to the head, so Haraket had better send to the Temple of Teth for a trepanning-priest, just in case. You go run ahead now—" He raised his voice as Vetch broke into a mad dash for the compound. "You lot! Stretch him on a bench—*carefully*, now—and bring him to the compound and Overseer Haraket!"

Vetch couldn't do anything about the injured Jouster—and in any case, he didn't really *care* what happened to the man—but once his errand was discharged, he ran to the landing-court where he could see the dragons in the sky, who were still wheeling and whirling around each other in a complicated ritual that was the equal of anything a bird could do. They soared and plunged, they twined around each other and broke apart, then—then they lunged for one another with a ferocity indistinguishable from rage.

It ended in a tangle of locked claws and a plunge to earth that must have terrified Seftu's rider out of a dozen years of life.

Caught together, neither willing to let go, they spun around a common center, whirling, wings held tightly to their sides, down to the unforgiving earth. At the very last minute just before the impact, they broke their hold.

Their wings snapped open as one, and the vertical plunge suddenly became horizontal as they streaked off in opposite directions, parallel to the ground.

Vetch never saw what happened to Seftu; presumably his Jouster got him back under control and brought him in. He had eyes only for Ari and Kashet, who had followed the entwined dragons down in their deadly plunge, and now deftly herded Coresan away from the hills above the King's Valley—where she *wanted* to go—and toward the compound. And she didn't want to go there; she kept snaking her head back and trying to snap at them. But Ari and Kashet were cleverer than she; by getting and staying above her, they forced her to fly lower and lower as she slowed, until she couldn't stay in the air any longer. And at that very moment, they were above the landing-court, and her training took over and she came in to ground.

Haraket had arrived without Vetch noticing; the moment Coresan touched the earth, he was there with two of the strongest slaves in the compound and three leading-chains. With Ari and Kashet hovering above to keep her from taking off again, Haraket hooked his chain into the ring on the front of her harness and the two slaves hooked theirs into the foot-loops on either side of the saddle. Together they led the dragon to her pen, while Ari and Kashet rose again and then landed and headed for Kashset's enclosure.

By that time, Vetch had guessed what they were about, and his last glimpse of them was as he sprinted through the gate in the wall, going for Kashet's pen himself. Seftu's dragon-boy was in the corridor, laden with food and drink; Vetch snatched what he wanted from the provender over the other boy's vehement protests, which he ignored. After all, the rider didn't *deserve* it; wasn't he half-responsible for the near-disaster?

When Ari and Kashet stumbled into Kashet's pen, Vetch was there ahead of him, waiting with a flask of palm-wine for Ari and a bucket of water for Kashet. But Ari waved off the wine and took the bucket of water instead, drinking as he had that day that Vetch had first seen him, and pouring the rest over his head and shoulders. Kashet went straight to his trough, which, as always, was full of clean water, and drank as deeply; Vetch was unharnessing him as soon as he stopped moving.

Ari shook his head like a dog, sending droplets of water flying. Vetch cast a look at him; he looked *terrible*. Weary and ill, and not at all as triumphant as Vetch thought he should be—

"Etat save me from ever having to do *that* again," he said, and sat down, right on the edge of the sandpit, head and shoulders sagging.

Vetch was torn between going to him and continuing to get the harness off of Kashet; he compromised by unbuckling the last strap and letting the saddle drop to the side, then going to Ari.

"Sir?" he ventured, not daring to touch the Jouster.

"I'll have that wine now, boy," came the muffled reply.

Vetch put the skin in his hand; he fully expected Ari to drain it, but the Jouster again surprised him, taking only a single mouthful before handing it back.

"That's better." He raised his head. "How is Reaten?"

That was Coresan's Jouster; Vetch recalled it as soon as Ari spoke the name. "He has a cracked skull, but the priest is certain that he will be all right," Vetch told him. "Sir—

how did you *do* that? One moment he was falling, the next, he was across your saddle! It looked like magic!"

"It's all Kashet's doing," Ari replied, but looked very pleased at Vetch's wide-eyed admiration. "I'll admit we've practiced just that move, in case something like this happened. This was the first time we've caught a man, though—it's always been bags of chaff before this. Have you ever seen a dragon take a goose in flight?" He glanced at Vetch, who shook his head. "No? Well, it's something they do in the wild, pulling their head and neck back, then snapping it forward while flying, like a heron catching a fish. I've taught Kashet to do that, only bring his head in *under* what we're trying to catch, then raise his head and fly up at the same time. If we've got the balance right, what we're aiming for slides right down his neck onto my saddle." He shook his head. "Needless to say, no one else can do it. Another of my little eccentricities that the others put up with in the past; none of them ever had the imagination to see that it could be used to rescue a falling rider. I suspect there won't be any more sniping remarks about it after this, though."

Vetch nodded, and watched as Kashet rolled in his hot sand-wallow. "Reaten won't be flying for weeks," he offered. "So the priest says."

"Just as well. Coresan will be impossible to handle for that long, or at least until she rids herself of her eggs. Let's hope he learned his lesson about paying attention to her behavior, anyway." Ari had a long pull on the wineskin; Vetch thought there was a grim satisfaction in his expression. But he was more interested in what Ari had said than in what his expression might imply.

"Eggs?" Vetch asked, wondering if he dared to think *he* might be able to get hold of one—if there were any at all. "She'll lay eggs now? How many? Who's going to mind them?"

"Nobody," Ari sighed. "What a waste! Of course, they'll probably be sterile—wild dragons mate a dozen times or more for a clutch of two or three and Coresan only mated once today—but you'd think that *someone* would be interested in trying to duplicate what I did when I was Haraket's helper! But no. This has happened before, and other than the one that hatched Kashet, the eggs were just taken away and left on the refuse-heap." His gaze turned scornful. "Of course, *warriors* can't be bothered with playing nursemaid to an egg and a dragonet—and they can't simply assign the task to their dragon-boy and expect to come take over from him when the dragon fledges. The dragon won't fly for just anyone, will he, Kashet? Like a falcon or a cheetah, a dragon is loyal only to the one who nurtures him—a dragon is *not* like a dog, who will hunt with any man who knows his commands."

Kashet rolled over on his back and twisted his long neck around, eyeing Ari for a moment, then snorting with what sounded like amusement.

Suddenly, a number of disparate bits of information came together for Vetch. That Ari was once a scribe—or at least, had studied to be a scribe. That he had "found" a dragon-egg—Vetch couldn't imagine anyone climbing into a nest after a dragon-egg! *That a Jousting dragon had escaped to mate and lay eggs at least once before this.*

Ari must have been a dragon-boy, then rose to become one of Haraket's helpers; perhaps he had been attending one of the Temple schools to be a scribe, when his family fell on hard times and could no longer pay for the schooling. *He* must have gotten hold of a fertile egg from one of those chance matings, perhaps from his own Master's dragon.

Vetch knew better than to blurt his conclusion out, though. Nor did he blurt out *his* reaction—that what Ari had done, *he,* Vetch could do. "You should rest, Master," was what he said instead. "Your room is ready; I've already seen to that."

"And whatever Haraket sent you to tell me is now of minimal importance," Ari said, and shook his head, crossly. "Evil spirits plague Reaten with boils! I'll have to take *his* patrols now, doubtless, while *he* lies abed, being made much of by all his noble friends! Get Kashet an extra treat; bullock hearts, if there are any. He more than deserves them. Then go to the kitchen and tell them I want my dinner in my room; I'm for a cool swim first, in the Atet-pool, and perhaps after that I'll feel less like strangling Reaten."

He levered himself up off the edge of the sandpit, and as he stalked off out of the pen, Vetch noticed that he was favoring one leg. He must have injured it somehow—either in the rescue, or when he and Kashet were bringing Coresan to earth. Typical of him not to have mentioned it.

Vetch did as he was told, and found that, not unexpectedly, the request for someone to bring Ari his supper nearly brought on a fight among the servants over who was to have the honor. Ari's very self-effacement in *not* lingering to be made a hero of, had had the effect of making him more of a hero than he would have been if he *had* stayed about to preen rather than bringing Coresan in. Or at least that was true amongst the servants. What those wealthy spectators had thought of Ari's heroic efforts today—well, Vetch couldn't begin to guess.

But there was another repercussion to all of this—when Vetch went to the butchers for Kashet's feed and his treat, there was a drama being enacted right in the center of the court. Reaten's dragon-boy refused, sweating and trembling, to go anywhere near his charge. He described, at the top of his lungs, to an enraptured and credulous audience in the butcher-court, how she had snapped at him and—so he claimed—nearly taken his leg off.

"Like a mad thing!" he cried, his voice cracking. "Mark me, she'll *eat* anyone she gets hold of! She nearly ate *me!* I swear it!"

"That is because she mistook you for a goat, with all of your silly bleating," said Haraket from the door to the courtyard, where he stood, legs braced slightly apart, arms crossed over his chest, a fierce and disapproving frown on his face. Vetch shrank back against the wall, but already his mind was awhirl with a possible idea. "What is all of this foolishness, Sobek?" Haraket continued. "*And* disobedience—saying you will not tend to your dragon—"

"And I won't!" Sobek cried hysterically, both hands clenched into fists, his face a contorted mask of fear and defiance. "I won't, you hear me! My father is a priest in the Temple of Epis, and he'll have something to say about this!"

"Your father is a cleaner of Temple floors, and *you* may go back to him in disgrace if you say one word further—" Haraket thundered dangerously, his brow as black as a rainy-season storm, and his eyes flashing. Vetch sucked in a breath; Haraket annoyed was dangerous enough, but Haraket enraged? *Was* he about to see Sobek beaten? If so, it would be the first time he'd seen *anyone* beaten, even the slaves, since he came to the compound.

But Sobek had been pushed too far; his fear was no act, and he had gone over the edge from fear into panic. He snatched the eye-amulet off his neck, and threw it to the pavement. "Send me back, then!" he screeched, as it shattered into a thousand pieces. "Go ahead! Better that, than to be torn apart! I care not, Haraket, I will cut papyrus, I will beg for my bread, rather than go into *that* killer's pen!"

"*Out!*" Haraket roared. "*Out of my compound, out of*

my life!" Step by step he advanced on Sobek, his face red with anger, so outraged by the dragon-boy's rebellion that he was about to lose control of himself. "You are *dismissed*, dragon-boy, *little* boy, little *coward!* Run back to your father, pathetic scum! Run away like the frightened child you are! Run! *Run!*"

Sobek ran; bolted for his life past Haraket, sandals slapping on the stone, fleeing for the outside world and presumed safety.

Silence flew over the courtyard, a silence broken only by the shuffling feet of the other dragon-boys. Hanging in the silence was the certain knowledge that *someone* would have to take care of Coresan until Haraket found another boy to tend her. And Coresan at her best was no Kashet—at her worst, well, she was evidently so unmanageable that Sobek had chosen disgrace over continuing to tend her.

This was the opportunity, all unlooked-for, that Vetch had not dared to hope would be granted to him. He leapt upon it and seized it with both hands. "Overseer?" he said, into the leaden silence. "I will tend Coresan along with Kashet, if someone else will mend harness, pound tala, and clean Jouster Ari's room for me. I will *need* that sort of help. Feeding, tending, and bathing two dragons will not be easy; it is hard enough at the best of times, but it will be much more difficult when one of them is Coresan, a dragon newly mated."

A collective sigh arose out of the huddle of dragon-boys, and Haraket's brow cleared a trifle. "You? Coresan is no Kashet, boy. She has always been a handful for Sobek, and as you said, she is going to lay eggs, which will make her even more difficult—"

"But I have been around females about to whelp all my life," he countered. "My father was a farmer. I believe that I can tame her a little. Perhaps more than a little." He allowed scorn to come into his tone for the first time ever. But Sobek was now, in Haraket's mind at least, in disgrace, and criticism of Sobek would fall on ears ready to hear it. And it was such a relief to be able to abuse one of those wretched Tian boys without fear of being punished for it! "Sobek never treated her properly; half the time he was afraid of her, and he never thought she was anything better than a dumb beast with a vicious streak. He never saw how clever she was, or treated her with any kindness. I'd have snapped at him myself."

Haraket rubbed his shaven head with the palm of one hand, now looking worried. "Sobek was—not entirely in the wrong, boy," he admitted. "Coresan could harm you, if you are not careful."

"Let me feed her, feed her now, Overseer," Vetch pleaded, urgently. A plan was forming in his mind, but he could only carry it out if *he* became Coresan's keeper, at least until she laid those eggs. "Please! Watch and see if I can handle her!"

Haraket took a deep breath, and Vetch felt a surge of triumph, knowing he had won—at least so far. "Very well. You may feed her. We will see—"

Vetch did not wait for Haraket to have second thoughts. He was out into the corridor before anyone could blink, his own sandals making the walls echo as he ran—but not, like Sobek, for the outside world. He had a chance; he had to make the most of it. Unlike Sobek, he had nowhere to go, nothing to lose, and the world to gain if he succeeded . . .

Haraket and two of the biggest of his slaves, trailing a curious and apprehensive crowd of dragon-boys, intercepted him on the way to Coresan's pen. He was wheeling a barrow heaped with tala-treated meat, as much as he could manage, and double Kashet's usual ration. If she was breeding, she'd be hungry, and if Sobek had been neglecting her because he was afraid of her and impatient to get away, he might not have been feeding her properly for some time—

He heard her hissing before he even reached her pen, and looking up, saw her head up above the walls, watching the corridor, swaying back and forth at the end of her long neck.

She ignored him—except for a voracious glare down at his laden barrow. *He* was not Sobek; she did not expect feeding from *him*.

But when he appeared in the door of her pen with his barrow heaped with fresh red meat, she reared up, her hiss of anger turning to a short bark of surprise. Then she went into a lunge that came up far short of where he stood, her chain snapping taut between her collar and the wall.

She was ravenous, and Vetch gritted his teeth when he realized that she was thin—not unhealthy, not yet, but that miserable excuse for a dragon-boy hadn't been feeding her nearly enough, just as he'd suspected! Hadn't he *seen* how much hungrier she was?

Like Jouster, like dragon-boy, it seemed; Sobek and Reaten deserved each other, for neither of them had noticed the changes in Coresan. It was possible that *none* of the trouble of this morning would have happened if they had only been paying proper attention to their dragons!

Vetch didn't leave the poor thing straining at the end of her tether for any longer than it took him to get up beside the barrow and begin tossing the biggest chunks of meat in it in her direction. She was quick; she saw the first one coming and snatched it right out of the air, snaked her head around to catch the second, and the third—

She paused to swallow; he kept the meat coming. Only when the barrow was half-empty did she pause, for a breath, then to turn her head to take a good long drink from her trough.

While she was drinking, he moved the barrow; when she looked up, the barrow was well within her reach, and Vetch stood behind it, making sounds that Kashet found soothing, a kind of "pish, pish" noise.

Now the tala that had been dusted over the meat she'd bolted had begun to take effect, taking the edge off her aggressive nature. She had eaten as much as she usually did, too, and although she was still hungry, she was no longer ravenous, and her mood had mellowed considerably. She arched her back and her neck, and eyed him with a great deal more favor.

"Come, my beauty," he said to her in a soft and coaxing voice. "See what I've brought you? There will be plenty of meat for you from now on, if you can be a good girl for me."

She snaked her head at him with a lightning-strike, and snapped a pair of jaws that could have taken off his head—

If his head had been what she was aiming for.

The jaws clashed a good foot above his head. He never moved. *She* was trying to see if he rattled as easily as Sobek; if he flinched, she'd bully him at every possible opportunity. He'd seen her with Sobek at the grooming-compound, where she snapped and lashed her tail at him, and he would jump and wince and insist that slaves put extra tethers on her. She reminded him of a goat on one of his masters' farms, who'd done the same to her herders until she got one who'd given her a good rap across the nose with his crook the first time she charged him.

"Come along, my beauty," he coaxed. "I'm tough and stringy—there's better fare for you in my barrow, if you're good."

She eyed him again, then abruptly buried her muzzle in the meat, and didn't stop until she'd eaten every morsel and licked the barrow clean. Only then did she raise her head and gaze at him with eyes that blinked with sleepy satiation.

"*There's* a good girl," he told her, and taking the chance that the tala was coursing through her veins, further tranquilizing her, he moved down and loosened her chain from the wall. "Come on," he said, tugging at the chain. "I know you want a good bath, and a proper oiling, don't you? That wretched Sobek can't have given you one in an age."

She was more restive by far than Kashet, who didn't need a chain, just a hand on his shoulder. And she kept snapping at the air above Vetch's head. But she still allowed him to lead her to the grooming-court without too much fuss.

Perhaps it was her bulging belly that was leading her . . .

He fastened her to the nearest ring in the wall, and began buffing and oiling her. Flakes of dead skin fell away as he rubbed, confirming his guess that Sobek hadn't been tending her properly. And *she* responded to his careful ministrations, slowly, but favorably, finally bending her head to permit him to tend to the delicate skin of her ears, her muzzle, and around her eyes.

When he led her back to her pen, she ambled along quietly beside him, and dove into the sandpit to wallow as soon as they reached it. He chained her up—she was *still* no Kashet, and he wasn't going to trust this good behavior until he knew how big a dose of tala he really needed to keep her tractable—but he gave her a much longer chain than Sobek had.

Haraket had followed him every step of the way; as he left her to her nap in the warm sand and turned to leave the pen, Haraket gave him an approving slap on his back that staggered him.

"Well done!" the Overseer said gruffly. "You *do* know your business. You tend your Kashet and this virago; that's enough work for any man or boy. I'll see to it that your other tasks are taken care of."

Vetch ducked his head, and murmured his thanks. This would *not* be easy; Coresan was going to test him every single time he entered her pen. She was intelligent and crafty, and she had learned how to disobey. Disobedience was a habit it would be hard to break her of.

But if all went well—

Vetch would have a dragon-egg. And then, well—then it would all depend on the gods of Altan, and whether here, in the heart of Tian, they would be strong enough to aid him.

No one, not even Haraket, really knew how long after mating it would take a dragon to lay her eggs. So he had a measure of time in which he could act before he had to admit that there *were* eggs and allow the slaves to take them away to discard them. Ari had been right; no one rushed forward to claim them in order to repeat Ari's experiment. The Jousters much preferred the old ways—hunting the nests of dragonets about to fledge, trapping them, and confining them, dosing them with tala, training them until they were broken to the saddle and accepted a rider and were grown enough to carry one.

Small wonder none of them loved their Jousters.

Vetch fed and groomed Kashet to within an inch of his life while Coresan slept; he had not forgotten his promise to get the treat of ox hearts. Kashet got a half-dozen of his favorite treats, and once fed, Vetch made sure that every inch of him gleamed with buffing and oil, telling him the whole time what a fine and brave, and above all, *clever* fellow he was. There was no doubt that he enjoyed hearing the tone of Vetch's voice, but Vetch had to wonder just how much of the words he also understood. The more time he spent with

Kashet, the more certain he became that the dragons were far more intelligent than any Jouster—except, perhaps, Ari—really guessed.

"I won't neglect you for Coresan, handsome one," he told the dragon, as they paced back to Kashet's pen, side by side. Kashet curved his neck, bringing his head down to Vetch's level. "And I won't neglect you for—" He didn't say it—*my egg, my dragonet*—he didn't dare think that far. "—for anything else, I won't neglect you."

As long as he was *here*. He could not promise more.

For the next three days, he gave Coresan double-rations, which (more than the tala, he suspected) greatly improved her temper. She swiftly put on weight until she was sleek again; she began to dig in her sand, as if she was looking for some perfect spot to nest. She had plenty of opportunity to do as she pleased, since she only left the pen with Vetch to be groomed. She still snapped at strangers, but she seemed to have accepted him and only tried to bully him on the first morning feeding. And even then, it was halfhearted.

Every morning Haraket asked if there were eggs yet. But it was better than a week later that the first egg appeared.

It was in a corner of the sandpit she had been paying special attention to last night, and if he had not been looking for it, he might not have seen it, for only the barest top curve showed above the sand. It was very hard, rather than leathery like a snake-egg, and weighed about the same as a five-year-old child. Coresan didn't seem to mind that he handled it, perhaps because she wasn't yet brooding.

When Haraket asked him about eggs, he just shook his head. Haraket took that as "there is no egg yet" and didn't ask anything further, much to his relief.

But the egg was on his mind all day. He had a choice of several courses of action, but he would have to decide what he was going to do soon, before someone else decided to check Coresan's pen on the theory that he wouldn't necessarily know what he was looking for. Just because he'd sorted Coresan didn't mean that he knew about dragon-eggs.

They didn't dare let her go broody—for one thing, she'd then be useless to a Jouster until the time had passed for her eggs to hatch. For another, she just *might* kill anyone she thought threatening the eggs, tala or no tala.

Meanwhile he had to make up his mind what he was going to do before she went broody.

He could take the chance that the first egg would be fertile, and carry it off. He already knew when—at night, when the Jousters were in their quarters, the dragon-boys at their recreations, and darkness would cover his actions. And he knew where he would take it—one of the empty pens on either side of Kashet's. There were three times the number of pens than there were dragons, plenty of empty pens where an egg could incubate in the hot sands undisturbed.

Or he could wait, hope that no one noticed, and have his choice of eggs. She could lay as many as four; he was giving her plenty of extra bone for the shells. But the more eggs that appeared, the more likely it was that someone would notice. The longer he waited, the more likely that someone would get impatient and take a look for himself to see what Coresan was up to.

Take the first, or wait? He wavered between the two actions all day. When Kashet and Ari came in, clearly tired from taking double-patrols, he still had not decided.

"If I didn't know he was flying twice as far as the others, I wouldn't guess it," Vetch said, as Ari handed him a lance and dismounted, as usual, with a pat on the shoulder for Kashet. "He's *tired*, but not as exhausted as he could be. I think he's in great condition."

"Well, perhaps it's because he was first-laid," Ari said with a smile. "Firstborn is supposed to be strongest, but when the young ones are taken by dragonet-hunters out in the wild, firstborn has usually fledged and gone, so they get whatever is left."

Then Ari strode off without looking back—which was just as well, for Vetch was still standing there with his mouth open for a long moment after he was gone.

There it was, the deciding factor. *Firstborn is the strongest.*

If that had not been enough, *all* of the conditions that night were perfect. The other dragon-boys all went out that night, for it was a full moon, and the father of one of them, a fisherman, had promised to take them out for night-fishing in the moonlight. The Jousters' quarters were full of music and voices; someone was having a party. The corridors outside the pens were flooded with light from the moon, and utterly deserted—and Coresan slept like a stone, probably exhausted from laying the first of her eggs.

Vetch dug the egg out of the hot sand with his bare hands. It was very warm, the texture very like that of a common pot. He lifted it very carefully, transferred it to a barrow, and trundled it to its new home without sight or sound of anyone or anything except a few bats flitting about the corridors in search of insects. The spirits of the dead were supposed to take the form of bats—was one of them his father, flitting a silent guardian over his son? Probably not. They were probably just bats. If his father returned, how could he *possibly* know that his Altan son was here, in the compound of the Tian Jousters? No, he would surely be flitting about the farm that had been stolen from him. Hopefully he was sending the worst possible dreams into the heads of those who had taken it.

Vetch reburied the egg in the corner of the empty pen least visible from the entrance. He would have to turn it at least twice a day to keep the growing dragonet from sticking to the inside of the shell. He would have to make certain that no one spotted him going into the pen. Then, if the egg was fertile, if it hatched, he would have to get food to it several times a day, also without being seen—

If, if, if. There were a lot of "ifs" standing between him and a fragile hope of success . . .

One thing at a time. One day at a time. There was no point in thinking past the next obstacle, which was how to slip away to turn the egg in the morning . . .

One small step at a time, on the path to what was nothing more than a hope at this point. That was all he dared to do for now. There were sixty mornings, sixty evenings, one hundred and twenty egg-turnings to get through before he had to worry about a nestling. If there was a nestling. If the egg was fertile, if the sand was hot enough but not too hot, if no one discovered it . . .

If, if, if.

———◆———◆———◆———

Reaten was back on his patrols—after a good long dressing-down from Haraket that had practically pinned his ears back. Coresan had laid three more eggs, which were duly taken away from her before she had a chance to go broody. She didn't seem to miss them at all, any more than she'd missed the one that Vetch had taken. Vetch didn't know what had been done with them, and tried not to think about them. After a month, Haraket found another dragon-boy for Coresan, another serf from a stolen farm like Vetch—presumably, having found that Vetch was such a good worker,

Haraket was willing to try another of the same type.

He'd chosen well, so far as Coresan was concerned—Fisk had been a goatherd; he might not be very bright, but he was eminently practical. Unlike Vetch, *he* hadn't a family to lose, as he was already an orphan, tending goats for a surly uncle. As a consequence, life in the Jousters' compound was an improvement, with only a single nonwandering creature to be in charge of, and much better food. He'd understood *exactly* what Vetch meant when he described Coresan's quirks and personality, he didn't let her bully him, and to Haraket's delight, the two of them took to each other with a great deal of mutual respect and even affection.

That released Vetch from his duties to Coresan, which was a great relief. Anyone could tend Kashet, but Coresan needed someone who understood her and *cared* about her. Haraket was overjoyed, and Vetch had overheard him speaking with Ari about finding more goatherd-serfs in the future to use as dragon-boys.

All this came just in time; the egg was starting to move. It was *definitely* fertile. He slipped away every night as soon as it was quiet to turn it and speak softly to the dragonet within the shell, and woke before dawn to turn it again. So far, no one had caught him at it.

Even though Ari came to the pen nearly every night, for a least a little while. Sometimes he spoke, more as if he was just thinking out loud, than as if he was talking to Vetch, but *what* he said—well, Ari was the one person Vetch couldn't think of as a *thing*, a "Tian enemy." He just couldn't hold that anger in Ari's presence. Maybe that was just as well; he had his egg to think of, and you couldn't nurture a young creature if you were angry all the time.

That egg would hatch soon, though. Now came the next hurdle, a successful hatching. He *had* to be there. He daren't

take any chances. Baby chickens thought that the first thing
that *they* saw was their mother—the same might be true of a
dragonet—

And that was when, once again, it seemed as if the Altan
gods *had* heard him and were answering him with subtle aid.

Just when the egg was due to hatch, the summer dry
decided to break, all out of season.

The egg was close, very close, to hatching, and Vetch was
checking it as often as he dared. Then, in the middle of
patrol-time, he noticed that the sky on the horizon seemed
unusually cloudy. He didn't think anything of it, until he
heard something that sounded like the rumbling of a thousand chariot wheels, and looked up again.

The clouds were boiling up before his very eyes, and with
bottoms as black as the soil the floods laid on the fields. As
if the hand of a god was shoving them along, they were
speeding toward Mefis.

And that storm sent the dragons back on the gust-front,
winging in just ahead of the lightning.

He wasn't the only servant to have noticed; Haraket ran
through the compound shouting for the boys, and cursing
everyone in his path. The landings were chaotic; the dragons
were clearly fighting their Jousters to get back to safety
before the storm struck, and there were near-collisions in the
air above the landing-court, actual collisions on the ground.
Kashet, secure and nothing near as nervous as the rest,
landed in his own pen. Ari helped Vetch to strip Kashet of
his saddle and harness and pull a canvas canopy over the
sandpit just as the first warning drops of the torrent to come
splattered into it. Then Ari raced for his own quarters, as
splatters turned to downpour. The canopies were clever
devices, fastened to fat bronze rings that were strung on two
ropes, running along two opposite walls of a pen. You

grasped two hanging straps and pulled it across the pit, where you fastened the straps to rings at the other end. This was the only way to keep the sandpits from turning into hot sand soup during the rainy season.

Kashet burrowed down into the sand as the rain poured down onto the canvas, sheeting down along the sides and into the drains along the edges of his pit.

And Vetch sprinted for the next pen.

He thanked his gods that the canvas was routinely pulled over the tops of the unused pens. His egg was safe from the downpour.

He checked it anyway to be sure, and in the brief time it took to get from one pen to the other, he was soaked to the skin. He peered through the murk from his vantage point in the doorway—and thought that his egg was rocking, but it was hard to tell. Without getting into the pen, all he could see was that it was all right.

Back he ran to Kashet's pen. He peeled off his sodden kilt and changed to a new one in the shelter of his own little awning. The edges of the awnings had become waterfalls, and the sky was so dark it seemed to be dusk, not mid-afternoon. Lightning flickered constantly, seeming to freeze droplets in midair for a moment, and thunder drowned out every other sound.

He was just grateful that the gust-front had been the only wind. A good blow could rip the canvas from its moorings, soaking and cooling the sands, and *that* might have spelled an end to his hopes.

Such fury couldn't last long; the sky lightened, the torrent lessened, the lightning and thunder passed into the distance, leaving behind only a steady rain, interrupted by brief surges of a heavier pelting. Vetch dashed across to the sandpit, the edges of which steamed from the rainwater that had escaped the drains and soaked into the sand along the perimeter. Kashet was in the middle, buried up to his flanks, his neck stretched along the top of the sand with his eyes closed. Vetch knew that pose. Nothing was going to get Kashet out of his warm wallow; not the sweetest bit of meat, not the coaxing of Ari, not the promise of a grooming and burnishing and oiling. Nothing. And at the moment, every other dragon in the compound was doing the same as Kashet.

Back he ran to his egg.

It *was* rocking! In fact, it had rocked itself right up out of the sand! It must be hatching!

No one was going anywhere in this mess; the dragons wouldn't stir, and the Jousters and dragon-boys were all in their respective quarters. Vetch waded out into the hot sand to the egg, which now was rocking madly. He could hear the dragonet inside knocking at the shell, and after turning it carefully, spotted a place where it was cracking. He took the hilt of his knife and pounded at it from the other side. This seemed to encourage the dragonet, it redoubled its efforts, and in a moment, it punched through!

A nostril poked up through the breathing-hole, and the dragonet rested for a while. Vetch let it be, just picking bits of broken shell away from the hole and snapping them off to enlarge it. That was harder than it sounded; the shell was like stone. But the more he opened it, the more the dragonet's muzzle protruded out, the nostrils flaring as it pulled in its first breaths of fresh air.

When the muzzle withdrew from the breathing-hole, the rocking and hammering started again from within the egg. Vetch watched to see where the cracks were appearing, and helped again, pounding with the hilt of his knife, and grateful that the thunder and rain was covering the sound of tapping.

Vetch confined himself to helping cracks along and chipping bits away from the airhole. He wasn't certain how much he could help the dragonet without hurting it by forcing the hatch; this wasn't one of his mother's chickens, after all, and even she had been careful with hatching eggs. There was a difference between *assisting* a hatch, and *forcing* it, a difference that could mean a dead chick or a live one.

He had to run off at one point to feed Kashet—the dragon's appetite wasn't diminished by the rain. The entire time he watched Kashet, he worried; what if the dragonet got into trouble? What if it hatched, and floundered out of the sand and got chilled?

But this was also an opportunity—he loaded his barrow with more meat than Kashet could eat. The top was the usual big chunks, but on the bottom was a thick layer of the smaller scraps and chopped bits. When a dragon needed a heavier dose of tala than you could get into it just by dusting the big pieces with the powder, the other dragon-boys would mix it with the chopped pieces and blood—

Well, that wasn't what he needed it for.

He fed Kashet to satiation, while the rain drummed on the canvas awning. Kashet yawned and dug himself back into his hot sand when he was done, and was asleep in moments. Vetch quickly checked the corridor for the presence of anyone else before he whisked the barrow out of Kashet's pen and into the one next door.

And found himself looking at a limp and exhausted dragonet, sprawled on the sand in an awkward mirror of Kashet's pose. The damp wings were half-under the poor thing, and at his entrance, the dragonet looked up at him and *meeped* pathetically. It could barely raise its head on its long neck; the head wavered back and forth like a heavy flower on a slender stalk.

Vetch parked the barrow under the awning and floundered out into the sand to the dragonet's side. It was bigger than he was, and heavier—twice his size and weight, he thought, though it was hard to tell. It was going to get a lot bigger before it was finished growing. He dug a trench in the hot sand and helped it to slide in, tucking the clumsy, weak limbs into comfortable positions, and spreading the wings out to dry. It was going to be a crimson red, like its parents; until it got a little older, its delicate skin was going to tear and bruise easily if he wasn't careful about it. Then he left the dragonet to bask in the heat and rest from the effort of hatching, heaped a plate with the chopped meat, and returned to it.

It opened its eyes when he returned, and its nostrils twitched as it caught the scent of the meat. Its head wavered up; the poor thing looked so weak! But the mouth opened, and the thin hiss that emerged had a great deal of *demand* in it.

He laughed. "All right, baby—don't be impatient!" he whispered, and dropped a piece the size of his palm in the open mouth.

He'd worried about whether the dragonet would be difficult to feed—in the next several minutes, he knew that this, at least, was *not* going to be a problem. The baby gaped, he dropped meat and bone in, the jaws snapped shut and the throat worked, and the mouth gaped again. It ate until its belly was round, the skin tight, and Vetch could not imagine how it could cram another morsel in.

That was when it stopped, closed its mouth, and *looked* at him, really looked at him for the first time since it had hatched. And then it sighed, laid its head in his lap, and closed its eyes and went immediately to sleep.

He thought his heart was going to melt. A pent-up flood of emotion threatened to overwhelm him; he squeezed his eyes shut to keep from crying, and just whispered tender nonsense into the ruby shells that were the dragonet's ears.

But he couldn't hold the tears back for very long; finally they started, and he wept silently, anger and grief mingling together in those tears, and nothing left to hold them back.

After a while, he ran out of tears.

Carefully, so as not to wake it, he began to stroke the head and ears, and as he petted the delicate skin of the brows, he knew this his dragonet was a female, for it did not have the bumps beneath the skin that would eventually form into a pair of skin-covered "horns."

"What shall I call you, baby?" he murmured to it. This wasn't a question he took lightly. Words had power, and names were the most powerful of all words. Words were what the gods used to shape the world, and whatever he named this little dragonet would shape her.

Then it came to him; from her colors, shading from yellow on her belly, through the scarlet of her body, to a deep plum along her spine and at the end of her tail and her ears. Like the colors of a sunrise—

"Avatre," he murmured. "Fire of the dawn. I name you for that."

She stirred in her sleep and pushed her forehead against his stomach, as though in approval. Avatre it was.

"Avatre," he sighed with content, and with rain drumming on the canvas above them, caressed the head that rested so trustingly in his lap.

Now for the next hurdles. Keeping her presence secret— and *keeping* her . . .

———◆———◆———◆———

Avatre grew at a rate that would have been alarming if Vetch hadn't expected it. Dragons fledged at the end of the dry season, for they absolutely required heat, and the nests that lay in the full sunlight during the dry season would be fully exposed to the rains and cold winds of the winter wet. A young dragon had to be up and out of his nest before the rain and wind came, so that he could follow his mother down into the warm volcanic caves for the winter.

Then he would spend the next two years reaching his full size. In the wild it often took even longer than that, for his growth depended on how well he ate. Here in the compound, of course, a dragonet never lacked for food, so he would achieve his full size in the minimum possible time.

So when Avatre doubled her weight nearly every day, he wasn't alarmed. He oiled her morning and evening to keep her skin supple and prevent it from tearing as she grew.

He knew how to do this because she wasn't the only young one in the compound; two older Jousters whose dragons were growing old had gone out last season and captured themselves replacements, and a new man, one of the Tian King's officers, had captured one as well and presented himself and his dragonet to be trained. With three other youngsters it was far easier to conceal Avatre's presence, especially as one of the others was also a red. If anyone stumbled across her, they would assume that she was one of the legitimate dragonets, not an interloper. The butchers kept plenty of chopped meat on hand, too, and no one seemed to notice that Vetch was taking some at each feeding, even though Kashet never got any tala.

And, luckily, no one was keeping track of the sheer *amount* of meat he was taking.

Ari wasn't paying a lot of attention to what he was doing, either. The Jouster was working hard of late; he was still covering the patrols that should have been taken by Reaten. That was all to the good; it kept him from noticing that Vetch was in and out of the pen next to Kashet's.

Excitement kept him from feeling too weary. And if his day was crowded from dawn to dusk, well, it was crowded with good things rather than miseries.

His one regret was that he didn't dare ask Ari for advice. If only he could have! But he had to blunder through on his own, with common sense and the information he picked up listening to the three boys who were tending the growing youngsters.

He learned that the dragons weren't allowed to carry a grown man until they were three, but that even a fledgling could carry the weight of a small boy. So for the first two years that they were in captivity, the young dragons were given saddles and harnesses, then taken out on long leads and goaded to fly with the dead weight of sandbags in the saddle.

So as soon as she was romping around the sands of her pen, he began getting her used to a weight on her back, improvising a harness and a small sandbag at first, then when he discovered where the dragonet harnesses were kept, purloining one and using that. She grew strong and agile, and hardly noticed the weight; he had to wonder, given how lively she was, if giving tala to the growing youngsters did more than simply make them easier to handle. She was going to be big, bigger than her mother Coresan, for certain, and females were always bigger than the males. She was quieter than the other youngsters, too; they *meeped* all the time, their tone rising in shrillness the closer it got to feeding-time, she only hissed happily when he appeared in the doorway and made no other sounds but a soft chuckling when she settled down for a nap with her head in his lap.

She began exercising her wings, too, flapping hard and making little jumps into the air. When *that* happened, he knew that the moment for fledging was close, and he kept the harness on her during daylight hours, except when he was giving her a bath. He rushed through the chores that took him away from the pens, too—heart in mouth, he listened all the time for some sign she had been discovered. He was so close to his goal—and yet, at any moment, the prize could be snatched away from him—

And for the first time since his father had been killed, he prayed, prayed to the Altan gods, to any god that would listen, that she *not* be discovered and taken from him—or that, if she was discovered, it at least be that she escaped into the free skies—

Even if *he* could not.

And perhaps the gods, aloof in the Land Beyond the Horizon, actually listened to him.

Because the moment of discovery—and the moment of first flight—came when he was with her.

He was, in fact, sitting on her back—not in a saddle, for there wasn't one that would fit her, but with his legs braced in the harness, his hand locked into the hand-brace at the back of the collar, while she made little bounds up and down the sands of her pen, flapping her wings wildly the whole time. *He* had come to enjoy these wild rides, even though he'd been terrified at first; the exhilaration had overcome the terror and now he was able to join in the sense of *fun* she had in these exercises. She was right in the middle of her pen, about to make a really big bound, and he was braced for it—

When a wild shout from the doorway of the pen startled them both.

"*Hoi!*" shouted one of the older dragon-boys, staring at them both. "*Haraket! Haraket! Come quick!*"

He didn't even think; he just reacted, by punching her in the shoulders with his heels. *She* just reacted—by leaping, not jumping, leaping for the sky, eyes focused up, neck outstretched, and wings working. *One* wing-flap. *Two*.

She was off the ground, with *him* still on her back. Then she was above the walls. Then *higher* than the walls—

There was more shouting down below; he clutched at the harness in sudden fear; she looked down at the waving, yelling humans below her. Then she glanced back at him, her eyes pinning with alarm; she seemed to understand the fear in him, and redoubled her efforts, which were showing more skill with every passing second. For the first time, Vetch was glad, *glad* that he was such a skinny weed—he was lighter than the sandbags, and she was having no trouble carrying him.

Now she was over the city, wings pumping furiously as she gained height; he clung on more by instinct than skill, and told himself not to look down.

But he did look back, and saw what he'd feared to see—dragons and Jousters in pursuit.

If they caught him—*he* wasn't a freeborn Tian. He was an Altan serf. They would never, ever permit him to be a Jouster.

They would never let him stay with her.

He would rather die than give her up. They had taken everything from him—they would not take this.

He made up his mind at that moment that if they caught him, if they started to force them down, he would jump. Better dead than lose the only thing he loved, the only family he had now.

No. Never.

He looked back again; there were three in pursuit of him. He bent over Avatre's neck, and whispered encouragement to her.

He had no goal in mind, but she, guided by instinct, was heading for the same hills that her mother had sought at the end of the mating flight. Those hills were riddled with caves and rich with game—and they marked the boundary of the lands that could truly be called "Tian." If they could reach the hills—

But the hills were a long way away, and there were three trained dragons in pursuit.

When they were halfway between the hills and the Great Mother River, he looked back again. Avatre was still flying strongly, showing no signs of tiring. And now there were only two dragons following.

When they reached the hills, he looked back again. One dragon had turned back, but the third was still in hot pursuit, and was closing the gap between them.

And the third was Kashet.

His heart felt as if it were being squeezed, and for a moment, he was blinded by tears. But he leaned over her neck again and begged Avatre to fly faster, harder—

She heard him, and he felt her trying to do as he asked. They topped the first set of hills, and below them he saw the ground of the second rising to meet them, horribly close—

And she was losing height as well. He felt her muscles beginning to tremble, and knew then that she was running out of strength.

And a shadow passed over them.

He knew without looking up that it was Kashet.

And with a sob, he pulled his legs free of the harness, overbalanced, and let go.

He screamed in utter terror as he fell. He couldn't help it. He waited for the scream and the horror to end in blackness.

Something hard struck him in the stomach instead, knocking what was left of his breath out of him and ending his scream in a gasp. He slid—then impacted a second time, and felt a strong arm grab him.

Avatre cried out above him—he'd never heard her cry

before, it sounded like a hawk—and she followed them down, floundering wearily through the air, as Ari and Kashet brought him down to the earth. *He* was crying, uncontrollably, sobbing with rage and thwarted hope, and the death of everything he had hoped for. He couldn't see, blinded by the tears as they landed, as Ari slid off first, then pulled him down to the ground—

—and held him while he wept.

He wanted to fight, but all the fight was out of him. There was nothing, literally nothing left but grief and hopelessness.

Or so he thought—until Ari took his shoulders and gave him a good hard shake.

"Stop it!" the Jouster commanded. "You don't really think I'm going to take you back, do you?"

For a moment, the words made no sense. Then when he *did* get the sense of them, he was so shocked that all he could do was stare.

"I have no intention of bringing you back," Ari repeated. "Especially not after seeing you try and kill yourself to keep from being caught. I may be a monster, but at least I'm not that sort of monster."

He might have said more, but just then Avatre came charging toward them, knocking Ari aside with her head, and clumsily putting herself between the Jouster and Vetch, hissing defiance. Ari put up both his hands, placatingly, but laughing all the same.

Especially when Kashet, full of dignity and twice the size of Avatre, interposed himself between the dragonet and his Jouster, looking down at her with an expression of weary condescension. Avatre, who had never seen another dragon except as a head over the top of the walls of her pen, just hissed at Kashet.

"Very brave," Ari chuckled. "I hardly think I need to worry about you encountering trouble. Here—"

He took a set of bags from the back of his saddle and tossed them to Vetch. "You'll have to hunt food for her—and to be brutally frank, if *I* were you, I would go and decimate a few Tian farms. It seems to me that you're owed a cow or two. But there's a bow and arrows in there, and a hatchet and a knife, other things you'll need. Especially if you decide to live in the hills—"

He didn't finish that sentence, he only looked at Vetch with curiosity.

"I never thought that far," Vetch confessed—because he hadn't. In all of his plans, he had never gotten any farther than this, the fledgling flight, and the escape from what were, after all, his captors. Never what he would do afterward, perhaps because an "afterward" seemed so improbable.

But he had a choice. He and Avatre could live wild.

Or he could go to Altan. There were Jousters there. He could join them.

"I don't know," he said, honestly. "I don't know."

Because the anger that had driven him was gone, at least for now. And with nothing driving him, he had no clear direction.

"Well, stay here for a moment," Ari ordered, and mounted Kashet again.

He was glad enough to follow those orders; when the Jouster and his dragon were back in the air and out of sight over a hill, he went to Avatre and wept on her neck for a moment, then led her to water for a long drink, which they both sorely needed. There were no hot sandpits here, but there were sun-warmed rocks, and they both curled up around some, eyes closed, giving in to exhaustion.

The sound of dragon-wings broke them out of their doze;

he looked up, and saw Kashet returning—with a fat wild sheep in his talons.

Vetch made a messy job of butchering it, but he managed, and Avatre gorged herself. Ari stood by and watched, offering occasional advice, but letting Vetch deal with the butchery and the cleanup afterward.

"You'll be all right," the Jouster told him. "There's a flock of sheep over the hill, and if you put your mind to it, you'll find a way to pen them up, or most of them, anyway. That will keep you two going until you make up your mind. Whatever you decide, do it for *her* sake," Ari added, firmly. "Nothing else. Nothing less."

"I won't," Vetch said, drawing himself up and looking Ari straight in the eyes.

"Good," Ari replied, and got into the saddle. "You and the dragonet got into trouble in these hills," he said, watching them meditatively. "You fell to your death; she flew on. It was very tragic, and I am going to have a *hell* of a time replacing you."

"I'm sorry, Ari—" he said, suddenly stricken with guilt. "I—"

"Don't be. *I'm* not." For the very first time in all of the time that Vetch had known him, Ari broke into a broad and unshadowed smile. "It's the best thing in the world, to see a young thing fly free. Your gods go with you, in whatever you decide, Vetch."

And he sent Kashet up into the sky, leaving Vetch and Avatre to watch, as they disappeared into the heavens that were, at last, no less bright than Vetch's hopes, and no lighter than his heart.

KING DRAGON

by Michael Swanwick

Those familiar with my earlier anthologies may be aware that I reserve the closing spot for the most unusual story in the collection, but this is the first time that guideline does not apply; in my opinion, every tale in *The Dragon Quintet* is worthy of the honor. "King Dragon" certainly qualifies for its dramatic plot, its beauty of language, and its startlingly unusual dragon. Michael Swanwick is the author of six novels and "an uncountable number of short stories." He has won the Hugo, Nebula, Sturgeon, and World Fantasy Awards. *Bones of the Earth*, a novel involving dinosaurs, time travel, and the ultimate fate of mankind, is currently available in paperback from HarperCollins Eos.

The dragons came at dawn, flying low and in formation, their jets so thunderous they shook the ground like the great throbbing heartbeat of the world. The village elders ran outside, half unbuttoned, waving their staffs in circles and shouting words of power. *Vanish*, they cried to the land, and *sleep* to the skies, though had the dragons' half-elven pilots cared they could have easily seen through such flimsy spells of concealment. But the pilots' thoughts were turned toward the west, where Avalon's industrial strength was based, and where its armies were rumored to be massing.

Will's aunt made a blind grab for him, but he ducked under her arm and ran out into the dirt street. The gun emplacements to the south were speaking now, in booming shouts that filled the sky with bursts of pink smoke and flak.

Half the children in the village were out in the streets, hopping up and down in glee, the winged ones buzzing about in small, excited circles. Then the yage-witch came hobbling out from her barrel and, demonstrating a strength Will had never suspected her of having, swept her arms wide and then slammed together her hoary old hands with a *boom!* that drove the children, all against their will, back into their huts.

All save Will. He had been performing that act which rendered one immune from child-magic every night for three weeks now. Fleeing from the village, he felt the enchantment like a polite hand placed on his shoulder. One weak tug, and then it was gone.

He ran, swift as the wind, up Grannystone Hill. His great-great-great-grandmother lived there still, alone at its tip, as a grey standing stone. She never said anything. But sometimes, though one never saw her move, she went down to the river at night to drink. Coming back from a nighttime fishing trip in his wee coracle, Will would find her standing motionless there and greet her respectfully. If the catch was good, he would gut an eel or a small trout, and smear the blood over her feet. It was the sort of small courtesy elderly relatives appreciated.

"Will, you young fool, turn back!" a cobbley cried from the inside of a junk refrigerator in the garbage dump at the edge of the village. "It's not safe up there!"

But Will didn't want to be safe. He shook his head, long blond hair flying behind him, and put every ounce of his strength into his running. He wanted to see dragons. Dragons! Creatures of almost unimaginable power and magic. He wanted to experience the glory of their flight. He wanted to get as close to them as he could. It was a kind of mania. It was a kind of need.

It was not far to the hill, nor a long way to its bald and grassy summit. Will ran with a wildness he could not understand, lungs pounding and the wind of his own speed whistling in his ears.

And then he was atop the hill, breathing hard, with one hand on his grandmother stone.

The dragons were still flying overhead in waves. The roar of their jets was astounding. Will lifted his face into the heat of their passage, and felt the wash of their malice and hatred as well. It was like a dark wine that sickened the stomach and made the head throb with pain and bewilderment and wonder. It repulsed him and made him want more.

The last flight of dragons scorched over, twisting his head and spinning his body around, so he could keep on watching them, flying low over farms and fields and the Old Forest that stretched all the way to the horizon and beyond. There was a faint brimstone stench of burnt fuel in the air. Will felt his heart grow so large it seemed impossible his chest could contain it, so large that it threatened to encompass the hill, farms, forest, dragons, and all the world beyond.

Something hideous and black leaped up from the distant forest and into the air, flashing toward the final dragon. Will's eyes felt a painful wrenching *wrongness*, and then a stone hand came down over them.

"*Don't look*," said an old and calm and stony voice. "*To look upon a basilisk is no way for a child of mine to die.*"

"Grandmother?" Will asked.

"*Yes?*"

"If I promise to keep my eyes closed, will you tell me what's happening?"

There was a brief silence. Then: "*Very well. The dragon has turned. He is fleeing.*"

"Dragons don't flee," Will said scornfully. "Not from anything." Forgetting his promise, he tried to pry the hand from his eyes. But of course it was useless, for his fingers were mere flesh.

"This one does. And he is wise to do so. His fate has come for him. Out from the halls of coral it has come, and down to the halls of granite it will take him. Even now his pilot is singing his death-song."

She fell silent again, while the distant roar of the dragon rose and fell in pitch. Will could tell that momentous things were happening, but the sound gave him not the least clue as to their nature. At last he said, "Grandmother? Now?"

"He is clever, this one. He fights very well. He is elusive. But he cannot escape a basilisk. Already the creature knows the first two syllables of his true name. At this very moment it is speaking to his heart, and telling it to stop beating."

The roar of the dragon grew louder again, and then louder still. From the way it kept on growing, Will was certain the great creature was coming straight toward him. Mingled with its roar was a noise that was like a cross between a scarecrow screaming and the sound of teeth scraping on slate.

"Now they are almost touching. The basilisk reaches for its prey . . ."

There was a deafening explosion directly overhead. For an astonishing instant, Will felt certain he was going to die. Then his grandmother threw her stone cloak over him and, clutching him to her warm breast, knelt down low to the sheltering earth.

When he awoke, it was dark and he lay alone on the cold hillside. Painfully, he stood. A somber orange-and-red sunset limned the western horizon, where the dragons had disappeared. There was no sign of the War anywhere.

"Grandmother?" Will stumbled to the top of the hill, cursing the stones that hindered him. He ached in every joint. There was a constant ringing in his ears, like factory bells tolling the end of a shift. "Grandmother!"

There was no answer.

The hilltop was empty.

But scattered down the hillside, from its top down to where he had awakened, was a stream of broken stones. He had hurried past them without looking on his way up. Now he saw that their exterior surfaces were the familiar and comfortable grey of his stone-mother, and that the freshly exposed interior surfaces were slick with blood.

One by one, Will carried the stones back to the top of the hill, back to the spot where his great-great-great-grandmother had preferred to stand and watch over the village. It took hours. He piled them one on top of another, and though it felt like more work than he had ever done in his life, when he was finished, the cairn did not rise even so high as his waist. It seemed impossible that this could be all that remained of she who had protected the village for so many generations.

By the time he was done, the stars were bright and heartless in a black, moonless sky. A night-wind ruffled his shirt and made him shiver, and with sudden clarity he wondered at last why he was alone. Where was his aunt? Where were the other villagers?

Belatedly remembering his basic spell-craft, he yanked out his rune-bag from a hip pocket, and spilled its contents into his hand. A crumpled blue-jay's feather, a shard of mirror, two acorns, and a pebble with one side blank and the other marked with an X. He kept the mirror-shard and poured the rest back into the bag. Then he invoked the secret name of the *lux aeterna*, inviting a tiny fraction of its radiance to enter the mundane world.

A gentle foxfire spread itself through the mirror. Holding it at arm's length so he could see his face reflected therein, he asked the oracle glass, "Why did my village not come for me?"

The mirror-boy's mouth moved. "They came." His skin was pallid, like a corpse's.

"Then why didn't they bring me home?" And why did *he* have to build his stone-grandam's cairn and not they? He did not ask that question, but he felt it to the core of his being.

"They didn't find you."

The oracle-glass was maddeningly literal, capable only of answering the question one asked, rather than that which one wanted answered. But Will persisted. "Why didn't they find me?"

"You weren't here."

"Where was I? Where was my Granny?"

"You were nowhere."

"How could we be nowhere?"

Tonelessly, the mirror said, "The basilisk's explosion warped the world and the mesh of time in which it is caught. The sarsen-lady and you were thrown forward, halfway through the day."

It was as clear an explanation as Will was going to get. He muttered a word of unbinding, releasing the invigorating light back to whence it came. Then, fearful that the blood on his hands and clothes would draw night-gaunts, he hurried homeward.

When he got to the village, he discovered that a search party was still scouring the darkness, looking for him. Those who remained had hoisted a straw man upside down atop a tall pole at the center of the village square, and set it ablaze against the chance he was still alive, to draw him home.

And so it had.

Two days after those events, a crippled dragon crawled out of the Old Forest and into the village. Slowly he pulled himself into the center square. Then he collapsed. He was wingless and there were gaping holes in his fuselage, but still the stench of power clung to him, and a miasma of hatred. A trickle of oil seeped from a gash in his belly and made a spreading stain on the cobbles beneath him.

Will was among those who crowded out to behold this prodigy. The others whispered hurtful remarks among themselves about its ugliness. And truly it was built of cold, black iron, and scorched even darker by the basilisk's explosion, with jagged stumps of metal where its wings had been and ruptured plates here and there along its flanks. But Will could see that, even half-destroyed, the dragon was a beautiful creature. It was built with dwarven skill to high-elven design—how could it *not* be beautiful? It was, he felt certain, the same dragon that he had almost seen shot down by the basilisk.

Knowing this gave him a strange sense of shameful complicity, as if he were in some way responsible for the dragon's coming to the village.

For a long time no one spoke. Then an engine hummed to life somewhere deep within the dragon's chest, rose in pitch to a clattering whine, and fell again into silence. The dragon slowly opened one eye.

"Bring me your truth-teller," he rumbled.

The truth-teller was a fruit-woman named Bessie Applemere. She was young and yet, out of respect for her office, everybody called her by the honorific Hag. She came, clad in the robes and wide hat of her calling, breasts bare as was traditional, and stood before the mighty engine of war. "Father of Lies." She bowed respectfully.

"I am crippled, and all my missiles are spent," the dragon said. "But still am I dangerous."

Hag Applemere nodded. "It is the truth."

"My tanks are yet half-filled with jet fuel. It would be the easiest thing in the world for me to set them off with an electrical spark. And were I to do so, your village and all who live within it would cease to be. Therefore, since power engenders power, I am now your liege and king."

"It is the truth."

A murmur went up from the assembled villagers.

"However, my reign will be brief. By Samhain, the Armies of the Mighty will be here, and they shall take me back to the great forges of the East to be rebuilt."

"You believe it so."

The dragon's second eye opened. Both focused steadily on the truth-teller. "You do not please me, Hag. I may someday soon find it necessary to break open your body and eat your beating heart."

Hag Applemere nodded. "It is the truth."

Unexpectedly, the dragon laughed. It was cruel and sardonic laughter, as the mirth of such creatures always was, but it was laughter nonetheless. Many of the villagers covered their ears against it. The smaller children burst into tears. "You amuse me," he said. "All of you amuse me. We begin my reign on a gladsome note."

The truth-teller bowed. Watching, Will thought he detected a great sadness in her eyes. But she said nothing.

"Let your lady-mayor come forth, that she might give me obeisance."

Auld Black Agnes shuffled from the crowd. She was scrawny and thrawn and bent almost double from the weight of her responsibilities. They hung in a black leather bag around her neck. From that bag, she brought forth a flat stone from the first hearth of the village, and laid it down before the dragon. Kneeling, she placed her left hand, splayed, upon it.

Then she took out a small silver sickle.

"Your blood and ours. Thy fate and mine. Our joy and your wickedness. Let all be as one." Her voice rose in a warbling keen:

> "Black spirits and white, red spirits and grey,
> Mingle, mingle, mingle, you that mingle may."

Her right hand trembled with palsy as it raised the sickle up above her left. But her slanting motion downward was swift and sudden. Blood spurted, and her little finger went flying.

She made one small, sharp cry, like a sea-bird's, and no more.

"I am satisfied," the dragon said. Then, without transition: "My pilot is dead and he begins to rot." A hatch hissed open in his side. "Drag him forth."

"Do you wish him buried?" a kobold asked hesitantly.

"Bury him, burn him, cut him up for bait—what do I care? When he was alive, I needed him in order to fly. But he's dead now, and of no use to me."

"Kneel."

Will knelt in the dust beside the dragon. He'd been standing in line for hours, and there were villagers who would be standing in that same line hours from now, waiting to be processed. They went in fearful, and they came out dazed. When a lily-maid stepped down from the dragon, and somebody shouted a question at her, she simply shook her tear-streaked face, and fled. None would speak of what happened within.

The hatch opened.

"Enter."

He did. The hatch closed behind him.

At first he could see nothing. Then small, faint lights swam out of the darkness. Bits of green and white stabilized, became instrument lights, pale luminescent flecks on dials. One groping hand touched leather. It was the pilot's couch. He could smell, faintly, the taint of corruption on it.

"Sit."

Clumsily, he climbed into the seat. The leather creaked under him. His arms naturally lay along the arms of the couch. He might have been made for it. There were hand-grips. At the dragon's direction, he closed his hands about them and turned them as far as they would go. A quarter-turn, perhaps.

From beneath, needles slid into his wrists. They stung like blazes, and Will jerked involuntarily. But when he tried, he discovered that he could not let go of the grips. His fingers would no longer obey him.

"Boy," the dragon said suddenly, "what is your true name?"

Will trembled. "I don't have one."

Immediately, he sensed that this was not the right answer. There was a silence. Then the dragon said dispassionately, "I can make you suffer."

"Sir, I am certain you can."

"Then tell me your true name."

His wrists were cold—cold as ice. The sensation that spread up his forearms to his elbows was not numbness, for they ached terribly. It felt as if they were packed in snow. "I don't *know* it! Will cried in an anguish. "I don't know, I was never told, I don't think I have one!"

Small lights gleamed on the instrument panel, like forest eyes at night.

"Interesting." For the first time, the dragon's voice displayed a faint tinge of emotion. "What family is yours? Tell me everything about them."

Will had no family other than his aunt. His parents had died on the very first day of the War. Theirs was the ill-fortune of being in Brocielande Station when the dragons came and dropped golden fire on the rail yards. So Will had been shipped off to the hills to live with his aunt. Everyone agreed he would be safest there. That was several years ago, and there were times now when he could not remember his parents at all. Soon he would have only the memory of remembering.

As for his aunt, Blind Enna was little more to him than a set of rules to be contravened and chores to be evaded. She was a pious old creature, forever killing small animals in honor of the Nameless Ones and burying their corpses under the floor or nailing them above doors or windows. In consequence of which, a faint perpetual stink of conformity and rotting mouse hung about the hut. She mumbled to herself constantly and on those rare occasions when she got drunk— two or three times a year—would run out naked into the night and, mounting a cow backwards, lash its sides bloody with a hickory switch so that it ran wildly uphill and down until finally she tumbled off and fell asleep. At dawn Will would come with a blanket and lead her home. But they were never exactly close.

All this he told in stumbling, awkward words. The dragon listened without comment.

The cold had risen up to Will's armpits by now. He shuddered as it touched his shoulders. "Please . . ." he said. "Lord

Dragon . . . your ice has reached my chest. If it touches my heart, I fear that I'll die."

"Hmmmm? Ah! I was lost in thought." The needles withdrew from Will's arms. They were still numb and lifeless, but at least the cold had stopped its spread. He could feel a tingle of pins and needles in the center of his fingertips, and so knew that sensation would eventually return.

The door hissed open. "You may leave now."

He stumbled out into the light.

An apprehension hung over the village for the first week or so. But as the dragon remained quiescent and no further alarming events occurred, the timeless patters of village life more or less resumed. Yet all the windows opening upon the center square remained perpetually shuttered and nobody willingly passed through it anymore, so that it was as if a stern silence had come to dwell within their midst.

Then one day Will and Puck Berrysnatcher were out in the woods, checking their snares for rabbits and camelopards (it had been generations since a pard was caught in Avalon but they still hoped), when the Scissors-Grinder came puffing down the trail. He lugged something bright and gleaming within his two arms.

"Hey, bandy-man!" Will cried. He had just finished tying his rabbits' legs together so he could sling them over his shoulder. "Ho, big-belly! What hast thou?"

"Don't know. Fell from the sky."

"Did *not!*" Puck scoffed. The two boys danced about the fat cobber, grabbing at the golden thing. It was shaped something like a crown and something like a birdcage. The metal of its ribs and bands was smooth and lustrous. Black runes adorned its sides. They had never seen its like. "I bet it's a roc's egg—or a phoenix's!"

And simultaneously Will asked, "Where are you taking it?"

"To the smithy. Perchance the hammerman can beat it down into something useful." The Scissors-Grinder swatted at Puck with one hand, almost losing his hold on the object. "Perchance they'll pay me a penny or three for it."

Daisy Jenny popped up out of the flowers in the field by the edge of the garbage dump and, seeing the golden thing, ran toward it, pigtails flying, singing, "Gimme-gimme-gimme!" Two hummingirls and one chimney-bounder came swooping down out of nowhere. And the Cauldron Boy dropped an armful of scavenged scrap metal with a crash and came running up as well. So that by the time the Meadows Trail became Mud Street, the Scissors-Grinder was red-faced and cursing, and knee-deep in children.

"Will, you useless creature!"

Turning, Will saw his aunt, Blind Enna, tapping toward him. She had a peeled willow branch in each hand, like long white antennae, that felt the ground before her as she came. The face beneath her bonnet was grim. He knew this mood, and knew better than to try to evade her when she was in it. "Auntie . . ." he said.

"Don't you Auntie me, you slugabed! There's toads to be buried and stoops to be washed. Why are you never around when it's time for chores?"

She put an arm through his and began dragging him homeward, still feeling ahead of herself with her wands.

Meanwhile, the Scissors-Grinder was so distracted by the children that he let his feet carry him the way they habitually went—through Center Square, rather than around it. For the first time since the coming of the dragon, laughter and children's voices spilled into that silent space. Will stared yearningly over his shoulder after his dwindling friends.

The dragon opened an eye to discover the cause of so much noise. He reared up his head in alarm. In a voice of power he commanded, "*Drop that!*"

Startled, the Scissors-Grinder obeyed.

The device exploded.

Magic in the imagination is a wondrous thing, but magic in practice is terrible beyond imagining. An unending instant's dazzlement and confusion left Will lying on his back in the street. His ears rang horribly, and he felt strangely numb. There were legs everywhere—people running. And somebody was hitting him with a stick. No, with two sticks.

He sat up, and the end of a stick almost got him in the eye. He grabbed hold of it with both hands and yanked at it angrily. "Auntie," he yelled. Blind Enna went on waving the other stick around, and tugging at the one he had captured, trying to get it back. "Auntie, stop that!" But of course she couldn't hear him; he could barely hear himself through the ringing in his ears.

He got to his feet and put both arms around his aunt. She struggled against him, and Will was astonished to find that she was no taller than he. When had *that* happened? She had been twice his height when first he came to her. "Auntie Enna!" he shouted into her ear. "It's me, Will, I'm right here."

"Will." Her eyes filled with tears. "You shiftless, worthless thing. Where are you when there are chores to be done?"

Over her shoulder, he saw how the square was streaked with black and streaked with red. There were things that looked like they might be bodies. He blinked. The square was filled with villagers, leaning over them. Doing things. Some had their heads thrown back, as if they were wailing. But of course he couldn't hear them, not over the ringing noise.

"I caught two rabbits, Enna," he told his aunt, shouting so he could be heard. He still had them, slung over his shoulder. He couldn't imagine why. "We can have them for supper."

"That's good," she said. "I'll cut them up for stew, while you wash the stoops."

Blind Enna found her refuge in work. She mopped the ceiling and scoured the floor. She had Will polish every piece of silver in the house. Then all the furniture had to be taken apart, and cleaned, and put back together again. The rugs had to be boiled. The little filigreed case containing her heart had to be taken out of the cupboard where she normally kept it and hidden in the very back of the closet.

The list of chores that had to be done was endless. She worked herself, and Will as well, all the way to dusk. Sometimes he cried at the thought of his friends who had died, and Blind Enna hobbled over and hit him to make him stop. Then, when he did stop, he felt nothing. He felt nothing, and he felt like a monster for feeling nothing. Thinking of it made him begin to cry again, so he wrapped his arms tight around his face to muffle the sounds, so his aunt would not hear and hit him again.

It was hard to say which—the feeling or the not—made him more miserable.

The very next day, the summoning bell was rung in the town square and, willing or not, all the villagers once again assembled before their king dragon. "Oh, ye foolish creatures!" the dragon said. "Six children have died and old *Tanarahumra*—he whom you called the Scissors-Grinder—as well, because you have no self-discipline."

Hag Applemere bowed her head sadly. "It is the truth."

"You try my patience," the dragon said. "Worse, you drain my batteries. My reserves grow low, and I can only partially recharge them each day. Yet I see now that I dare not be King Log. You must be governed. Therefore, I require a speaker. Someone slight of body, to live within me and carry my commands to the outside."

Auld Black Agnes shuffled forward. "That would be me," she said wearily. "I know my duty."

"No!" the dragon said scornfully. "You aged cronies are too cunning by half. I'll choose somebody else from this crowd. Someone simple . . . a child."

Not me, Will thought wildly. *Anybody else but me.*

"Him," the dragon said.

So it was that Will came to live within the dragon king. All that day and late into the night he worked drawing up plans on sheets of parchment, at his lord's careful instructions, for devices very much like stationary bicycles that could be used to recharge the dragon's batteries. In the morning, he went to the blacksmith's forge at the end of town to command that six of the things be immediately built. Then he went to Auld Black Agnes to tell her that all day and every day six villagers, elected by lot or rotation or however else she chose, were to sit upon the devices pedaling, pedaling, all the way without cease from dawn to sundown, when Will would drag the batteries back inside.

Hurrying through the village with his messages—there were easily a dozen packets of orders, warnings, and advices that first day—Will experienced a strange sense of unreality. Lack of sleep made everything seem impossibly vivid. The green moss on the skulls stuck in the crotches of forked sticks lining the first half-mile of the River Road, the salamanders languidly copulating in the coals of the smithy forge, even the stillness of the carnivorous plants in his Auntie's garden as they waited for an unwary frog to hop within striking distance . . . such homely sights were transformed. Everything was new and strange to him.

By noon, all the dragon's errands were run, so Will went out in search of friends. The square was empty, of course, and silent. But when he wandered out into the lesser streets, his shadow short beneath him, they were empty as well. It was eerie. Then he heard the high sound of a girlish voice and followed it around a corner.

There was a little girl playing at jump rope and chanting:

> "Here-am-I-and
> All-a-lone;
> What's-my-name?
> It's-Jum-ping—"

"Joan!" Will cried, feeling an unexpected relief at the sight of her.

Jumping Joan stopped. In motion, she had a certain kinetic presence. Still, she was hardly there at all. A hundred slim braids exploded from her small, dark head. Her arms and legs were thin as reeds. The only things of any size at all about her were her luminous brown eyes. "I was up to a million!" she said angrily. "Now I'll have to start all over again."

"When you start again, count your first jump as a million-and-one."

"It doesn't work that way and you know it! What do you want?"

"Where is everybody?"

"Some of them are fishing and some are hunting. Others are at work in the fields. The hammermen, the tinker, and the Sullen Man are building bicycles-that-don't-move to place in

Tyrant Square. The potter and her 'prentices are digging clay from the riverbank. The healing-women are in the smoke-hutch at the edge of the woods with Puck Berrysnatcher."

"Then that last is where I'll go. My thanks, wee-thing."

Jumping Joan, however, made no answer. She was already skipping rope again, and counting "A-hundred-thousand-one, a-hundred-thousand-two . . ."

The smoke-hutch was an unpainted shack built so deep in the reeds that whenever it rained it was in danger of sinking down into the muck and never being seen again. Hornets lazily swam to and from a nest beneath its eaves. The door creaked noisily as Will opened it.

As one, the women looked up sharply. Puck Berrysnatcher's body was a pale white blur on the shadowy ground before them. The women's eyes were green and unblinking, like those of jungle animals. They glared at him wordlessly. "I w-wanted to see what you were d-doing," he stammered.

"We are inducing catatonia," one of them said. "Hush now. Watch and learn."

The healing-women were smoking cigars over Puck. They filled their mouths with smoke and then, leaning close, let it pour down over his naked, broken body. By slow degrees the hut filled with bluish smoke, turning the healing-women to ghosts and Puck himself into an indistinct smear on the dirt floor. He sobbed and murmured in pain at first, but by slow degrees his cries grew quieter, and then silent. At last his body shuddered and stiffened, and he ceased breathing.

The healing-women daubed Puck's chest with ocher, and then packed his mouth, nostrils, and anus with a mixture of aloe and white clay. They wrapped his body with a long white strip of linen.

Finally they buried him deep in the black marsh by the edge of Hagmere Pond.

When the last shovelful of earth had been tamped down, the women turned as one and silently made their ways home, along five separate paths. Will's stomach rumbled, and he realized he hadn't eaten yet that day. There was a cherry tree not far away whose fruit was freshly come to ripeness, and a pigeon pie that he knew of which would not be well-guarded.

Swift as a thief, he sped into town.

He expected the dragon to be furious with him when he finally returned to it just before sundown, for staying away as long as he could. But when he sat down in the leather couch and the needles slid into his wrists, the dragon's voice was a murmur, almost a purr. "How fearful you are! You tremble. Do not be afraid, small one. I shall protect and cherish you. And you, in turn, shall be my eyes and ears, eh? Yes, you will. Now, let us see what you learned today."

"I—"

"Shussssh," the dragon breathed. "Not a word. I need not your interpretation, but direct access to your memories. Try to relax. This will hurt you, the first time, but with practice it will grow easier. In time, perhaps, you will learn to enjoy it."

Something cold and wet and slippery slid into Will's mind. A coppery foulness filled his mouth. A repulsive stench rose up in his nostrils. Reflexively, he retched and struggled.

"Don't resist. This will go easier if you open yourself to me."

More of that black and oily sensation poured into Will, and more. Coil upon coil, it thrust its way inside him. His body felt distant, like a thing that no longer belonged to him. He could hear it making choking noises.

"Take it all."

It hurt. It hurt more than the worst headache Will had ever had. He thought he heard his skull cracking from the pressure, and still the intrusive presence pushed into him, its pulsing mass permeating his thoughts, his senses, his memories. Swelling them. Engorging them. And then, just as he was certain his head must explode from the pressure, it was done.

The dragon was within him.

Squeezing shut his eyes, Will saw, in the dazzling, pain-laced darkness, the dragon king as he existed in the spirit world: sinuous, veined with light, humming with power. Here, in the realm of ideal forms, he was not a broken, crippled *thing*, but a sleek being with the beauty of an animal and the perfection of a machine.

"Am I not beautiful?" the dragon asked. "Am I not a delight to behold?"

Will gagged with pain and disgust. And yet—might the Seven forgive him for thinking this!—it was true.

Every morning at dawn Will dragged out batteries weighing almost as much as himself into Tyrant Square for the villagers to recharge—one at first, then more as the remaining six standing bicycles were built. One of the women would be waiting to give him breakfast. As the dragon's agent, he was entitled to go into any hut and feed himself from what he found there, but the dragon deemed this method more dignified. The rest of the day he spent wandering through the village and, increasingly, the woods and fields around the village, observing. At first he did not know what he was looking for. But by comparing the orders he transmitted with what he had seen the previous day, he slowly came to realize that he was scouting out the village's defensive position, discovering its weaknesses, and looking for ways to alleviate them.

The village was, Will saw, simply not defensible from any serious military force. But it could be made more obscure. Thorn-hedges were planted, and poison oak. Footpaths were eradicated. A clearwater pond was breached and drained, lest it be identified as a resource for advancing armies. When the weekly truck came up the River Road with mail and cartons of supplies for the store, Will was loitering nearby, to ensure that nothing unusual caught the driver's eye. When the bee-warden declared a surplus that might be sold downriver for silver, Will relayed the dragon's instructions that half the overage be destroyed, lest the village get a reputation for prosperity.

At dimity, as the sunlight leached from the sky, Will would feel a familiar aching in his wrists and a troubling sense of need, and return to the dragon's cabin to lie in painful communion with him and share what he had seen.

Evenings varied. Sometimes he was too sick from the dragon's entry into him to do anything. Other times, he spent hours scrubbing and cleaning the dragon's interior. Mostly, though, he simply sat in the pilot's couch, listening while the dragon talked in a soft, almost inaudible rumble. Those were, in their way, the worst times of all.

"You don't have cancer," the dragon murmured. It was dark outside, or so Will believed. The hatch was kept closed tight and there were no windows. The only light came from the instruments on the control panel. "No bleeding from the rectum, no loss of energy. Eh, boy?"

"No, dread lord."

"It seems I chose better than I suspected. You have mor-

tal blood in you, sure as moonlight. Your mother was no better than she ought to be."

"Sir?" he said uncomprehendingly.

"I said your mother was a *whore!* Are you feeble-minded?
Your mother was a whore, your father a cuckold, you a bas-
tard, grass green, mountains stony, and water wet."

"My mother was a good woman!" Ordinarily, he didn't
talk back. But this time the words just slipped out.

"Good women sleep with men other than their husbands
all the time, and for more reasons than there are men. Didn't
anybody tell you that?" He could hear a note of satisfaction
in the dragon's voice. "She could have been bored, or reck-
less, or blackmailed. She might have wanted money, or
adventure, or revenge upon your father. Perchance she bet
her virtue upon the turn of a card. Maybe she was overcome
by the desire to roll in the gutter and befoul herself. She may
even have fallen in love. Unlikelier things have happened."

"I won't listen to this!"

"You have no choice," the dragon said complacently.
"The door is locked and you cannot escape. Moreover I am
larger and more powerful than you. This is the *Lex Mundi*,
from which there is no appeal."

"You lie! You lie! You lie!"

"Believe what you will. But, however got, your mortal
blood is your good fortune. Lived you not in the asshole of
beyond, but in a more civilized setting, you would surely be
conscripted for a pilot. All pilots are half-mortal, you know,
for only mortal blood can withstand the taint of cold iron.
You would live like a prince, and be trained as a warrior. You
would be the death of thousands." The dragon's voice sank
musingly. "How shall I mark this discovery? Shall I . . . ?
Oho! Yes. I will make you my lieutenant."

"How does that differ from what I am now?"

"Do not despise titles. If nothing else, it will impress your friends."

Will had no friends, and the dragon knew it. Not anymore. All folk avoided him when they could, and were stiff-faced and wary in his presence when they could not. The children fleered and jeered and called him names. Sometimes they flung stones at him or pottery shards or—once—even a cowpat, dry on the outside but soft and gooey within. Not often, however, for when they did, he would catch them and thrash them for it. This always seemed to catch the little ones by surprise.

The world of children was much simpler than the one he inhabited.

When Little Margotty struck him with the cowpat, he caught her by the ear and marched her to her mother's hut. "See what your brat has done to me!" he cried in indignation, holding his jerkin away from him.

Big Red Margotty turned from the worktable, where she had been canning toads. She stared at him stonily, and yet he thought a glint resided in her eye of suppressed laughter. Then, coldly, she said, "Take it off and I shall wash it for you."

Her expression when she said this was so disdainful that Will felt an impulse to peel off his trousers as well, throw them in her face for her insolence, and command her to wash them for a penance. But with the thought came also an awareness of Big Red Margotty's firm, pink flesh, of her ample breasts and womanly haunches. He felt his lesser self swelling to fill out his trousers and make them bulge.

This too Big Red Margotty saw, and the look of casual scorn she gave him then made Will burn with humiliation. Worse, all the while her mother washed his jerkin, Little Red Margotty danced around Will at a distance, holding up her skirt and waggling her bare bottom at him, making a mock of his discomfort.

On the way out the door, his damp jerkin draped over one arm, he stopped and said, "Make for me a sark of white damask, with upon its breast a shield: Argent, dragon rouge rampant above a village sable. Bring it to me by dawn-light tomorrow."

Outraged, Big Red Margotty said: "The cheek! You have no right to demand any such thing!"

"I am the dragon's lieutenant, and that is right enough for anything."

He left, knowing that the red bitch would perforce be up all night sewing for him. He was glad for every miserable hour she would suffer.

Three weeks having passed since Puck's burial, the healing-women decided it was time at last to dig him up. They said nothing when Will declared that he would attend—none of the adults said anything to him unless they had no choice— but, tagging along after them, he knew for a fact that he was unwelcome.

Puck's body, when they dug it up, looked like nothing so much as an enormous black root, twisted and formless. Chanting all the while, the women unwrapped the linen swaddling and washed him down with cow's urine. They dug out the life-clay that clogged his openings. They placed the finger-bone of a bat beneath his tongue. An egg was broken by his nose and the white slurped down by one medicine woman and the yellow by another.

Finally, they injected him with 5 cc of dextroampheta-mine sulfate.

Puck's eyes flew open. His skin had been baked black as silt by his long immersion in the soil, and his hair bleached white. His eyes were a vivid and startling leaf-green. In all respects but one, his body was as perfect as it had ever been. But that one exception made the women sigh unhappily for his sake.

One leg was missing, from above the knee down.

"The Earth has taken her tithe," one old woman observed sagely.

"There was not enough left of the leg to save," said another.

"It's a pity," said a third.

They all withdrew from the hut, leaving Will and Puck alone together.

For a long time Puck did nothing but stare wonderingly at his stump of a leg. He sat up and ran careful hands over its surface, as if to prove to himself that the missing flesh was not still there and somehow charmed invisible. Then he stared at Will's clean white shirt, and at the dragon arms upon his chest. At last, his unblinking gaze rose to meet Will's eyes.

"*You* did this!"

"No!" It was an unfair accusation. The land mine had nothing to do with the dragon. The Scissors-Grinder would have found it and brought it into the village in any case. The two facts were connected only by the War, and the War was not Will's fault. He took his friend's hand in his own. "*Tchortyrion* . . ." he said in a low voice, careful that no unseen person might overhear.

Puck batted his hand away. "That's not my true name anymore! I have walked in darkness and my spirit has returned from the halls of granite with a new name—one that not even the dragon knows!"

"The dragon will learn it soon enough," Will said sadly.

"You wish!"

"Puck . . ."

"My old use-name is dead as well," said he who had been Puck Berrysnatcher. Unsteadily pulling himself erect, he wrapped the blanket upon which he had been laid about his thin shoulders. "You may call me No-name, for no name of mine shall ever pass your lips again."

Awkwardly, No-name hopped to the doorway. He steadied himself with a hand upon the jamb, then launched himself out into the wide world.

"Please! Listen to me!" Will cried after him.

Wordlessly, No-name raised one hand, middle finger extended.

Red anger welled up inside Will. "Asshole!" he shouted after his former friend. "Stump-leggity hopper! Johnny-three-limbs!"

He had not cried since that night the dragon first entered him. Now he cried again.

In midsummer an army recruiter roared into town with a bright green-and-yellow drum lashed to the motorcycle behind him. He wore a smart red uniform with two rows of brass buttons, and he'd come all the way from Brocielande, looking for likely lads to enlist in the service of Avalon. With a screech and a cloud of dust, he pulled up in front of the Scrannel Dogge, heeled down the kickstand, and went inside to rent the common room for the space of the afternoon.

Outside again, he donned his drum harness, attached the drum, and sprinkled a handful of gold coins on its head. *Boom-Boom-de-Boom!* The drumsticks came down like thunder. *Rap-Tap-a-Rap!* The gold coins leaped and danced, like raindrops on a hot griddle. By this time, there was a crowd standing outside the Scrannel Dogge.

The recruiter laughed. "Sergeant Bombast is my name!" *Boom! Doom! Boom!* "Finding heroes is my game!" He struck the sticks together overhead. *Click! Snick! Click!* Then he thrust them in his belt, unharnessed the great drum, and set it down beside him. The gold coins caught the sun and dazzled every eye with avarice. "I'm here to offer certain brave lads the very best career a man ever had. The chance to learn a skill, to become a warrior . . . and get paid damn well for it, too. Look at me!" He clapped his hands upon his ample girth. "Do I look underfed?"

The crowd laughed. Laughing with them, Sergeant Bombast waded into their number, wandering first this way, then that, addressing first this one, then another. "No, I do not. For the very good reason that the Army feeds me well. It feeds me, and clothes me, and all but wipes me arse when I ask it to. And am I grateful? I am *not.* No, sirs and maidens, so far from grateful am I that I require that the Army pay me for the privilege! And how much, do you ask? How much am I paid? Keeping in mind that my shoes, my food, my breeches, my snot-rag—" he pulled a lace handkerchief from one sleeve and waved it daintily in the air—"are all free as the air we breathe and the dirt we rub in our hair at Candlemas eve. How much am I *paid?*" His seemingly random wander had brought him back to the drum again. Now his fist came down on the drum, making it shout and the gold leap up into the air with wonder. "Forty-three copper pennies a month!"

The crowd gasped.

"Payable quarterly in good honest gold! As you see here! *Or* silver, for them as worships the horned matron." He chucked old Lady Favor-Me-Not under the chin, making her blush and simper. "But that's not all—no, not the half of it! I see you've noticed these coins here. Noticed? Pshaw! You've noticed that I *meant* you to notice these coins! And why not? Each one of these little beauties weighs a full

Trojan ounce! Each one is of the good red gold, laboriously mined by kobolds in the griffin-haunted Mountains of the Moon. How could you not notice them? How could you not wonder what I meant to do with them? Did I bring them here simply to scoop them up again, when my piece were done, and pour them back into my pockets?"

"Not a bit of it! It is my dearest hope that I leave this vil- lage penniless. I *intend* to leave this village penniless! Listen careful now, for this is the crux of the matter. This here gold's meant for bonuses. Yes! *Recruitment* bonuses! In just a minute I'm going to stop talking. I'll reckon you're glad to hear that!" He waited for the laugh. "Yes, believe it or not, Sergeant Bombast is going to shut up and walk inside this fine establishment, where I've arranged for exclusive use of the common room, and something more as well. Now, what I want to do is to talk—just talk, mind you!—with lads who are strong enough and old enough to become soldiers. How old is that? Old enough to get your girlfriend in trouble!" Laughter again. "But not too old, neither. How old is that? Old enough that your girlfriend's jumped you over the broom, and you've come to think of it as a good bit of luck!

"So I'm a talkative man, and I want some lads to talk *with*. And if you'll do it, if you're neither too young nor too old and are willing to simply hear me out, with absolutely no strings attached . . ." He paused. "Well, fair's fair and the beer's on me. Drink as much as you like, and I'll pay the tab." He started to turn away, then swung back, scratching his head and looking puzzled. "Damn me, if there isn't some- thing I've forgot."

"The gold!" squeaked a young dinter.

"The gold! Yes, yes, I'd forget me own head if it weren't nailed on. As I've said, the gold's for bonuses. Right into your hand it goes, the instant you've signed the papers to become a soldier. And how much? One gold coin? Two?" He grinned wolfishly. "Doesn't nobody want to guess? No? Well, hold onto your pizzles . . . I'm offering *ten gold coins* to the boy who signs up today! And ten more apiece for as many of his friends as wants to go with him!"

To cheers, he retreated into the tavern.

The dragon, who had foreseen his coming from afar, had said, "Now do we repay our people for their subservience. This fellow is a great danger to us all. He must be caught unawares."

"Why not placate him with smiles?" Will had asked. "Hear him out, feed him well, and send him on his way. That seems to me the path of least strife."

"He will win recruits—never doubt it. Such men have tongues of honey, and glamour-stones of great potency."

"So?"

"The War goes ill for Avalon. Not one of three recruited today is like to ever return."

"I don't care. On their heads be the consequences."

"You're learning. Here, then, is our true concern: The first recruit who is administered the Oath of Fealty will tell his superior officers about my presence here. He will betray us all, with never a thought for the welfare of the village, his family, or friends. Such is the puissance of the Army's sorcerers."

So Will and the dragon had conferred, and made plans.

Now the time to put those plans into action was come.

The Scrannel Dogge was bursting with potential recruits. The beer flowed freely, and the tobacco as well. Every tavern pipe was in use, and Sergeant Bombast had sent out for more. Within the fog of tobacco smoke, young men laughed and joked and hooted when the recruiter caught the eye of that lad he deemed most apt to sign, smiled, and crooked a beckoning finger. So Will saw from the doorway.

He let the door slam behind him.

All eyes reflexively turned his way. A complete and utter silence overcame the room.

Then, as he walked forward, there was a scraping of chairs and putting down of mugs. Somebody slipped out the kitchen door, and another after him. Wordlessly, a knot of three lads in green shirts left by the main door. The bodies eddied and flowed. By the time Will reached the recruiter's table, there was nobody in the room but the two of them.

"I'll be buggered," Sergeant Bombast said wonderingly, "if I've ever seen the like."

"It's my fault," Will said. He felt flustered and embarrassed, but luckily those qualities fit perfectly the part he had to play.

"Well, I can *see* that! I can see that, and yet shave a goat and marry me off to it if I know what it means. Sit down, boy, sit! Is there a curse on you? The evil eye? Transmissible elf-pox?"

"No, it's not that. It's . . . well, I'm half-mortal."

A long silence.

"Seriously?"

"Aye. There is iron in my blood. 'Tis why I have no true name. Why, also, I am shunned by all." He sounded patently false to himself, and yet he could tell from the man's face that the recruiter believed his every word. "There is no place in this village for me anymore."

The recruiter pointed to a rounded black rock that lay atop a stack of indenture parchments. "This is a name-stone. Not much to look at, is it?"

"No, sir."

"But its mate, which I hold under my tongue, is." He

took out a small lozenge-shaped stone and held it up to be admired. It glistered in the light, blood-crimson yet black in its heart. He placed it back in his mouth. "Now, if you were to lay your hand upon the name-stone on the table, your true name would go straight to the one in my mouth, and so to my brain. It's how we enforce the contracts our recruits sign."

"I understand." Will calmly placed his hand upon the black name-stone. He watched the recruiter's face, as nothing happened. There were ways to hide a true name, of course. But they were not likely to be found in a remote river-village in the wilds of the Debatable Hills. Passing the stone's test was proof of nothing. But it was extremely suggestive.

Sergeant Bombast sucked in his breath slowly. Then he opened up the small lockbox on the table before him, and said, "D'ye see this gold, boy?"

"Yes."

"There's eighty ounces of the good red here—none of your white gold nor electrum neither!—closer to you than your one hand is to the other. Yet the bonus you'd get would be worth a dozen of what I have here. *If*, that is, your claim is true. Can you prove it?"

"Yes, sir. I can."

"Now, explain to me again," Sergeant Bombast said. "You live in a house of *iron*?" They were outside now, walking through the silent village. The recruiter had left his drum behind, but had slipped the name-stone into a pocket and strapped the lockbox to his belt.

"It's where I sleep at night. That should prove my case, shouldn't it? It should prove that I'm . . . what I say I am."

So saying, Will walked the recruiter into Tyrant Square.

It was a sunny, cloudless day, and the square smelled of dust and cinnamon, with just a bitter under-taste of leaked hydraulic fluid and cold iron. It was noon.

When he saw the dragon, Sergeant Bombast's face fell.

"Oh, fuck," he said.

As if that were the signal, Will threw his arms around the man, while doors flew open and hidden ambushers poured into the square, waving rakes, brooms, and hoes. An old hen-wife struck the recruiter across the back of his head with her distaff. He went limp and heavy in Will's arms. Perforce, Will let him fall.

Then the women were all over the fallen soldier, stabbing, clubbing, kicking, and cursing. Their passion was beyond all bounds, for these were the mothers of those he had tried to recruit. They had all of them fallen in with the orders the dragon had given with a readier will than they had ever displayed before for any of his purposes. Now they were making sure the fallen recruiter would never rise again to deprive them of their sons.

Wordlessly, they did their work and then, wordlessly, they left.

"Drown his motorcycle in the river," the dragon commanded afterward. "Smash his drum and burn it, lest it bear witness against us. Bury his body in the midden-heap. There must be no evidence that ever he came here. Did you recover his lockbox?"

"No. It wasn't with his body. One of the women must have stolen it."

The dragon chuckled. "Peasants! Still, it works out well. The coins are well-buried already under basement flagstones, and will stay so indefinitely. And when an investigator comes through looking for a lost recruiter, he'll be met by a universal ignorance, canny lies, and a cleverly planted series of misleading evidence. Out of avarice, they'll serve our cause better than ever we could order it ourselves."

A full moon sat high in the sky, enthroned within the constellation of the Mad Dog and presiding over one of the hottest nights of the summer when the dragon abruptly announced, "There is a resistance."

"Sir?" Will stood in the open doorway, lethargically watching the sweat fall, drop by drop from his bowed head. He would have welcomed a breeze, but at this time of year when those who had built well enough slept naked on their rooftops and those who had not burrowed into the mud of the riverbed, there were no night-breezes cunning enough to thread the maze of huts and so make their way to the square.

"Rebels against my rule. Insurrectionists. Mad, suicidal fools."

A single drop fell. Will jerked his head to move his moon-shadow aside, and saw a large black circle appear in the dirt. "Who?"

"The greenshirties."

"They're just kids," Will said scornfully.

"Do not despise them because they are young. The young make excellent soldiers and better martyrs. They are easily dominated, quickly trained, and as ruthless as you command them to be. They kill without regret, and they go to their deaths readily, because they do not truly understand that death is permanent."

"You give them too much credit. They do no more than sign horns at me, glare, and spit upon my shadow. Everybody does that."

"They are still building up their numbers and their courage. Yet their leader, the No-name one, is shrewd and capable. It worries me that he has made himself invisible to your eye, and thus to mine. Walking about the village, you have oft enough come upon a nest in the fields where he slept, or scented the distinctive tang of his scat. Yet when was the last time you saw him in person?"

"I haven't even seen these nests nor smelt the dung you speak of."

"You've seen and smelled, but not been aware of it. Meanwhile, No-name skillfully eludes your sight. He has made himself a ghost."

"The more ghostly the better. I don't care if I never see him again."

"You will see him again. Remember, when you do, that I warned you so."

The dragon's prophecy came true not a week later. Will was walking his errands and admiring, as he so often did these days, how ugly the village had become in his eyes. Half the huts were wattle-and-daub—little more than sticks and dried mud. Those that had honest planks were left unpainted and grey, to keep down the yearly assessment when the teind-inspector came through from the central government. Pigs wandered the streets, and the occasional scavenger bear as well, looking moth-eaten and shabby. Nothing was clean, nothing was new, nothing was ever mended.

Such were the thoughts he was thinking when somebody thrust a gunnysack over his head, while somebody else punched him in the stomach, and a third person swept his feet out from under him.

It was like a conjuring trick. One moment he was walking down a noisy street, with children playing in the dust and artisans striding by to their workshops and goodwives leaning from windows to gossip or sitting in doorways shucking peas, and the next he was being carried swiftly away, in darkness, by eight strong hands.

He struggled, but could not break free. His cries, muffled by the sack, were ignored. If anybody heard him—and there had been many about on the street a moment before—nobody came to his aid.

After what seemed an enormously long time, he was dumped on the ground. Angrily, he struggled out of the gunnysack. He was lying on the stony and slightly damp floor of the old gravel pit, south of the village. One crumbling wall was overgrown with flowering vines. He could hear birdsong upon birdsong. Standing, he flung the gunnysack to the ground and confronted his kidnappers.

There were twelve of them and they all wore green shirts.

He knew them all, of course, just as he knew everyone else in the village. But, more, they had all been his friends, at one time or another. Were he free of the dragon's bondage, doubtless he would be one of their number. Now, though, he was filled with scorn for them, for he knew exactly how the dragon would deal with them, were they to harm his lieutenant. He would accept them into his body, one at a time, to corrupt their minds and fill their bodies with cancers. He would tell the first in excruciating detail exactly how he was going to die, stage by stage, and he would make sure the eleven others watched as it happened. Death after death, the survivors would watch and anticipate. Last of all would be their leader, No-name.

Will understood how the dragon thought.

"Turn away," he said. "This will not do you nor your cause any good whatsoever."

Two of the greenshirties took him by the arms. They thrust him before No-name. His former friend leaned on a crutch of ash-wood. His face was tense with hatred and his eyes did not blink.

"It is good of you to be so concerned for our *cause*," No-name said. "But you do not understand our *cause*, do you? Our *cause* is simply this."

He raised a hand, and brought it down fast, across Will's face. Something sharp cut a long scratch across his forehead and down one cheek.

"*Llandrysos,* I command you to die!" No-name cried. The greenshirties holding Will's arms released them. He staggered back a step. A trickle of something warm went tickling down his face. He touched his hand to it. Blood.

No-name stared at him. In his outstretched hand was an elf-shot, one of those small stone arrowheads found everywhere in the fields after a hard rain. Will did not know if they had been made by ancient civilizations or grew from pebbles by spontaneous generation. Nor had he known, before now, that to scratch somebody with one while crying out his true name would cause that person to die. But the stench of ozone that accompanied death-magic hung in the air, lifting the small hairs on the back of his neck and tickling his nose with its eldritch force, and the knowledge of what had almost happened was inescapable.

The look of absolute astonishment on No-name's face curdled and became rage. He dashed the elf-shot to the ground. "You were *never* my friend!" he cried in a fury. "The night when we exchanged true names and mingled blood, you lied! You were as false then as you are now!"

It was true. Will remembered that long-ago time when he and Puck had rowed their coracles to a distant river-island, and there caught fish which they grilled over coals and a turtle from which they made a soup prepared in its own shell. It had been Puck's idea to swear eternal friendship and Will, desperate for a name-friend and knowing Puck would not believe he had none, had invented a true name for himself.

He was careful to let his friend reveal first, and so knew to shiver and roll up his eyes when he spoke the name. But he had felt a terrible guilt then for his deceit, and every time since when he thought of that night.

Even now.

Standing on his one good leg, No-name tossed his crutch upward and seized it near the tip. Then he swung it around and smashed Will in the face.

Will fell.

The greenshirties were all over him then, kicking and hitting him.

Briefly, it came to Will that, if he were included among their number, there were thirteen present and engaged upon a single action. We are a coven, he thought, and I the random sacrifice, who is worshiped with kicks and blows. Then there was nothing but his suffering and the rage that rose up within him, so strong that though it could not weaken the pain, it drowned out the fear he should have felt on realizing that he was going to die. He knew only pain and a kind of wonder: a vast, world-encompassing astonishment that so profound a thing as death could happen to *him,* accompanied by a lesser wonder that No-name and his merry thugs had the toughness to take his punishment all the way to death's portal, and that vital step beyond. They were only boys, after all. Where had they learned such discipline?

"I think he's dead," said a voice. He thought it was No-name, but he couldn't be sure. His ears rang, and the voice was so very, very far away.

One last booted foot connected with already broken ribs. He gasped, and spasmed. It seemed unfair that he could suffer pain on top of pain like this.

"That is our message to your master dragon," said the distant voice. "If you live, take it to him."

Then silence. Eventually, Will forced himself to open or
eye—the other was swollen shut—and saw that he was alor
again. It was a gorgeous day, sunny without being at all ho
Birds sang all about him. A sweet breeze ruffled his hair.

He picked himself up, bleeding and weeping with rag
and stumbled back to the dragon.

——— ——— ———

Because the dragon would not trust any of the healin;
women inside him, Will's injuries were treated by a fluffe
who came inside the dragon to suck the injuries from Will
body and accept them as her own. He tried to stop her a
soon as he had the strength to do so, but the dragon ove
ruled him. It shamed and sickened him to see how painful
the girl hobbled outside again.

"Tell me who did this," the dragon whispered, "and w
shall have revenge."

"No."

There was a long hiss, as a steam valve somewhere dee
in the thorax vented pressure. "You toy with me."

Will turned his face to the wall. "It's my problem and n
yours."

"You *are* my problem."

There was a constant low-grade mumble and grumble
machines that faded to nothing when one stopped payir
attention to it. Some part of it was the ventilation system, fo
the air never quite went stale, though it often had a fla
under-taste. The rest was surely reflexive—meant to keep th
dragon alive. Listening to those mechanical voices, fadir
deeper and deeper within the tyrant's corpus, Will had
vision of an interior that never came to an end, all the nig]
contained within that lightless iron body, expanding inwar

in an inversion of the natural order, stars twinkling in the vasty reaches of distant condensers and fuel-handling systems and somewhere a crescent moon, perhaps, caught in his gear train. "I won't argue," Will said. "And I will never tell you anything."

"You will."

"*No!*"

The dragon fell silent. The leather of the pilot's couch gleamed weakly in the soft light. Will's wrists ached.

The outcome was never in doubt. Try though he might, Will could not resist the call of the leather couch, of the grips that filled his hand, of the needles that slid into his wrists. The dragon entered him, and had from him all the information he desired, and this time he did not leave.

Will walked through the village streets, leaving footprints of flame behind him. He was filled with wrath and the dragon. "*Come out!*" he roared. "Bring out your greenshirties, every one of them, or I shall come after them, street by street and house by house." He put a hand on the nearest door, and wrenched it from its hinges. Broken fragments of boards fell flaming to the ground. "Spillikin cowers herewithin. Don't make me come in after him!"

Shadowy hands flung Spillikin face-first into the dirt at Will's feet.

Spillikin was a harmless albino stick-figure of a marsh-walker who screamed when Will closed a cauterizing hand about his arm to haul him to his feet.

"Follow me," Will/the dragon said coldly.

So great was Will's twin-spirited fury that none could stand up to him. He burned hot as a bronze idol, and the heat went before him in a great wave, withering plants, charring house-fronts, and setting hair ablaze when somebody did not flee from him quickly enough. "*I am wrath!*" he screamed. "*I am blood-vengeance! I am justice!* Feed me or suffer!"

The greenshirties were, of course, brought out.

No-name was, of course, not among their number.

The greenshirties were lined up before the dragon in Tyrant Square. They knelt in the dirt before him, heads down. Only two were so unwary as to be caught in their green shirts. The others were bare-chested or in mufti. All were terrified, and one of them had pissed himself. Their families and neighbors had followed after them and now filled the square with their wails of lament. Will quelled them with a look.

"Your king knows your true names," he said sternly to the greenshirties, "and can kill you at a word."

"It is true," said Hag Applemere. Her face was stony and impassive. Yet Will knew that one of the greenshirties was her brother.

"More, he can make you suffer such dementia as would make you believe yourselves in Hell, and suffering its torments forever."

"It is true," the hag said.

"Yet he disdains to bend the full weight of his wrath upon you. You are no threat to him. He scorns you as creatures of little or no import."

"It is true."

"One only does he desire vengeance upon. Your leader—he who calls himself No-name. This being so, your most merciful lord has made this offer: Stand." They obeyed, and he gestured toward a burning brand. "Bring No-name to me while this fire yet burns, and you shall all go free. Fail, and you will suffer such torments as the ingenuity of a dragon can devise."

"It is true."

Somebody—not one of the greenshirties—was sobbing softly and steadily. Will ignored it. There was more Dragon within him than Self. It was a strange feeling, not being in control. He liked it. It was like being a small oracle carried helplessly along by a raging current. The river of emotion had its own logic; it knew where it was going. "Go!" he cried. "Now!"

The greenshirties scattered like pigeons.

Not half an hour later, No-name was brought, beaten and struggling, into the square. His former disciples had tied his hands behind his back, and gagged him with a red bandanna. He had been beaten—not so badly as Will had been, but well and thoroughly.

Will walked up and down before him. Those leaf-green eyes glared up out of that silt-black face with a pure and holy hatred. There could be no reasoning with this boy, nor any taming of him. He was a primal force, an anti-Will, the spirit of vengeance made flesh and given a single unswerving purpose.

Behind No-name stood the village elders in a straight, unmoving line. The Sullen Man moved his mouth slowly, like an ancient tortoise having a particularly deep thought. But he did not speak. Nor did Auld Black Agnes, nor the yage-witch whose use-name no living being knew, nor Lady Nightlady, nor Spadefoot, nor Annie Hop-the-Frog, nor Daddy Fingerbones, nor any of the others. There were mutters and whispers among the villagers, assembled into a loose throng behind them, but nothing coherent. Nothing that could be heard or punished. Now and again, the buzzing of wings rose up over the murmurs and died down again like a cicada on a still summer day, but no one lifted up from the ground.

Back and forth Will stalked, restless as a leopard in a cage, while the dragon within him brooded over possible punishments. A whipping would only strengthen No-name in his hatred and resolve. Amputation was no answer—he had lost one limb already, and was still a dangerous and unswerving enemy. There was no gaol in all the village that could hope to hold him forever, save for the dragon himself, and the dragon did not wish to accept so capricious an imp into his own body.

Death seemed the only answer.

But what sort of death? Strangulation was too quick. Fire was good, but Tyrant Square was surrounded by thatch-roofed huts. A drowning would have to be carried out at the river, out of sight of the dragon himself, and he wanted the manna of punishment inextricably linked in his subjects' minds to his own physical self. He could have a wine-barrel brought in and filled with water, but then the victim's struggles would have a comic element to them. Also, as a form of strangulation, it was still too quick.

Unhurriedly, the dragon considered. Then he brought Will to a stop before the crouching No-name. He raised up Will's head, and let a little of the dragon-light shine out through Will's eyes.

"Crucify him."

To Will's horror, the villagers obeyed.

It took hours. But shortly before dawn, the child who had once been Puck Berrysnatcher, who had been Will's best friend and had died and been reborn as Will's Nemesis, breathed his last. His body went limp as he surrendered his name to his revered ancestress, Mother Night, and the exhausted villagers could finally turn away and go home and sleep.

Later, after he had departed Will's body at last, the dragon said, "You have done well."

Will lay motionless on the pilot's couch and said nothing.

"I shall reward you."

"No, lord," Will said. "You have done too much already."

"Haummn. Do you know the first sign that a toady has come to accept the rightness of his lickspittle station?"

"No, sir."

"It is insolence. For which reason, you will not be punished but rather, as I said, rewarded. You have grown somewhat in my service. Your tastes have matured. You want something better than your hand. You shall have it. Go into any woman's house and tell her what she must do. You have my permission."

"This is a gift I do not desire."

"Says you! Big Red Margotty has three holes. She will refuse none of them to you. Enter them in whatever order you wish. Do what you like with her tits. Tell her to look glad when she sees you. Tell her to wag her tail and bark like a dog. As long as she has a daughter, she has no choice but to obey. Much the same goes for any of my beloved subjects, of whatever gender or age."

"They hate you," Will said.

"And thou as well, my love and my delight. And thou as well."

"But you with reason."

A long silence. Then, "I know your mind as you do not. I know what things you wish to do with Red Margotty and what things you wish to do *to* her. I tell you, there are cruelties within you greater than anything I know. It is the birthright of flesh."

"You lie!"

"Do I? Tell me something, dearest victim. When you told the elders to crucify No-name, the command came from me, with my breath and in my voice. But the form . . . did not the _choice_ of the punishment come from you?"

Will had been laying listlessly on the couch staring up at the featureless metal ceiling. Now he sat upright, his face white with shock. All in a single movement he stood, and turned toward the door.

Which seeing, the dragon sneered, "Do you think to leave me? Do you honestly think you _can?_ Then try!" The dragon slammed his door open. The cool and pitiless light of earliest morning flooded the cabin. A fresh breeze swept in, carrying with it scents from the fields and woods. It made Will painfully aware of how his own sour stench permeated the dragon's interior. "You need me more than I ever needed you—I have seen to that! You cannot run away, and if you could, your hunger would bring you back, wrists foremost. You _desire_ me. You are empty without me. Go! Try to run! See where it gets you."

Will trembled.

He bolted out the door and ran.

The first sunset away from the dragon, Will threw up violently as the sun went down, and then suffered spasms of diarrhea. Cramping, and aching and foul, he hid in the depths of the Old Forest all through the night, sometimes howling and sometimes rolling about the forest floor in pain. A thousand times he thought he must return. A thousand times he told himself: Not yet. Just a little longer and you can surrender. But not yet.

The craving came in waves. When it abated, Will would think: If I can hold out for one day, the second will be easier, and the third easier yet. Then the sick yearning would return, a black need in the tissues of his flesh and an aching in his bones, and he would think again: Not yet. Hold off for just

a few more minutes. Then you can give up. Soon. Just a little longer.

By morning, the worst of it was over. He washed his
clothes in a stream, and hung them up to dry in the wan
predawn light. To keep himself warm, he marched back and
forth singing the *Chansons Amoreuses de Merlin Sylvanus*,
as many of its five hundred verses as he could remember.
Finally, when the clothes were only slightly damp, he sought
out a great climbing oak he knew of old, and from a hollow
withdrew a length of stolen clothesline. Climbing as close to
the tippy-top of the great tree as he dared, he lashed himself
to its bole. There, lightly rocked by a gentle wind, he slept at
last.

Three days later, Hag Applemere came to see him in his
place of hiding. The truth-teller bowed before him. "Lord
Dragon bids you return to him," she said formally.

Will did not ask the revered hag how she had found him.
Wise-women had their skills; nor did they explain themselves. "I'll come when I'm ready," he said. "My task here is
not yet completed." He was busily sewing together leaves of
oak, yew, ash, and alder, using a needle laboriously crafted
from a thorn, and short threads made from grasses he had
pulled apart by hand. It was no easy work.

Hag Applemere frowned. "You place us all in certain
danger."

"He will not destroy himself over me alone. Particularly
when he is sure that I must inevitably return to him."

"It is true."

Will laughed mirthlessly. "You need not ply your trade
here, hallowed lady. Speak to me as you would to any other.
I am no longer of the dragon's party." Looking at her, he saw
for the first time that she was not so many years older than
himself. In a time of peace, he might even have grown fast

enough to someday, in two years or five, claim her for his own, by the ancient rites of the greensward and the midnight sun. Only months ago, young as he was, he would have found this an unsettling thought. But now his thinking had been driven to such extremes that it bothered him not.

"Will," she said then, cautiously, "whatever are you up to?"

He held up the garment, complete at last, for her to admire. "I have become a greenshirtie." All the time he had sewn, he was bare-chested, for he had torn up his dragon sark and used it for tinder as he needed fire. Now he donned its leafy replacement.

Clad in his fragile new finery, Will looked the truth-teller straight in the eye.

"You *can* lie," he said.

Bessie looked stricken. "Once," she said, and reflexively covered her womb with both hands. "And the price is high, terribly high."

He stood. "Then it must be paid. Let us find a shovel now. It is time for a bit of grave-robbery "

It w evening when Will returned at last to the dragon. Tyran Square had been ringed about with barbed wire, and a loudspeaker had been set upon a pole with wires leading back into his iron hulk, so that he could speak and be heard in the absence of his lieutenant.

"Go first," Will said to Hag Applemere, "that he may be reassured I mean him no harm."

Breasts bare, clad in the robes and wide hat of her profession, Bessie Applemere passed through a barbed-wire gate (a grimpkin guard opened it before her and closed it after her) and entered the square. "Son of Cruelty." She bowed deeply before the dragon.

Will stood hunched in the shadows, head down, with his hands in his pockets. Tonelessly, he said, "I have been broken to your will, great one. I will be your stump-cow, if that is what you want. I beg you. Make me grovel. Make me crawl. Only let me back in."

Hag Applemere spread her arms and bowed again. "It is true."

"You may approach." The dragon's voice sounded staticky and yet triumphant over the loudspeaker.

The sour-faced old grimpkin opened the gate for him, as it had earlier been opened for the hag. Slowly, like a maltreated dog returning to the only hand that had ever fed him, Will crossed the square. He paused before the loudspeaker, briefly touched its pole with one trembling hand, and then shoved that hand back into his pocket. "You have won. Well and truly, have you won."

It appalled him how easily the words came, and how natural they sounded coming from his mouth. He could feel the desire to surrender to the tyrant, accept what punishments he would impose, and sink gratefully back into his bondage. A little voice within cried: *So easy! So easy!* And so it would be, perilously easy indeed. The realization that a part of him devoutly wished for it made Will burn with humiliation.

The dragon slowly forced one eye half-open. "So, boy . . ." Was it his imagination, or was the dragon's voice less forceful than it had been three days ago? "You have learned what need feels like. You suffer from your desires, even as I do. I . . . I . . . am weakened, admittedly, but I am not all so weak as *that!* You thought to prove that I needed you—you have proved the reverse. Though I have neither wings nor missiles and my electrical reserves are low, though I cannot fire my jets without destroying the village and myself as well, yet am I of the mighty, for I have neither pity nor remorse. Thought you I craved a mere boy? Thought you to make me dance attendance on a soft, unmuscled half-mortal mongrel fey? Pfaugh! I do not need you. Never think that I . . . that I *need* you!"

"Let me in," Will whimpered. "I will do whatever you say."

"You . . . you understand that you must be punished for your disobedience?"

"Yes," Will said. "Punish me, please. Abase and degrade me, I beg you."

"As you wish," the dragon's cockpit door hissed open, "so it shall be."

Will took one halting step forward, and then two. Then he began to run, straight at the open hatchway. Straight at it—and then to one side.

He found himself standing before the featureless iron of the dragon's side. Quickly, from one pocket he withdrew Sergeant Bombast's soulstone. Its small blood-red mate was already in his mouth. There was still grave-dirt on the one, and a strange taste to the other, but he did not care. He touched the soulstone to the iron plate, and the dragon's true name flowed effortlessly into his mind.

Simultaneously, he took the elf-shot from his other pocket. Then, with all his strength, he drew the elf-shot down the dragon's iron flanks, making a long, bright scratch in the rust.

"What are you doing?" the dragon cried in alarm. "Stop that! The hatch is open, the couch awaits!" His voice dropped seductively. "The needles yearn for your wrists. Even as I yearn for—"

"Baalthazar, of the line of Baalmoloch, of the line of Baalshabat," Will shouted, "I command thee to *die!*"

And that was that.

All in an instant and with no fuss whatever, the dragon king was dead. All his might and malice was become nothing more than inert metal, that might be cut up and carted away to be sold to the scrap-foundries that served their larger brothers with ingots to be reforged for the War.

Will hit the side of the dragon with all the might of his fist, to show his disdain. Then he spat as hard and fierce as ever he could, and watched the saliva slide slowly down the black metal. Finally, he unbuttoned his trousers and pissed upon his erstwhile oppressor.

So it was that he finally accepted that the tyrant was well and truly dead.

Bessie Applemere—hag no more—stood silent and bereft on the square behind him. Wordlessly, she mourned her sterile womb and sightless eyes. To her, Will went. He took her hand, and led her back to her hut. He opened the door for her. He sat her down upon her bed. "Do you need anything?" he asked. "Water? Some food?"

She shook her head. "Just go. Leave me to lament our victory in solitude."

He left, quietly closing the door behind him. There was no place to go now but home. It took him a moment to remember where that was.

"I've come back," Will said.

Blind Enna looked stricken. Her face turned slowly toward him, those vacant eyes filled with shadow, that ancient mouth open and despairing. Like a sleepwalker, she stood and stumbled forward and then, when her groping fingers tapped against his chest, she threw her arms around him and burst into tears. "Thank the Seven! Oh, thank the Seven! The blessed, blessed, merciful Seven!" she sobbed over and over again, and Will realized for the first time that, in her own inarticulate way, his aunt genuinely and truly loved him.

And so, for a season, life in the village returned to normal. In the autumn the Armies of the Might came through the land, torching the crops and leveling the buildings. Terror went before them and the villagers were forced to flee, first into the Old Forest, and then to refugee camps across the border. Finally, they were loaded into cattle cars and taken away to far Babylonia in Faerie Minor, where the streets are bricked of gold and the ziggurats touch the sky, and there Will found a stranger destiny than any he might previously have dreamed.

But that is another story, for another day.

AFTERWORD
Have I Got a Dragon for You!

If you look up dragons on the Internet, one popular search engine will offer considerably more than one million Web sites to choose from. Not all of them, of course, relate to the fabulous monsters that are the stars of this book, but even after ruling out antique firearms, brand names, flying lizards, speech recognition software, and sports teams, there still remain a plethora of pages to ponder.

It would therefore be both impossible and pointless for me to attempt to provide a comprehensive listing of novels and movies about dragons; there are simply too many, and not only don't I know them all, I don't like all of those I know. I cannot speak with authority on Fritz Lang's silent film classic, *Siegfried,* which I have not seen, or Anne McCaffrey's highly regarded dragonrider novels—every work of hers that I *have* read was excellent, but mea culpa, I haven't gotten around to that series (though I do own them). As for dragon stories I do not care for, I cite two films, *Dragonslayer* and *Pete's Dragon,* the former because it gratuitously and I felt tastelessly killed off one of its most engaging characters. The latter film, despite its charming dragon, is sluggishly paced and runs too long, at least in its initial theatrical issue; when reissued, its running time was variously trimmed. Nor is there much point in listing cornerstone works like *Beowulf* or J. K. Rowling's Harry Potter books, in which dragons figure importantly, since nearly every reader knows them; likewise, popular-tangential phenomena such as the old TV show *H. R. Pufnstuf,* or Peter Yarrow's song, "Puff the Magic Dragon."

The following recommendations, therefore, are merely a few of my own quirky suggestions of dragon books, films, and Web sites that I have found especially engaging.

colba.net/~tempest1/dragons.htm is an attractive and informative Web site devoted to dragon lore. A rather nice version of the old song "My Lady Greensleeves" plays as you browse.

Dove Isabeau, a powerful fable by Jane Yolen, is magnificently illustrated by Dennis Nolan Harcourt. Jane, who is one of fantasy literature's finest writers, has written many books and stories about dragons, all of them well worth reading, but this is a particular favorite of mine. Dove, its title character, is a sweet young woman whose evil stepmother casts a spell on her and turns her into a dragon that devours many of the men who would be Dove's suitors. A prince comes to her aid, but the ordeal she endures as a dragon changes her life forever. Though intended as a children's book, *Dove Isabeau* darkly resonates for readers of all ages.

draconian.com is another of many fine Web sites devoted to "dragonology." It includes interesting pages about the history and physiology of dragons and even offers the opportunity for the user to adopt a dragon.

Dragon, Dragon is the first of three volumes of magical short stories by John Gardner, author of *Nickel Mountain, October Light, The Sunlight Dialogues,* and *The Wreckage of Agathon.* Ostensibly written for children but definitely intended to be enjoyed by adults, this funny, urbane, and satirical trio of books also includes *Gudgekin the Thistle Girl* and *The King of the Hummingbirds.* "Dragon, Dragon" is the droll story of a really annoying dragon who virtually dies laughing. Gardner wrote the critically acclaimed novel *Grendel,* which tells the Beowulf legend from the monster's point of view. One chapter of it is devoted to a memorable scene between Grendel and a sage and world-weary dragon.

Dragonheart (1996) is a splendid film starring Dennis Quaid as a knight who first tries to kill, but subsequently befriends, a personable dragon named Draco, whose voice is supplied by Sean Connery. When first released, its coming-attractions trailer gave me the impression that it was cute and slight, and I ignored it, but when I recently rented it on videotape, I was surprised at its scope and power. It is funny and suspenseful, with characters one cares about, and its ending is the stuff of legends: ennobling, sad, and exhilarating.

Dragonheart: A New Beginning is a direct-to-DVD sequel made by the same production team that created *Dragonheart.* Though intended for a younger audience, and slightly impaired, in my opinion, by a few gross scenes, it is a good sequel to its superior predecessor. Beginning some eighty years after the events of the first film, it reveals that though the earlier dragon was supposedly the last of its species, a dragon egg was discovered in its old cave. From it hatches a gentle dragon (voice supplied by Robby Benson) who has to be taught how to fly and other dragonly lessons by a stable boy who aspires to knighthood. One of the film's special virtues is a fascinatingly ambiguous villain named Osric.

Farmer Giles of Ham features J. R. R. Tolkien's "other" dragon, Chrysophylax, whose path crosses that of the titular hero, who has already successfully dealt with an obstreperous giant. Tolkien's better-known dragon is Smaug, the bane of the dwarves who enlist the hobbit Bilbo Baggins to help take back some of their treasure that Smaug has stolen from them; this, of course, is the story of *The Hobbit,* the acclaimed prequel to *Lord of the Rings.* If Chrysophylax has been comparatively overlooked, this is the time to rectify that, for 2002 marked the fiftieth anniversary of *Farmer Giles of Ham*'s first publication, and a new edition has been released. It includes the original droll illustrations by Pauline Baynes, as well as Tolkien's earlier draft of the story, plus notes for a sequel he never wrote.

Jack the Giant Killer (1962) is one of those old Saturday matinee costume adventure films whose special effects—monsters, witches, and the like—are in the tradition of Ray Harryhausen's Sinbad fantasy films. Torin Thatcher makes a marvelous villain, and at the climax, his name, Pendragon, proves to be quite apt.

The Reluctant Dragon was first published in 1898 as part of *Dream Days,* a classic collection of evanescent essays by Kenneth Grahame. This gentle tale of a decidedly un-dragonly dragon and the knight who would rather be his friend than his assassin, was made into an amusing 1941 Walt Disney film. The movie is worth viewing, with its inside look at the Disney studio's mode of animation, voicing, and storyboard development. Its star is the great humorist Robert Benchley, and if you look closely, you'll notice that one of the writers is played by a young Alan Ladd. The dragon sequence comes at the end of the film.

Shrek (2001) is the winner of the first Academy Award for Best Animated Feature. Children love its quirky tale of an ogre who rescues a princess from a dragon, but it is just as much fun for adults. The story contains many delightful surprises, one being the unexpected way in which the dragon is tamed.

Sleeping Beauty (1959) is Walt Disney's fairly straightforward retelling of the fairy tale. When it was first released, it was the most expensive animated feature film ever made. Originally shown in a widescreen process, it was visually spectacular, and its final confrontation between the hero and the villain who turned into a dragon was, and still is, quite scary.

urbandragons.com is a whimsical and funny Web site comic strip by C. S. McDonald and Sandy Turner. Its comedic dragons remind me a little of Walt Kelly's *Pogo*, as well as Burr Tillstrom's Oliver J. Dragon, of the late lamented TV show *Kukla, Fran, and Ollie*. The Urban Dragons Web site features a large bestiary of variant dragon species, including the Baseball Dragon, the Barbecue Dragon, the Jazz Dragon, the Literary Dragon, and the Yuppie Dragon. The comic strip itself began on September 22, 1999, and is still running online. Don't miss it, especially if you want to know where your missing socks go—and what dragons do with them!

ABOUT THE AUTHORS

ORSON SCOTT CARD is the author of the SF classic, *Ender's Game*, as well as dozens of other bestselling novels, including *Shadow of the Hegemon*. He lives in Greensboro, North Carolina.

MARVIN KAYE is the author and editor of more than forty books, including *The Game Is Afoot: Parodies, Pastiches, and Ponderings of Sherlock Holmes* and *The Resurrected Holmes: New Cases from the Notes of John H. Watson, M.D.* He lives in New York City.

MERCEDES LACKEY is a full-time writer and has published numerous novels and stories, including the bestselling Heralds of Valdemar series. She lives in Oklahoma with her husband and collaborator, artist Larry Dixon, and their flock of parrots.

TANITH LEE has written fifteen children's books, forty-two adult novels, and nearly two hundred short stories. She has won the World Fantasy Award and the August Derleth Award for her work. Tanith Lee lives in England with her husband.

ELIZABETH MOON is a native Texan who has a degree in both History and Biology, spent three years in the Marine

Corps, and has been nominated for a Hugo Award. She lives in Florence, Texas, with her family.

MICHAEL SWANWICK has received the Hugo, Nebula, Theodore Sturgeon, and World Fantasy Awards for his work. *Stations of the Tide* was honored with the Nebula Award and was also nominated for the Hugo and Arthur C. Clarke Awards. "The Edge of the World" was awarded the Theodore Sturgeon Memorial Award in 1989. It was also nominated for both the Hugo and World Fantasy Awards. "Radio Waves" received the World Fantasy Award in 1996. "The Very Pulse of the Machine" received the Hugo Award in 1999, as did "Scherzo with Tyrannosaur" in 2000.